To Touch the Whale

To Touch the Whale

a novel

Lynne Ann Mitchell

Published by Rabbit Hole Productions
April 2009

Written 1995-1998.
Small hand bound edition created by author in 1998.
Manuscript sat in a closet collecting dust 1998-2009.

Copyright © 2009 by Lynne Ann Mitchell

Published by Rabbit Hole Productions
www.rabbitholeproductions.com

First Paperback Edition: April 2009

The characters and events portrayed in this book are fictitious. Any similarity to real persons, living or dead, is coincidental and not intended by the author.

Library of Congress Cataloging-in-publication Data
To Touch the Whale / Lynne Ann Mitchell

Library of Congress Control Number: 2009903034

ISBN: 978-0-578-01802-7 (paperback)

For those who went before us— Nini, Dana & Rabbit.

Acknowledgments

I am grateful to the many people who made this work possible—for inspiration, encouragement, love and hope, and for a little aggravation too— what better form of motivation can there be? Thanks to—my wonderful husband and number one supporter, Shawn, to Grandma-Billie Fletcher, Jessica, Diana, Laurie, Sharon & Lindsey, Betty Mitchell, Debbie, Don, Carmen & Clay, Bill & Becky, Frank, Donna Dunson, Steve Stern, and Michelle Schneider, and to The West Florida Literary Federation—*for those few readings I gave a long, long time ago.*

Section One

Is it possible
To place a soul onto paper,
And have it still seem—
A soul?

1

At the first moment of life, we are born struggling for breath. The first sound we make is a scream. The sound of our voice is our only expression. We are struck down by our own fear, and by the lights, and movement, and sounds which charge out at us, rough hands, monstrous sizes and shapes— *How do we possibly survive our first hour?— except that we do.*

Mother chewed us up and down like we were bones. She was always trying to get inside us, to the marrow of us, and crack us between her teeth. The way she looked, just standing there even, doing nothing but watching us with her eyes, felt like teeth marks. Like the way it felt when Jessie would get mad and sink her teeth into the nearest flesh, a hand, or the soft part of an arm, wet and red, indented curves of each baby tooth. There was always a bruise afterwards. For days you could point to it and say, "See, this is what you did." Mother's words wore us down, the way old shoes wear out through the sides, revealing tender fleshy parts, filling in with sand, sharp stones. When we walked, it was on tiptoe, quietly, and soft as Bible leather.

I was born three weeks premature. I always said I was early, because I couldn't wait to get away from my childhood, and from the darkness I found inside my mother. My mother was born with a heart, but over time she began to loose pieces of it. While each of us children were still living inside her, she lost the last remaining pieces.

It was the only time I would be forced to be that close to her, and to her heart that beat too fast from fear. It would have sounded like a war drum to my tiny ears, beating faster and faster, the sound of it moving each cell into place as I was made. Its rhythm would become my rhythm as I learned how to move, and when I learned this, I beat tiny feet and hands against her, inside. I beat her and kicked her until she had no choice, but to let me go.

Karen, who is the one most like our mother, was born one year later, three weeks overdue. Karen is of a selfish nature, and has always thought any good thing should be hers. As a baby, still inside the womb, I believe she held herself very close to our mother's heart, pulling in it's secrets, and eating up any kind words that might have ever been said. She was learning the secrets of how to be just like her. When Karen was born, she weighed ten pounds. It was all those possibilities, that she had stolen, and eaten up.

Jessie, the youngest, arrived at the scheduled time five years after Karen, but was born a girl instead of a boy, like our mother insisted she would be. A friend of our mother had held a pendulum on a long string over her stomach. It swung to the right, which made her a boy, so our mother told everyone to buy only boy clothes, and boy colors for her next child. When grandma asked her, what she would do if it turned out to be a girl? She'd said matter-of-factly, "Then they'll be my maids, and I'll never lift another finger to do anything."

Jessie must have been trying hard to figure out what she was supposed to be. She got all turned around, and tried to come out the wrong way—feet first. I imagine that's the way a boy would have come out, feet first and kicking. When the doctor reached in to turn her around, she refused to believe she was to be a girl. How could she please our mother as a girl? She intended to stay in until she got it right, and grabbed hold of the little piece of our mother's heart that was left. When the doctor pulled, she pulled, and that last piece came loose and was set adrift, without anything to anchor it in place.

This is why, whenever our mother tried to say a nice thing, or a loving word, she couldn't. Karen had eaten up all the things she had intended to say, and Jessie had broken it and set it loose, so she couldn't think up any more. Me, well, I had kicked it, and knocked it off center to begin with. And I wouldn't have been able to hear anything even if she did. I was running too fast. All I could hear was the wind in my ears. All I could feel was the crash of waves, as I washed out of my mother and into the world, and was set adrift on my own.

I don't believe our mother knows her heart is missing.

It's someplace other than she thought it was.

Raw Umber Violet.

Mother's face, so much smaller than the body, seems to exist separately and alone. "Don't you talk to me like that—" she says, grating voice. The words that fly out of her and into me, are cool and crisp. Her face appears as a fossil embedded on a wide expanse of ice and rock, two shining bits of granite shaped like eyes. Inside, I feel a tingling shiver to have evoked such a dangerous spirit.

Because I am the oldest, I can get away with more, so I say things that I know will make waves. Then I stand back and watch whatever happens. "Like what— grown up, or truthful?" I ask. I follow her around the room with my eyes. I want to see who she thinks she is.

The trailer living room does not give her much room to move around in. It is more like she is standing in one spot, a huge weather vane that changes directions. A metallic grinding sound comes from the floor when she swings around. "All figured out..." Her voice is full of contempt. "You think it's so much this, or that. You really don't have the faintest idea about any of it."

"Oh, I have a pretty good idea."

"You don't know anything—"

"Some things I know. *Enough.*"

"Well, so what!" snap-cold air. Winter frost. "I don't answer to you."

"Who then?"

The eyes that fix on me have a frozen, liquid color to them, old ice that has existed a long time. I imagine things are hidden inside, frozen in place, like animals that fall into ravines and become trapped. "I did whatever it took to make it through those days." she says. "I was the best damn thing you had."

"Not much to say of yourself then—"

"Watch your mouth!" snake quick, her skin turning in shades of red. A silence, follows. Neither of us it seems, knows which way to turn. Other sounds, like passing cars and dogs barking, become too loud. The trailer walls are too thin to keep the outside where it belongs and I'm sure the neighbors can hear us.

I sit on the couch trying to look casual, in control. At seventeen, I believe I can pull off such a look of confidence. I think of filling the room with as many words as I can think up— a battery of insults, cruel innuendoes, a thousand direct-hit memories that would bring her crumbling down in an avalanche. But I can think of only one thing, an image...the color of tarnished brass.

"Can you even remember what she looked like?" I ask finally. The tone is even and perfectly smooth. "That day. Her hair was still wet from the pool. The tangles were nearly impossible to take out once it was dry. Twisted up, like wires." Through the screen door, hot air blows, banging the curtain rod back and forth. It fills the room with a suffocating heat. "Or—" the words are careful, slow, "the way she looked when she was afraid?" Fearful, clinging hands trying to hide behind me...is what I remember. "It seems strange that as small as she was, she was always trying to make herself smaller. As though the size of pin— would be enough for you not to find her."

She is looking away at blank walls. Nothing on them but shadows. "It must have taken a lot of effort to stop yourself." I say. "Karen— she's just like you. And Jessie— there's some of you there too." I say this to her back, since she won't turn around. She has wedged herself between the curio shelf and the end table. "There's a lot of you in me too." This is not something I want to admit, but know is true. "It takes everything I have to keep it in. The indifference, the anger, rage so big— I can't even find the edge of it. It keeps me from people. I can't get too close now. It just might come unleashed— strike out before I notice."

Through clenched teeth, she says, "You want to blame me for your faults now?"

"I want you to face yours—"

"You always did think you could see things that no one else could." Hard, unyielding sounds.

"Only what's in front of me."

"Oh, go on then!" Her voice is feverish, rising and dropping suddenly. Daring me. "Change the whole world— Go on!" She goes over to the door, kicks the suitcases over. "What are you waiting for? I know a lot more than you," she says. Her hands mold into soft fists, clinch the side of the chair beside me. "How far do you think you'll get? You think you can see the future and it's just the way you want it. Everything goes right for you, doesn't it? Well, I *know* the future—" a cracked open smile. "And I can't wait for it to happen to you. It'll wipe that smirk right off your face!"

She spits out the future in a wave. "The world'll beat you down! Your children will wear you down! The job will push you down! Your husband won't understand! Friends don't understand—" she screams over the furniture and distance. "There is no escape—You won't get far. My mother doesn't have the answers. Oh I know, you've always gone behind my back to her. Now she thinks she has you—that you're hers—but you're mine, and you always will be!"

"You shouldn't be so jealous of your own mother." I say this to the side, forcing myself to remain still.

"What's to be jealous of? My mother never understood anything, and nobody! What makes you think she listens to you? I was nothing to her from the moment I ran off and got married to your father. So what, if he turned out to be good for nothin'. She just had to rub it in my face. So what, about what she wanted for me— What I wanted, was different. I wasn't about to get stuck like her. Always looked down on me, like I was nothin'. I deserved more than that. She wanted a boy, and I beat her out, by being born a girl. Then I go and have nothin' but girls too! Ha! Go ahead—" she screams. "Run— cause that's what you're doing. Running from a life that will catch you and beat you till there's nothing left. And those happy, laughing children—looking up to you— only you'll look back knowing what's out there. Waiting with all it's cruel, little miseries. I made it easy on you! Life's a hard woman, just like me. Just like you..." A sharp finger points into my shoulder. I feel a shock at the unexpected touch, force my head to turn and look at her. "A hard woman don't break down in lost dreams." The finger still hangs in mid air. "She survives them! Did your sweat little faces ever look up at me, and ask what my dreams were? No. My time was up. You reminded me day after day of that fact. Go on. The clocks ticking! Your time's almost up. Those dreams are slippin' fast. Don't think I don't hear the fear in you. You're afraid! Afraid you've already lost it..." She points to the door and the fallen suitcases. "Go on, attack me for my mistakes. Yours are there, chasing you over that cliff— "

Looking at me through gray, red circled eyes, she hisses, teeth holding on. "Nothing ever changes for long, or for better! You remember that!" Young bones resisting, I move towards the door, slowly, cautiously. An ice cold, wind blows out of her. I am careful not to touch her. To do so, would weld our skins together, frozen in place. I would never get away.

From out of her, words are falling like heavy stones. "That's all you're ever going to get— *ever!*"

2

Every time I looked out at the world, it's as though I were a camera lens, with it's upside-down and backward vision. Only my right-way image was on the inside. I figure that's why I sometimes say words backwards, or put two words together in a nonsense way when I try to talk. In my head it was right. When I tried to express it on the outside it was wrong.

When I say I am not like other people, I am. I just don't show it. Instead, I move along as a shadow, watching the scenes around me, detached, invisible, collecting each day into me, and saving them up in the cells and thought-spaces of my body. From time to time, I forget who I am, not the *who* I have become, where I live, or anything like that— I forget that I am a participant in this life.

My internal view, is my most powerful view. Carved along my bones, etched deep for permanence and absolute clarity is the long history of my family. Every ache and pain I suffered over the years, I attributed to that history. When it rained, and the ache in my legs would travel down to my feet, I would think of my mother. When I was tired and frustrated, and my arms would weigh down, I would feel the oppressing weight of my sister, Karen. Tensed up hands would be my grandparents, hers the right hand, his the left. And a slow stiffness along the neck, that might start behind the eyes, work its way downward, pulling a throbbing pain, gathering in intensity until it drove me down completely, to bed, or someplace dark and quiet, I suffered this pain in solitude. It was not something I would admit to, or show to the outside world. It was just something I lived with everyday. This would be Jessie, my little sister, my shadow.

When I paint, it's as though some of my insides spilled out without me knowing it. First, I paint it inside— then it turns out I have also painted it on the outside, only it's not as mixed-up as when I try to talk, on account that it sort of slipped out unnoticed. I guess you could say the canvas was a sheet of film my thoughts imprinted themselves on. Where in the long moments of life, a flash of inspiration came along and illuminated my darkness, and a painting was born.

There is a process of elimination to each of my creations. Separating each element, I find buried beneath, some aspect of my history. It took sometime before I noticed it was there— hiding behind this color or that shape. In eliminating each layer, I thought I might one day find myself, nestled in the core— a small nucleus of thought, housed in the bones of my bones... If I took away my mother, took away my sisters, took away my past, my husband, my ideals, my world— there I would sit— child-sized, a grain of existence.

My art is something which must work its way out slowly, stretching out tentative hands, feeling its way along as a blind person would to read. To me, art must be lived, and through that experience, living becomes an art. Both are transitional. There is a beginning, a middle, and an end. Neither art, or life, come easily to me, but I am driven to do each, again and again, compelled to find some satisfactory point, that will bring me to some understanding, some feeling of completeness.

There are two things I learned as a child, that I could not imagine. Two things, that were said to exist, but that I could not see in my head. When I try to imagine infinity, I come to an edge in the mind. It is the only limit I have ever found. Starting off with a center point, a dark glass sphere for this universe, this space and time, vast distances of stars and moons, galaxies stretching out in a velvety blackness. My hand follows along this, feeling it as a soft fabric, except where the stars are. They are each a bright, sharp edge, knife sharp. I feel between the stars until it bends downward and becomes circular. Then another universe appears around the first, then another around that. Then another around that.

18

Each one bigger than the last. On and on, until I just stop, because I cannot see something that is supposed to keep going, forever. *Infinite.*

Perfection is the second thing I could never imagine, and from experience, learned was not possible. I could try to be perfect, and something would still be wrong. Usually things I would not be able to see myself, but my mother always could, or someone like her. I had never met a perfect person, so I could not imagine that such a person did exist. As a child I asked my grandmother if there was such a thing as perfect people. She said angels were perfect. But I had never seen an angel either, and I was looking for something more along the lines of a ten year old, long legged, awkward, shy, but not shy, since that would be an imperfect trait, and wanted more than anything in the world to be understood— but then a perfect person would be able to make everyone understand them.

I have to this day, yet to meet such a person, and still cannot imagine infinity beyond a certain wavering edge, beyond a multitude of transparent spheres, each enveloping the other. When I paint, it's as though I move backwards through the glass walls of my history, a house of mirrors, that send reflections of me in every direction. I am looking for things that I might have missed, some vital clue to who I am. Searching for doorways that will lead me through the labyrinth of my being, to explain how I came to be this person I am now. An exact point may not exist, like infinity, it wavers and hints, but never comes into view.

I have brought with me canvas, paints and brushes. They are my tools. Like a gardener's tools of shovel, rake, and good top soil, I have to discover myself by digging. I hope to plant new and better things once I find a good place. It is dark in the beginning, so I cannot use my eyes. I must feel my way across the surface, slowly and blindly, each step a painful fall backwards. As I go along it becomes lighter. I begin to see things that I couldn't before. I move towards the light so I can see better what has eluded me. Discovering myself a piece at a time, feeling my way between the cold, sharp edges, and old, dark roots.

3

Traffic downtown was heavy. It moved slow, both lanes packed with cars trying to maneuver through the narrow streets and the maze of one-way alleys. On either side, the people moved faster by sidewalk than those driving. Stopped by another red light, I rolled down the window. A blast of hot air pushed in against my face. Next to me, a white painted-sign was swinging back and forth. *Southern fried chicken, French fries, hot dogs, grilled fish or steak*— it read. The smell of cooking grease was what drifted out of the storefront.

The people moved past in waves. Hurrying, looking in shop windows, pushing babies in strollers, the sun-glassed faces reflected black across the eyes of strangers. I leaned against the door, hanging an elbow out and waited, wondered to what places they were all going?

A young couple in shorts and matching T-shirts walked by, close together, laughing. They looked freshly pressed, without a wrinkle of worry. Their laughter stirred an envious feeling in me. I could almost smell the suntan oil and warm sand they must smell of. The guy leaned closer to the girl and whispered something to her. She laughed again and smiled back. I could imagine how they felt up close, like worn Levi jeans and soft cotton. They seemed immuned to humidity, and strolled along as though it were a cool seventy degrees, instead of a blistering ninety-seven.

Older, heavier people walked past too, but they seemed further apart, whispering or silent, some with frowns on their expressions. Most had gone past some internal melting point, tugging at wet clothes that had reshaped itself around them. The heat had settled their spirits down around their ankles, where it flared out in loose cuffs, swimming around thick ankles, creamy skin, brown spotted, hints of blue underneath. They pointed at various things and talked quietly among themselves, moved slow, as though lost, or that things were different now from the last time they were here, rearranged and shuffled in some new order.

The locals and business people were easily picked out. They always seemed to be calling out to someone across the street or to a passing car. They bore the heat and damp clothes with some defiance. To them, it was something earned and bravely carried. They stood, eating lunch with one hand, waving flies away with the other. They contrasted with the tourists who moved too slow, holding up the flow of people, unsure, giddy and staring too long at things, that to the rest of us were common sights.

The light turns green finally, but I make it only to the next light and have to stop again. This time I hear louder voices in the crowd. Shouting in a harsh, rusty tone, the sounds repeat themselves like a rhythm, rising, falling away, then returning. Several cars ahead of me make it across and I inch forward to get a better view of these people. They are different from anyone else on the street. They seem out of place and look strange to be standing, dressed in suits and Sunday dresses. Some of the men's jackets are off and the sleeves rolled up above their elbows. Their hands are held high, waving black, leather Bibles over their heads. The skin is pale on their arms, their faces and hands, red and sunburned. I have seen them before. They do not wear sunglasses like everyone else, seeming to prefer eye to eye contact, even on the brightest days. Their children are dressed as smaller versions of themselves. Thin, with long faces and too serious expressions. Each of them holds a poster overhead, showing pictures that say, 'This is hell.' Figures are bent in poses of torment, screaming faces turned upward. The upraised hands are trying to hold back the black drawn lines of flame that are burning around them.

They are all shouting at the people walking, and the cars inching. Holding out their signs to them, shouting their words that also seem out of place, about sin and damnation. They shout. They point. They slap

22

their worn Bibles. They look angry and hot. As traffic moved forward my open window is presented to them. I think about rolling up the window, but before I do a man in a baby blue suit, wet with perspiration, moves in. "You!" he shouted. His voice is hoarse and rough from yelling. "Repent for your sins!" Long lines of sweat are running down each side of his face, out of his hair, down into the gray sagging collar at his neck. His whole body shivers under his rage, as though boiling, forcing it's way out through his pores. "You have sinned against God— *Repent!*" His eyes, accusing. Annoyance flashed through me, thinking he knew anything about me, or what I might have done, then settled into a tapping finger at the car seat.

After thirty years, I had learned ways of dealing with my accusers, to shut out their words, the cold looks full of suggestion, their pointing fingers. In one quick motion, I reached over and turned the radio on. Rock and Roll now matched the level of his voice. He looked repulsed, tried to shout louder, but all that was left were his jerking, angry motions. Sweat was raining down from his skin, pouring into his own shadow, a dark thunderstorm surrounded by hot light, sidewalk glare. Spinning on wet heels, Sundays-best, he stormed away, leaving me to be damned with the rest.

Together their voices rose up above the sun-lit people, made the heat worst, so that the whiteness of their skin, turned like mirrors, reflected the sun into sharp beams. Around them, the temperature is more like a 103.

The blue suited man passed by my window again. He pointed his Bible at me as if it were a gun. I could tell by his eyes he'd shoot me with it if he could, and say it was for my own good. I started tapping my fingers to the music on the radio, looking ahead as though I didn't see him. "Come on, come on— *Change*—" I said to myself. I wanted to move away from the voice calling after me, and the crowded streets, and the smells, the people, from the confining spaces of city streets. "I don't have to take this..." I waved my hands as though I were talking to someone. I was not thinking of the man now. I was thinking of where I was going. Around me, the heat was closing in, suffocating. I stretched out the shirt neckline, held it open, fanning. When I let go, it stayed limp and out of shape.

Then in a rush, all the cars went forward. Engines roared in the race for the open highways. The trees raced by, the cars even faster, a blur of movement and sound. I felt like I'd been released from something more too. There was a sense of guilt, escaping panic. "You can't turn back now." I tell myself. "It's done."

Quickly, I changed lanes to get around a slower car. The man's voice had creeped back into my head. Instantly I was angry. "Shut up." I said out loud.

Make me.

"I will."

Try.

I turned the radio up even louder.. "See—"

The music comes out like blue, watery bubbles, rising, rising. Inside me, something turned in quick, a bolt slamming shut on a door. I gripped the stirring wheel tighter, eyes forward, dug my fingernails deep into the rim.

Aqua Marine Blue.

Lying on the bottom of the pool looking up, I can hear blood in my ears. It sounds like water running down a sink drain, or rain. The water does not hurt my eyes like it does Karen's, so I can open my eyes under the water. I see the legs of people sitting along the edge of the pool. Their legs are pale looking, like the wicks of candles hung down in lamp oil. Leading up to wavering candle flame bodies, the legs dance misshapen images of the people above. Behind them is the deceptively blue sky. It should be a red sky. It is very hot up there where the people are.

When I have to go up for air, I think I will burst into flames too, my waxy, white arms burning through to the middle, cut off from my body, my head from my neck, and my wrinkled feet coming off at the ankles. I will rattle like pieces of glass in a paper bag when I move, all the pieces of me, hung together just barely, by a center most string. I will stay like this until I jump back into the water— where I become liquid and weightless and melt back into one shape.

"Kath- rine- get- up- here- now-"

A strangely formed head is making sounds on the other side.

I blow bubbles of leftover air to the head. The bubbles capture the brilliant white light, swirling with hints of blue from the pool walls, each one carrying a piece of me to release on the other side, bursting around the candle flame people who remain unaware that I have just breathed on them.

"Don't- make- me- come- and- get- you-" The head trembles at the pool edge, looking down at me. "The- count- of- three!"

"One-"

Bubbles.

"Two-"

Bubbles.

"Three!"

I'm rising.

I have no more air to hold me down.

I rise. Knowing the flames will devour what's left of me.

4

Most people prefer the Gulf, where the sand is white and the waves are blue and rough. On the Sound side, people take younger children to first introduce them to the water— to stick babies feet in, while holding their arms stretched out over fearful heads, screaming at the first chill of water on their toes.

The line that the coast makes from Gulf to bay is a jagged edge of coves, inlets, and shore. Each is distinct in the natural beauty that unkempt things have, and in the temper that such places must occasionally extend to remain so. Through unpredictable winds, hidden currents, sand dunes that shift underfoot, each summer storm rearranges the land and water's edge to something always new and different.

It would be a wavering edge of movement, if one tried to measure it's exact shape. A map would fail to show the snake-jointed curves, the spine-like hills of each sand dune. A person could easily get lost in such a wilderness place, or eaten alive by mosquitoes, or never come back from a seashell collecting walk. The wild beauty, leads and pulls one just a little further on. *One more mile, then I'll turn back.* Sometimes, the feet just want to keep walking and not turn back. Some internal instinct takes hold along the coast, urges us to ignore the fear of getting lost, or being alone in an unfamiliar place— and to just let the feet keep going, following the wild, shifting land, and blue shimmering waters.

The land in some places reached out straight and long, as if a bridge that lead no where, but stopped at some point, three sides cutting against the waves of the gulf. Each side was lined with huge rocks, storm fencing, posts nailed in deep, a staked claim of territory. Houses side by side along the borders, show where it has won against the ocean's pull. Only when the ocean throws up a hurricane does it get to take back, pulling the sand out from under the neatly painted houses, as it sometimes did, and laying them down flat, like cards on a table. It was a tenuous gamble to live next to the rough, blue waters and shifting sands. But it was a risk many were willing to take to live on the edge. On the Gulf side, the line of houses was as long as the shore itself.

In other places the land does not go out straight or bold, but curls back, the tail of a long J, with the inside, a protective space. It's facing waters form the bays. There the water is dark, the dip and cresting movement, gentle and rocking, shadow colors. Foam, made from the churning motion of under currents, pushed up against the sand, was the color of old paper. The bay gives the impression of something older, more settled. The inside places of things, where even wild places such as this, become a little less wild, soft edged, and seemingly safe.

Down off the main strip road, toward the end of this tamer ocean, a place developers hadn't stolen yet and cleared out as their own, was the place I was looking for. Practically hidden in a forest of drooping pines and heavy moss, whose pristine white waterfront was stained brown and black by broken oyster shells, and hermit crabs with their long spiny legs and dull shells. A single piece of scrap wood beside the main road indicated the turnoff. It was easy to miss. Painted in faded, red block letters, it's only advertisement was the word 'rentals'.

For eight years I had never seen the sign. Before, it was always a left at Belview and Fifth, where one day instead of left, I went right, down Jackson, down towards the edge of town, and in the direction of the water. I didn't consciously make the choice, it just kind of slipped out unnoticed, and I was driving 55 down a different life.

At each bump, the car seat squeaked loudly beneath me. The sound of it has also been a constant in the eight years I have been married. It sometimes became so loud, I thought it would pull loose and bounce me right out the window. John was always trying to oil, or tighten the bits and pieces underneath. I liked it. I always felt like I was riding along on a fair ride, the squeaks and groans following me down the roads everywhere I went. It was a language of complaints. It said. "Don't drive that fast. Take turns slower. Loose ten pounds. Why'd you have to take that way? I'm tired. Fix me. Oil me. Don't ignore me..."

It was a natural opening for me to tell it my own problems as we drove along. Why should I leave a terrible job— I'd only have to spend energy looking for another one— and that one could turn out to be worst? Why watch what I eat— I'll only put it back on— Why should I care? What would be the point of it all? Eventually, I learned to turn up the volume, with the radio, or out-loud talking, and to tune out all the 'whys' in my head. It was just that easy.

The person I was ten years ago had all about slipped away. And the person I was fifteen years ago I couldn't even remember. Something had to be done. I'd felt it for a long time, but simply couldn't bring myself to change one single bit of my life before this point. When I left college, I was supposed to become a full fledged, working artist. There wasn't a person back then, that doubted I would be successful at being just-that. They said I would make it. Said, I had what it took, that my work would take me far. But somewhere crossing those steps, leading down the front entryway, and crossing a mere three state lines to return home, I had decided not to believe them, and choose the futility's over the possibilities.

Strange how a simple change in direction can inspire fear. Already I could feel my stomach twisting in unseen knots, in worries and un-thought-of consequences. "So what?" I tried to fend off the feelings, pretend nothing mattered, as though I were like the land, protecting my insides, bending down over the stirring wheel. Held tight. "It's not like anybody cares what I do. Do they?" I answered myself. The car seat squeaked louder, bouncing. *Do-they? Do-they? Do-they?* It repeated.

For each day that I had lived and dreamed in school— I died triple, beneath the eyes of time clocks, electric bills, and the expectations of a thousand grabbing hands on my time. Life as I thought it would be, slowly and painfully slipped out across the cement cracked streets, into blazing hot, Florida skies, that cooked up my dreams and ate them. I could not remember the person I was fifteen years ago. That dream lie in the gullet of a giant, wind swept bird.

5

His face was a curved, yellow-old mirror. Tiny cracks pulled at the skin on each side, the edges worn smooth, reflective. The face of a stranger.

Around the eyes, finely drawn arrows turned in like clock numbers. Looking in a direction, from two o'clock or four—the eyes had a particular expression marking time. But it was the three to nine shifting, the sly time between the two, viewing me in the center at one second intervals that caused me to keep my distance. I felt sure he could see through to the back of my head, through my eyes, and I knew I should close them before he saw too much.

I began wondering, how did I get myself into this—watching those eyes, feeling the back of my neck, beads of sweat rolling down my face. I squinted to keep an eye on him. His were like two matches burned down to the end, threatening to the surrounding areas, looking for something to catch fire. Yellow and gold in the sunlight, shimmering as cat's eyes do. Something about the eyes of old people, how they could see from two places at once, from somewhere back then, to here now. It gave off the effect of knowing twice as much when they looked without speaking. I had the feeling he was doing that to me. Telling me something from just his eyes. From the way the light hit, I wasn't very sure I wanted to know what it was.

"I'm Katherine." I said, "—glad to meet you."

The eyes lessened their intensity, deciding something. Judging as if a scale, twelve to six— moving up and down, and back. The arrows were shiny. Oiled like clock-work pieces.

Beside him was Annie, not as much a stranger, and not as old. She stood, smiling and shaking her head. "Katherine is a painter." she said. "She'll be staying in number four. Katherine, this is your neighbor, Harold Amos Tenor."

He didn't move. Staring again, just over the top of my head. I brushed aside wet hair, looked at Annie instead. It was a relief to look at her. All soft edges, warm eyes, not fire gold, like his. Hers were dark, bay colored, laughing bright. "Amos..." she said. "Quit giv'n the girl the stare. You'll frighten her off before she's had a chance to settle in." He didn't move to look at her, and I had the odd sensation I was getting smaller, shrinking to the size of a ten year old. She planted both hands on her hips, rolled back her eyes, started laughing. "Don't worry." She looked at me. "He can hear just fine. His head just don't always get the message."

Annie was a round woman, with tiny arms and tiny feet. She rolled on the heels of her shoes as she stood looking at him. With each expression her features changed. One moment she was birdlike, a delicate finch in the way she tilted her head to speak, the next moment, with a hearty laugh and slap of her hands she was a loaf of fresh baked bread, brought out steaming hot and rising with a robust expression and sound, at once familiar and inviting. She could move incredibly fast, as I'd seen when she first gave me a tour of the place a week ago. With her white jogging shoes, twin red racing stripes down the sides, she'd fly over the sand and oyster shells beneath her. She had suggested that I bring a pair. She had been very thoughtful about suggestions on how to make my stay here comfortable.

In appearance, he was just the opposite of her. He stood about two feet past her head, and was all miles of tanned skin and bones. White hair hung down straight, just touching the tops of his shoulders. He stood very still beside her, and slightly hunched, as though the wind might be balancing him in an upright position, and had two of the largest hands I'd ever seen. They hung suspended at his sides, fingers wide apart, waiting.

"She's going to have herself some relaxin' time away from the crowds and noise of the other side." Annie told him. She wagged a finger under his nose. "I know you can hear me in there. Let her be—or I'll put you out." She threatened him, smiling, then turned back her warmth towards me. "Come on, I'll show you in." She hop-skipped past and started down the beach, white shoes kicking up sand as she went. "I opened up the windows this morning—" she went on, chirping back blissfully in her small bird face. I gave him one last look, then carefully followed. He was an ancient massive tree and I was Dorothy in Oz who had just picked the unlucky apple. "The sea air should have brushed her clean by now." Annie's voice pulled me along.

"I hope you like the salt air? There's an awful lot here to take in." Following after her, I was still trying to decide if I'd made a mistake. All I could think of was the silent Amos propped up against the wind.

As she reached the cottage, she flew up the four front steps, and was brushing some dead palm branches off the porch. It rattled loudly as she kicked it off. "Dang wind," she was saying to herself. "Can't keep nothing where it belongs, always blowin' things around, stirrin' up the dead." The place was small, very old, the paint that had once covered the wood, long gone except what was left in the cracks. It was situated just enough distance from the water to keep dry when the waves rolled up on the shore. It sat on cement stilts two feet above the ground. Underneath, a graveyard of oyster shells and branches could be seen through the wooden porch slats. At the front of the cottage, there were two small windows. One of the panes was missing and had an old piece of tin shoved into it's place. Lopsided, it looked like a giant patched eye that rattled when the wind blew against it.

Huge, green fists of leaves waved over the tops of everything, roof, porch, sand paths on either side. Everything was topped in green and midmorning shadow. With the air hot and dry, the feel of the brittle wood steps, every crevice filled with sand, and covering all of this, the wide canopy of green, I imagined for a moment I might be in a desert garden. I stood looking up at all this, trying to let it sink in; let it fill up some part of me. "I've lived here my whole life," I said to her. She was fishing in one of her pockets, apparently searching for the key. "Not this close to the water, but close enough, to smell it on a good day." She was busy pulling out all sorts of things from her pocket, but no key. "Annie..." I said. She insisted I call her that, wouldn't even give me a last name to call her by. Said to stay, a person has to call you by the name that mattered most. She had never known a Katherine. She had said it several times out loud, tasting the sound of it. Said it had a nice way of rolling of the tongue. Told me she was sure it tasted something like mint tea. "I could look for someplace else to stay. If this is an inconvenience or anything." I was thinking about Amos and looking for an excuse not to stay.

"Oh don't be silly." she said. A large ring of keys was finally pulled out. "Amos is just havin' his fun. He's doing what he calls, readin' a person. He likes to do that to my guests when they first arrive. I think he does it to put the fear in them. Make sure they don't do anything up to no good." She lauqhed. "I keep telling him he can't tell nothin' by starin' at a person. But he says the only reason we're still here, is cause he's kept all the psychos out. 'Word of mouth', he says— *gets around.*" She was trying out each of the keys in the door. "I say, the only thing getting 'round here, is that I keep up a crazy, old koon who should be locked up for starin' at people as if he had no sense. But don't worry, once your here for a spell, he won't mind you at all."

"If you're sure?"

"Sure as pie." She tilted her head towards his direction. "Just give him some distance for awhile. It'll wear off him. You're lucky. Some folks he doesn't take too with his stare. And he gets started in with a dose of *'clearin'*. Clears them out all right. Right out of a payin' stay. Yellin' a lot of nonsense and such. You can't understand a word he says. And with him hollerin' up a storm in their tracks like he was a devil. He doesn't do that too often. But boy, it sure is a sight to see." She pointed back towards the dock. "See that rat nest pile out there? Sticks, shells, rocks—Lord knows what else. That's his. Just leave that alone, and you'll have no problem. It's his collection. He's an artist too. Very temperamental though. Carves things. Maybe he'll show you some of his work sometime?"

"How long have these houses been here?" I asked. She stopped trying the keys to think about my question.

"My husband and I built here— it would be about forty— forty three years ago. Back then, we had ten rentals. Lost a few over the years to the weather."

The tin window rattled in a strong gust of wind. I laid a hand against the frame. When I took it away, paint chips blew off. "Sixteen years longer than I was born." I said. Another lifetime older. I ran my fingers over the wood, carefully, as one would an antique in a shop. Anything that existed before me was something of a treasure. If it had lasted this long, a feeling of legacy, simple survival, made it special. I liked old things and places, even old people, if they didn't have fire eyes, stared back too closely, too near.

"Tom, that was my husband's name." Annie said. "This place was his treasure. His place to be. He'd rebuild them every time the wind or water tore them down, until he just got too old to keep it up. Four is all that's left now. Every day, from the day we first moved here, he would go out and walk this shore, just down that way. Once every morning, and once in the evening. He called it his 'daily prayer to God." I looked at the shore below. The water washed in around the rocks where a group of seagulls stood, calling out loudly to each other.

"The Lord took him just five years back." she said. She was looking out at the water, smiling. "He always said we had ourselves a piece of heaven right here." For a moment she was quiet, lost in her own thoughts. "He knew when he was about to go. He told me I didn't have to stay, that I could sell it and move up state to live with our son. And I did think about it for a while, after he was gone. But I just couldn't bring myself to do it. It took me about twenty years to know this place as he did. Now it's apart of me too. He's still here, in heaven, singin' on the wind. His footprints down there, say'n the Lord's Prayer. One day I might leave, but not yet."

She seemed smaller than before. Her presence was loosing its stranger quality, and I was beginning to feel I knew her, or at least a part of her. It was her voice, low, as though it came from some place deep, a steady tide that swelled upwards with heavy sounds. I liked the way her words filled out, with rich full sounds. I decided right there, that I liked this person, Annie.

"I appreciate you letting me stay here. And I'll be sure and stay out of Mr. Tenor's way—"

"Amos" she said.

"Amos's way."

"He'll warm up. Just wait. It's a strange way of meeting people. But it's his."

"I hope so."

"I'll make sure of it." Then she smiled a secret smile, unlocked the door, and handed me the key. "If you need anything, I live in the first house down the way. Amos has the second one. The third is empty at the moment. This one has the best view of the ocean and the bay. I thought you'd like it best for your painting. Just holler if there's a problem—or you need anything."

"Only time." I said.

"Plenty of that. Take all you want."

"I will. Thanks." And with that she was speeding back down the beach, leaving her deep tennis shoe marks in one long straight line behind her.

I stood where I was for a few moments, unable to turn and cross the threshold. This new life was beginning to feel nice. I didn't know how to handle that. Guilt started to form around the edges, hard crusted, encompassing. I wished John could be here too. Hurting him was the only regret I had. I wished he could be here. This was the first time in eight years I'd ever really been without him. I closed my eyes for a moment. If I could just get through the first couple of days, I'll make it. But I hurt all over— guilt magnified to fit around every thought, made me heavy.

Out across the bay the sun was setting. It fell along the horizon in a dying, fire red. I held my breath as the last glowing crest sank below the water, off the edge of the world. *It has grown tired of me too.* I thought, and was turning away, closing in a bank of clouds.

"No..." I said to it. "You're not leaving me. I've left you."

Cerulean Blue.

The edge of the world. I step off the shore, off the edge of a continent, into something different.

I turn and look back at my mother. There, lying on shore, burned red, staring dead up at the sun, my mother was a few feet from here, and a hundred worlds away. I turn from her and dive under the water, flying

36

away fast. She is a foreign land, too strange to comprehend, best to set sail for something else.

Instantly, swimming hard, with effort to stay below the surface, I skim the sandy bottom. It is a constant struggle to stay below. Not like fish, who cut through the water with flattened sail bodies, who hovered or glided on watery breezes. My body wanted to float. Head pointed downward, feet trailing above. Or feet down, head pulled up, as though it were filled with air, and the space between my ears, a balloon. I want to sail along the bottom like a fish. Instead, I jab below the surface, like a spear, only to find myself rising again and again. I am anchored to the sky and air. No matter how hard I try. I cannot be a fish. I cannot embed myself into the invisible ocean heart.

I stay under the water as long as I can, rising when I have to fill my lungs, then retreating back to my other world, happy to float weightless, wrapped in the shifting light and sandy veils. A sting ray is hiding, just there, laying beneath the sand like a pancake. It's tail stretched out to a sharp point, almost invisible, with only a slight ridge showing against the bottom. I watch as a puff of sand explodes above it, then a dark wing shape heading for deeper water.

"Kath-eee..." a voice cuts through the layers around me, sounding very far off. I ignore it. The sounds break, falling in pieces through the water. "Kath-e!- You- have- to- watch- Jes- sie-"

Digging my hands deep into the sand, I try to hold myself at the bottom, face the deeper ocean. Out there, where I'm not big enough to swim—dark places, where I know I wouldn't be able to see, even if I could. Nothing moves. No beckoning response. No sign where the sting ray had flown. Just blueness, stretching into blackness.

A gust of wind slaps me hard in the face as I surface.

"Kathy— now!" My mother's voice. "Now—" Her beet red body charges the surf. "Don't make me come out there and get you!"

I swim slowly to the shore keeping the water at my chin, walking crab fashion beneath the water when I touch sand, purposely slow. Her large body sways against the bright sky. Hands on hips, feet planted apart, neck stiff and pulled in like a turtles. I see her anger dancing around her like a flame, giving her the illusion of movement, as if she were a crumpled up piece of paper thrown into a fireplace. The flames lick up her dry sides, eating up her limbs as they bend and distort under hot orange tongues of her bathing suit. She is gone in a moment, her life extinguished in the time it takes me to reach the shore. She has gone without another word to me, to lie back down on the sand.

The ocean puddles around my feet, running down my legs and arms over chill bumped skin. Jessie looks up at me. Her face is small, oblivious in her other-worldliness, a four-year-old's face. For a long moment I don't move, just watch the way my shadow cuts across the center, between nose and chin. She squints, sand dots on both cheeks, breathing loud child-sized breaths through her nose. She laughs at me staring at her. Two bright, blue eyes, the color of Blue Jay feathers, dark against the lighter, draw me back from the invisible edge where I stood— where once it seemed, I stood, then ran, then flew to some other, darker place.

6

"We always have our breakfast out here, weather permitting." Annie said.

I stepped up on the dock carefully. She and Amos sat in two rocking chairs, between them a lantern on a small table, with breakfast laid out in it's circle of light. "Come on over." she said. "Have a seat." Their shadows, as they rocked, ran back and forth across the wood. I moved to sit at the side, leaning against an old dock post nearest Annie. "So how was your first night?" she asked. "Not too hot, I hope? It gets mighty hot if you're not used to it. Most people 'round here swear they can't live without their air conditioner. Don't step outside all summer long I suppose." She took a sip of coffee, pressed a cloth against her neck, dabbed gently. Next to her, Amos, who was still not saying anything and staring, not at me, but out to the dark horizon, over the distant city's direction. His rocking chair groaned at the joints, slowly, steadily. "Tom didn't trust the 'cool air'." Annie went on. "Never had any put in. I guess I might do it one day. But then people in the old days didn't have air conditioners and they managed. Would you like some coffee? It might be too strong for you. We drink it black with no sugar and no cream. I have some milk though—"

I said no.

"We were just getting ready—" she said, glanced over at Amos. "—to say good morning."

I took out an orange I had brought, offering some first to Annie, then to Amos. He didn't look at my held out hand or at me.

"Amos—" Annie said. "Amos!" She rolled up a paper and smacked him on the knee. "Amos, Katherine is talkin' to you."

He moved only a little. "Who?" he asked.

"Katherine, here. She's asking if you want any?"

"Who's Katherine?"

"Our guest. She's sitting right beside you."

"Oh. I thought she wasn't going to be here till next Friday?"

"No, she's here now."

"When she get here?"

"She just got here."

"Oh." he said again, and continued to stare straight ahead

"Don't mind him." Annie told me. "He's being stubborn this morning."

I peeled back the tough skin, separated the pieces, took a bite, looked around at my first morning. It was still too dark to really see. But I could hear the shore birds, the waves hitting against the dock posts, the rocking chairs. Annie sipped coffee, fanned herself. Amos sat rubbing the ends of his elbows, staring still. Out across the water, a slight glow was just beginning to form at the horizon, over the tops of the trees. "There she is—" Amos then said, pulled himself up from his chair. A smile rose on his face too.

Quickly, Annie reached over and turned off the portable light. "There she is." she answered him. Her face, barely lit, I could just make out that she winked an eye at me.

Having straightened himself up, pressed down his shirt front as though he were about to meet someone, Amos said, his voice hardly a whisper, "*Mother...* it's nice to see you today. You're looking fine as ever."

I squinted at the rising sun, then back at him, then at her. She just rocked and fanned, smiling at me as though she knew I would figure it out. "*She* sure does, Amos." she said.

Only when the sun had completely risen above the horizon, over the trees and reflected water, did he sit back down. Then he said, "How 'bout it Annie? Here we are again."

"Yep." she answered. "Another day, and I still have to look at your grumpy, old face."

"Won't be too much longer now."

"Whatever you say..." She poured herself another cup of coffee, then said to me, "This is just a little something we do everyday. To make sure we're still alive and kicking." Amos took a piece of toast from the table and took a large, noisy bite. "Every morning and every evening at sunset you'll find us right out here. We'd welcome your company if you're up. Don't hesitate to come on down."

"Sure." I said.

"As long as Amos here sees the sun, he thinks everything in the world can be right. Or at least he's still here to say it is anyway." She looked at him, but he was busy working on a bowl of strawberries.

I felt very out of place and wished I could think of something to say. "You know," I said hesitantly, afraid of sounding stupid, but going ahead anyway under the circumstances, "When I was a child, I thought the sun had two sides." Glanced briefly at Amos. "At night, I believed it turned inside itself and looked out the other side and became the moon... and lit up the sky like a night-light."

Amos put down the coffee pot he had picked up. He swung around and looked straight at me. "Why Katherine—" he said, as though seeing me for the first time. "How's it going? God, it's been a long time."

Annie laughed. Shook her head, as though she just couldn't believe him sometimes.

"Good to see ya, Amos" I said.

"Have some coffee." he said. "You like it with a little cream right?" It was true, I did. "Thought so." he said and began pouring some in a third mug. "Now, what's this I hear about you— you're a painter?"

7

The shadows of seagulls pass over me and I look up to see them fly silently past only ten feet away. They each landed on an ancient post reaching out of the water. I had made my way through the woods, without reaching the ocean or finding the old paths that Annie had told me of. The seagulls, I imagined, knew the way. They could fly there and back. They had returned now to watch me, sitting on their perches over the bay. Their knowing cries rose and fell like laughter in the shimmering, midday heat.

Once to right, and once to the left, the shore unraveled it's speckled fabric of sand and shell. Through tall, stiff cat-tails, over piles of driftwood, with each step, my ankles would sink into holes, made loud sucking sounds when I pulled away. Small trees stood in the water, roots exposed, and I had to hold onto the tops of growing things to walk without slipping. Black mud covered the bottom of my shoes.

It had been years since I walked in white sand, seen the rough, blue waves of the other side. The unmistakable scent of Gulf waters drifted over the bay. In the distance, behind me, it was visible where the bay opened to it.

I reached down and took off my shoes, sloshed them back and forth in the water. It was much hotter than before, so I waded out in the shallow water, knee deep, back in the direction I had come before. More laughing gulls passed overhead. Behind them, dark clouds were beginning to form. I imagined they were responsible for this too, so I kept my eyes on the land, ignored them, waited for the rain.

Just inside the trees to my right, standing tall and unmoving between the reeds and cattails was a heron. The blue and gray mixture of it's body was a color I craved. In front of me were sandpipers looking for food, white, like the seagulls, but smaller. They stepped through the shallow's edge, racing up ahead of me, poked their long black beaks into the water as they went.

When I stood still, like the heron, and the reeds and the leaning posts, I could hear things I hadn't heard before. First far away, then up close. Sounds that fell together, pulsing and clicking, and buzzing, rising in a stream of sound that filled the scorching hot air with a hypnotizing rhythm. It was as though I had become invisible to nature, and for one moment she had forgotten I was there, and gone about her business, singing and growing, unaware that I could hear her. I could easily feel apart of this...I thought to myself. A seedling thought, small and insignificant.

Around me, the past pulled up, like a line cut loose of it's anchor. Memories returned— of what it was like, revealing another time, similar surroundings. I am a child again and my sisters are with me. We are at a place where the wind carried the sound of our voices away, running through the grasses, tumbling down dunes. Our squeals of falling head first down the hills of sand could easily be mistaken for the sound of seagulls. Where, if Karen reached out, hidden in a mass of sea oats and scratches, animal-like, at my leg, I could yank her out and make a run for it, stay hidden among the soft, warm sides of another dune. Or we could all three take off running to jump over invisible cliffs to fall safely, buried up to our ankles, or knees, in the sand below. Jessie was the biter, the best defense for the youngest. Karen pulled hair and I was always the fastest runner with the longest legs. It was hard to tell if we were fighting or playing.

Overhead, sounds of thunder. I knew I should go back. It was dangerous to be out here in a storm. I went back up to the shore, sat down to put my shoes on, watched the heron fly off over the water, then back towards shore, in the direction of the ocean. I could remember looking away, even then, my eyes following the line of the shore, as far as I could see, wishing I could follow it. *Away.* But what did that mean? I didn't know if there was such a thing. How far was it? Where did it go? To my eye, the shore traveled to an ever sharpening point, beyond what I could see, or know.

Even now, I did not know where it led.

Cadmium Yellow.

"Do fish breath?" Jessie asks me.

"Yes." I tell her. "They breath water."

"Can you breath water?"

"No. I have to hold my breath."

"Will I ever be able to do that?"

"You will have to wait till you're bigger. You'd be just a little pebble out there in those waves. That current probably suck you right out in a second. How would I be able to find you then?"

"I'd yell real loud."

"Wouldn't be loud enough. The ocean sucks out sound too. Makes everything different and funny sounding. Do you know what whales sound like? Like, lost babies. So many babies get washed out there, crying terribly. The whales hear 'em, remember it. Cry for the lost babies that no one hears and has to leave behind."

"I'm not a baby." she says, squints upwards with pink checks and nose.

"How would I be able to tell out there? You just wait till you're bigger."

She said, after thinking this over, "I want to build a castle."

"The sand's too wet here. We'll have to look for a better place."

Jessie pulls herself up, her yellow and white one piece bathing suit sagging at the bottom. She takes her shovel in one hand and her pail in the other. Her legs are sugar coated and red.

"Kathee...Katheee!" Karen yells out from the water behind us. I do not turn around to look at the two sets of dragon eyes I know are floating there. One pair red, enormously drawn eyes of plastic, the other green, with a crooked grin stretched across from corner to corner, laughing at me because I have to stay on shore and watch Jessie.

We walk down the beach until we find a small pond left by the surf. Cut off from the rest of the water, it is filled with minnows. Jessie's shadow cast over the silver flecks swimming in all directions at once. "Here fishy, fishy..." she says to them.

The sand was claiming back it's territory. It was too late for some of the minnows. They lay dead. Their little bodies dried up like bacon, sunken-in places where their eyes used to be. Some of the minnows were lying on their sides flopping around, as if the earth, had just that second, sucked up the last of the water through a straw somewhere underneath. Jessie reaches out tentatively to touch one that was stranded by her foot. It jumps and so does she.

"They won't bite." I say, and show her to prove it. "See...they're just trying to get back to the water."

She sniffs and puckers her face. "It smells." she says.

I flip a few by me into the water. I know it won't make much difference for long. They swim in shallow circles, looking for ways out in between the grass blades, became stranded again. Soon all the water will be gone. All the minnows will be cut off. The land will claim back their dead bodies left here by the ocean, and turn them into dust, and sunken in places of it's own.

"Let's build your castle." I say.

Out in the water, Karen riding the waves on her dragon, lets loose a yell of joy.

The body on shore turns over again.

I scope up an armful of sand and begin building my first wall.

8

Flashes of light shattered the gray sky. Rolling thunder sounds, electric fear that tingled my skin in it's own lightning swiftness, with each clash the feeling shot through me, through every nerve and bone. I moved up to higher ground, made a flat place on the grass, laid down on it, looked up at charcoal-black clouds. The hot smell of rain was so thick, it felt like a blanket across my skin. When the rain started, I felt this too, through my clothes, over chill-bump skin, hitting me from hundreds of raindrop size places. Inside, they felt like a hundred tiny wounds, soft bruises. With eyes closed, I imagined little hands pounding away at my skin.

How can I heal them all? I wondered.

"You can't." comes the answering voice. *Vincent's.*

"Then why try?" I turn and look beside me, imaging I see him. He looks back thoughtful and knowing.

"To feel." he said. Rain is settling in his eyes. It runs down his face, into soft green places.

Another flash of lightning. This time I don't jump.

"How do I feel?"

He looks up into the rain, thinks a moment, then says, *"First with your eyes."*

I look up too. I let the rain fall there without closing them.

"Then with your hands."

I feel the wet grass under my fingers. I pull it into a handful and hold it tight.

"Then with your heart."

I turn to him. He is gone. I let go of the grass.

"I don't know how to do that." I said. "I don't have a heart, remember?"

. . .

Words come naturally as I look closely into brushstrokes of shadow and highlight, signature markings of raised paint, like fingerprints. Techniques of impasto, chiaroscuro, glazes, skin tones— I could not get enough of looking, imagining that if I could peer long enough, and close enough, I would be able to see back to the moment it was created.

I fell into looking, right down to the last page. When I was done, I felt skimmed across, like a pebble over a pond. There was the recognizable, plop, plop, plop, disappearing underneath, and I was added to. Breathing in their histories, following the scent of oils and pigment, turpentine, primed canvas, the lines of my thought become the lines of their chalk as they sketch out their next creation. They are my teachers and I am their hungry student.

Certain artists I am drawn too for reasons that cannot be expressed by words alone. Their paintings hold me and we have conversations together. It is in French pastures I see Lenardo Da Vinci. Paul Gaugain is sitting on the steps of his hut in Tahitti. On her rooftop is Georgia O'Keefe, behind, a background of Southwest mesas, Indian colors. Mary Cassat is in the parlor, painting her brother's children. And Vincent Van Gogh, he is always alone, wandering through the dunes of Aries, or walking down a country path, carrying his sketchbook, smiling sometimes, mostly just looking in amazement at all he sees. I follow him, watching as he goes along. When he sees me, he smiles and we walk together. It is as though we have always been friends, walking together, talking about the colors of different leaves.

All I have to do is call his name, a whisper— *"Vincent..."* and I am gone from this life to his.

"I'm here—" a voice in the distance will call out.

. . .

"The water will catch fire and pour towards us like melted butter." Annie said. Unlike the sunrise, which was mostly over land, she promised the setting was a prize to be had. The sky was already darkening with pink and oranges. Coffee was poured, rockers rocking. Amos took out a long pipe to smoke. Annie was wiping up spilled coffee that had dripped down the side of her cup. I held mine in my hands feeling the warmth, relaxed back in my chair, let the rich tobacco smell, the scent of rain that had passed earlier, the moist air of approaching night— all tie itself together under my nose.

"Since you will be with us for a while, you'll get to meet my grand-daughters." Annie said to me. "Coming down from Nevada."

"Oh boy." Amos said less than enthusiastic.

"Oh *girls.*" Annie corrected him. "Two of them. Identical twins."

"Double trouble." Amos puffed. A line of smoke circled around his head.

"Hush. You love them girls like they were your own."

"I don't admit to any such a thing." he said.

"They make you six years old the minute they walk in that door."

"Six was not a good time for me. I prefer sixty."

"Sixty, my foot." she said. Then to me, she says, "They are sweet as they can be. Even if they only have a father to raise them for it. My son has done a fine job. Divorced three years and they're still running fine."

"Men don't make good mothers." Amos said.

"If you pinch them, you could make a cake from the sugar that pours out."

"You pourin' on the sugar some." he said.

She crossed her arms, hugging herself across the middle. "Sure— I'm a grandmother. I'm intitl'n to be."

"He's a fine boy." Amos said, reached down to tap the pipe over the rim of his foot.

"He is." Annie agreed. "We'll all be children again when they're here."

"I don't recall you talking about a nice childhood." Amos said to her.

"That don't mean I can't have a good one now."

"Pigtails and jump ropes."

"Well not that much. Just the feelings. And the way of seeing things the way they do."

"Maybe Katherine don't want to be a kid?"

"You don't have to, if you don't want, honey."

"Childhood was not something I'd want to relive." I said.

Amos stated towards Annie's direction, "Katherine does not like pigtails and jumping rope."

"No" I said. "I do not like the feelings."

"Well," Annie said. "Then you go ahead and be grown up like you are. They get along just as well with that. Joseph will be on with you. Serious type. Takes after his father."

"Katherine- does- not- like- games." Amos said, stated each word precisely. "She has better things to do."

As the sun fell lower, Amos laid his pipe on the ground beside him and stood up. With hands together, he reached out toward the sun as if to catch it. His voice trembled, as he whispered, "*Mother*". Then his hands, caught by the wind, fell back to his side, slowly, a released embrace. Annie rocked and smiled, sharing the feeling and vision with him. There was sadness in his word this time, as if having to say good-by again was almost too much to bare.

In me, there is the same sense. That it is almost too much to bare. But it is without the soft feeling Amos has in his voice. I am glad when the last bit of light is gone from the sky. I don't want them to see me. I might reveal too much. Things that can't be taken back, once out.

. . .

I drove to the nearest corner store and waited in front of the pay phone. I stared at it as though John might call on his own, just at that moment, knowing I was there. I even got out of the car, walked over and picked it up.

I listened to the sound. Constant, continuous, mono sound. It sounded like a heart monitor in a hospital. A flatline. Somebody was dead, it said. The heart had ceased to speak. Only the alarm on the monitor was just a warning in some cases. People could be brought back to life. I held the phone wondering if some stranger's soul might pass by, pick up on the other side? A ghostly voice asking, *Who is this?*

When I'm not with John, he is like a ghost. He ceased to be real. "John...", I said into the cradled phone, even though no one was there. I saw my voice being squeezed into the space of the telephone wire. Traveling to him through miles of suspended web across the city, creeping into his head as he answered. He'd hear my voice, wonder why I still walked the earth?

I hung up the phone. I wasn't ready for him to hear me so clearly, so close. I'd go back, if I did. He'd call me back, and I would leave this place. I couldn't risk going back yet. I was still *dead.*

9

A t one time, my mother was the space around me. The inner walls of her flesh pushed in against me, held me in place. As I grew to put my newly made ears up against her tender places, I could hear the red tides of blood that ran through her and me, washing us together of impure and unnecessary things. And, even after I had long been in the outside world, she was still the same swirling, moving space around me. Invisible, but felt, holding me in place, pushing against me. Still, I could hear the blood rising. Between every breath we stood connected. I am trapped in orbit around her, caught in her Saturn rings, circling, shimmering debris. A hand shoots out to grab me back if I move away. Gravitational pull, strong and suffocating. Where the constant weight of unseen things will pull you crashing back in a fiery grasp, if you are not fast enough and strong enough to get away. To break free is to fly. Better than a bird flies. So much, much better.

. . .

Annie's smile pulled the strongest.

I studied it for possibilities. The subtle areas that made a smile—smile, or the eyes laugh. The charcoal lines suggested these things, but painting them would be very difficult. I traced the edge of her face with my finger. Maybe facing forward a little more, so that both eyes were seen? Her youthful smile, her gray-black hair just touching shoulders, turned forward, laughing at something unseen, the bay beyond, some trees to the left side— warm colors, sun-lit edges.

I wondered if I would be able to do it? Could I throw myself into it? Would I know instinctively what colors to choose, what brush size would work the best? In my head I could see it perfectly. It was deceptively simple. Even a dark frame already surrounded it, contrasted beautifully with the warm colors. And there is the feeling that I have completed it already, the work over, the struggle done. Then slowly, moving backwards to see how I might have arrived at this point— How did I get those skin tones just right? Were there mistakes? Did I manage to cover up the bad choices? How did I finally get the nose right? Noses are very difficult things. The shape had to be balanced between the eyes, the angle just right, and the place—under the nose, over the lips, that curve was also difficult to create— too harsh a line would ruin the whole face, age her by twenty years.

"Don't—" I told myself. "Don't think about it." Outside it was night time again. Another day wasted. The wind picked up, filled the room with the smell of the bay.

I always thought of cities as tired places, worn out like people. I closed my eyes and imagined the city dropping off it's sweat beside the bay, blowing out it's exhaustion as a breeze, flooding sorrows, occasional joy, down muddy banks, into the brown, shallow tides and washes. As a child, I liked to breath it in and hold it on my tongue. I held the taste of it now, tried to picture my own sorrows sliding off into the darkness, let my mind take off it's heavy burden and just exist, like a seabird, or a dolphin. I would not mind a sleek dolphin body, fitting in between the waves, swimming fast under the moon at night. For one moment, I felt the sensation of moving fast, water sliding against smooth skin, weaving myself between water and air.

Shadows jumped back and forth over the walls. The lamp shade tilted on a loose screw. "Too hot to think." I said to myself, lifted up the shirt end so the wind would blow underneath. It puffed up several times, but left me hot as before. I rubbed the damp place over my stomach.

This place, under my skin— nothing inside now, but one day a soul would be there, growing little fingers, little toes, pulsing heart no bigger than a fingernail. Would I feel it? I wondered. A life growing inside me? I pictured John's hand touching my stomach, saying things close so that the baby could hear. What would he feel with his hands on either side. A rounded, filled out me? Now the skin was flat. I could feel each rib, see down to my toes. My breasts were not mother-sized, but they were warm and soft. Holding the pillow against my skin I could imagine what it would be like. Or making a baby, holding John. So tender. He was always watching my eyes, always wanting to know what I felt. I knew he wanted children. He had said it before.

"What names would you pick?" he asked me. But I could not imagine names. All I could see were two baby eyes looking at me— needing more than names, more than clothes and changing, feeding times, a proper way to hold, to kiss, rock to sleep. More than what I could ever give. A name was an avalanche of meaning I was not ready for.

"I can't think of any." I said to him.

He had several lined up on each side, girls and boy names. Solid names of his future faces. Jonathan, Patrick, Michael, Grace, Hannah, or Michelle. He smiled as though he could already see them. They came easily out of him, his family, our love. Togetherness.

I could think of many reasons to wait, just a little longer. I didn't feel old enough. I didn't know enough. I turned on my side, looked out the window. Somewhere, he must be lying in bed, wondering if there ever will be a when? "I don't know." I said, held onto the pillow, tried to feel comfort in it. Looked out into the darkness, the stars, the sound of waves. Maybe if I knew Annie's easy smile? Maybe, then? I hugged the pillow tighter, thought of it as John, my chin sunk down into it's middle.

I knew I was here to run away. Not to decide, or choose. But to be suspended from all those things that I was a part of. I was not here to remember if I could paint. I had run out into the darkness, in a place where night was really night, no streetlights, or kitchen lights left on for the one who had to work late, no porch light here. *Waiting.*

To see what? To see if I would go back? To waiting unnamed babies, waiting husband, waiting jobs that would pay the bills. All this was out there. I was here, half naked, laying next to an open window, looking out at stars. Lonely. But then, everything in it's difference, was lonely, in it's isolation in being what it was.

I was as yet, nothing.

No such thing, as nothing...

A star then. Hovering, bright star, beyond this place I was born to— *Grandfather's stars.*

But loneliness descends in me even more at this thought. No matter how close together the stars were in the sky— they were still, thousands of light years apart. Surrounded in the vast, swirling, darkness of space.

10

"You're a *southerner.*" Annie said. "Storytelling is as natural as breathing to folks here. Only three kinds of people does it best— the old, the very young, and Southerners! It comes out as it should with them, without too much effort, or reason. Just a good place to sit, and someone to sit with." She made herself comfortable, settled back deep in her chair, the arms molding into her on each side, looked out towards the horizon. "What good is a life untold?" she asked. "It disappears like the morning fog. No one sees just when it goes. It just does.

"Sometimes when I sit out here at night, I can hear their words. In-between the crickets and the waves, set back on the silence— a whisper that says, everything that was, is, and will be. The same questions a girl asked her mama a hundred years ago, are still asked today. The same fear. Same doubt. Same longing. Nothin's new 'round here. Just looks different.

"Alive." she said. "In it's people. Living memories of good times and bad. With the slow, heavy heat simmering each generation, letting it rise up through the tall pines on cool mornings, pushing it up over the damp banks, over dunes in it's stormy seasons. Its people become a part of the land here, forming it, reshaping it to be their own— Look over there at those trees. Can you see the residue and sap of those who were here just before us? The air we breath is made up of their spoken words. This sand was once the road they walked down. This shade, the very same they sat under. That bark is written with the language of time, theirs and ours. Makes every word I've said, already come out one way or 'nother. Said before. Their voice— mine, overlapping in the grooves. *That's* storytelling."

"Some's just not worth it." I said. "Telling or knowing."

She only laughed. "They're all worth something. But—" She cocked her head away, looked at me from the side. "Some things just need to be said. Have a way of finding a way out, even if you don't want 'em to." She grinned slow, eyes reflecting off the water. "Things closed up under a lid, stay good only for a certain time. Then turn bad, and have to be thrown out."

I pulled out paints and lined them in order. Nothing was coming out of me. I wouldn't let it. Not one word. Positioned easel for best light.

"This place is a southern place. Warms the soul when it's lost. That's Tom saying that." she said. "Warms the soul..." she said again more slowly. "I'd say that to you."

I smiled but didn't say anything. Took out several brushes. Lined them in order of size.

"My story," she then said. "Comes from a place that was not home, or heaven. Just a beginning place, where I was a little girl running barefoot across wide, smooth, country fields. I had neither mother, nor father. God had taken them early, when I was just three or so..."

Choosing my colors, by the sound of her voice, and the movement of light across her skin, I began with the foundation planes of her face. Painting the hills and valleys between the rise of her forehead, and the graceful slope of her dark neck, down her two arms resting on the chair. She looked out over the shore that was now her home, a smile half drawn on her face. Memories appearing just over the crest of her eyes. She watched an old life play out again. Showing me how a person's story comes out, without too much effort, or reason.

"A neighbor woman took me in to raise with her own children." she began. "She already had three girls and two boys. They were old enough to be working on the farm, so she took me in to help with the house. I was the youngest then, and not liked much by my new siblings. They took me in stride, as something they had to live with. Like having chicken pox, or the measles, they figured I'd go away at some point.

"Trouble started, when I found God— or God found me, or more like we bumped into each other 'round a corner, neither of us expecting the other. 'Excuse me, God.' I'd say. 'Excuse me, Annie.' He'd say. And then, when we'd gone on our own ways, I found that he'd left me with this gift. An accidental miracle, stuffed down in me like a pocket. Course I didn't know where God lived, so I couldn't give it back. And there I was, twelve years old, and knowing next to nothin' about the world outside the farm, with this special thing inside me. I never could say just what it was. And really, I didn't even know it was there, till the day it jumped out.

"Hard work was the only language I knew. My brothers worked the field with their father. My sisters worked the barn and the animals, and Lily and I worked the house. School was allowed only to the age of ten by our father, so that world had two years back, faded away from me. My only continuing education was in learning my place.

"My new father was a rough man, and taught his children to follow his example. As I was not one of his children, I was always on the outer edge of the swing, not one to do the swinging. Lily, his wife of seventeen years and my adopted mother, moved between the edge and the inner curve of that fist. She could take it, or give it, depending on which way she leaned. Running or playing dead, were my usual two choices. I learned to be grateful for what I'd been given, and to be fast.

"Back then, people were simple in their lives. I saw them as livin' in a patchwork quilt. Everyone was a different square, cut from some place else, and sewn up next to each other. *Different.* Lily said the only thing that held us all together was God. 'He was the thread', she said. 'He's the only thing that could cross any of us and get away with it.' When I asked her why it was this way, she would always tell me, 'That's just the way it is, Annie. No other reason to it.' And I was supposed to except that, as that was the general answer she gave for most things.

"People might know what went on across the road, but it weren't in their way to go on about it. Certain invisible lines were not crossed by them. You were expected to take care of your own, which also seemed to mean, in any way you wanted, or cared to.

"There's no set way to put pieces together when you sew up a quilt. You just take up two pieces, and there it is. Just like that. That's the way it was with small town lives. Basically good, with rock hard cores, and a unique ability to take bad things in stride, until they could find a way to make it seem the best thing, even if it wasn't. They went to church on Sundays, worked the week, and kept a family. Nothing made their lives special or different. Nothing made them want to be. They just endured, like strands of wheat standing against the weather. They lived and died along a straight line. Each generation replacing the last. Each following the example of the previous.

"But the day came, when I was set apart. When I became something different to them.

"It was in church, a hot May, leading into a hot June, where we sat faithfully, as we had each Sunday, on smooth, worn wooden benches, listening to the ever forgiving word of God. And as the goodness settled around our tired bones, we'd forgive God for making the days so hot, and walk home so long. Because it was our place to do so, we were grateful that we had a place to go home to, and families around us, and work to keep us through the hard times. It was on one of these days, the Reverend had asked me to join in the choir up front.

"The whole thing probably wouldn't even have happened the way it did, except that Mrs. Minnie, one of the town ladies, was sitting in the front row, right in front of me, with her newborn.

"I stood there in my cleanest dress, two damp places under my arms, and my feet slippin' in my shoes. I didn't like being in the front where everyone was watchin' me. I didn't like the idea that I was going to be singin' in peoples faces, instead of the back of their heads. I wanted to sit down, but instead I had to stand up.

"When the Reverend said, 'To sing the Lord's praise—' I opened my mouth, without any choice, and started to sing with the choir, to words I'd only mouthed before. And I looked right at her, Mrs. Minnie, the way she held her tiny baby to her, the way the baby was looking at her, smiling, clenching a tiny fist against a breast. And Mrs. Minnie, waving her paper fan with one hand, holding the baby to her with the other, smiling back, as though they were holdin' each other with those smiles.

"I don't remember what I was singing, or that I was.

"All I knew was this mother and child. All I could see was this picture of them, as though the rest of the world had been cut out around them, and left them like a Christmas card stuck on a blank wall. When

Mrs. Minnie looked up at me, something just burst right out. Singin' I guess, as I still couldn't hear anything except my heart beating and my ears ringing. But I knew then, there was something— something inside me, that had been missing the moment before, and all the moments before that. Like the knot on the last stitch, or a missing button that you try to fasten and it's no where to be found. All at once everything seemed to come unraveled and nothin' wanted to hold like it had. Something I had just witnessed and been touched by, when Mrs. Minnie had looked up at me.

"When it started, Lily told me later, the voice that had come out of me, there came sounds unlike any she'd ever heard, or anyone else, from the way they all looked. 'Words that floated up high on the air, then settled down low, she'd said. 'Words that couldn't stand still to the others...and took on a way of soundin' that reached deep inside a person, and made them want to weep, or start wanderin' on to someplace they never been.' The rest of the choir let off singing almost immediately, and everyone was looking at me.

"I say it like it was a separate thing, the voice, and it felt like it was. Separate from me, a voice whose direction I might have looked around to see where came from, except I couldn't move. I was glued down. My feet were two cast irons nailed to the floor. It was just that when I saw them, I felt something huge, and dark inside me, an emptiness, like a large hole left after the tree has been torn out in a storm. I seemed hungry for something I didn't even know I was hungry for. As the words came out, I was filled up, slowly, like sugar pouring down into a sugar bowl, smooth as water, and warm as fire.

"I believe now, it was love that I felt. Maybe I'd reached out and tasted it, seeing her like that, for her child. Like my real mother must have done once. Arms that must have held me. Eyes that must have looked at my face with such kindness and sweat gentleness.

"Love had, for one moment, filled up the hole inside me.

"But with love, also came pain, which I had not been aware of before. Not pain like a hit. But an empty pain. Pain in me where something else should be. And though love filled me, pain slowly leaked it out.

"Singing gave me two arms that let me reach out, to reach for my mother from a long buried place inside me. But she wasn't there. She never would be. And, when the arms pulled back, they became arms of pain. I didn't know what my real mother looked like. But I knew I should. So I sang like a mountain! It was as though Moses had taken his staff to the back of my head, and out flew music.

"Tears came out of my eyes, but I did not know this. I just kept singing, song after song, until finally the Reverend walked over, and put his hand on my shoulder, and said, 'The Lord walk among us this day.' and I stopped and looked around, and wanted more than anything to go and sit down. The congregation answered 'Amen!', with a sort of amazed silence following the sound.

"Then the Reverend said, 'And the Lord sends angels to sing among us today.' And the silence raised up again with 'Praise Him!'

"When the Reverend moved his hand away from my shoulder, I did not hesitate, but took my escape down the center isle, to the door and all the way home, as fast as two feet could carry me, with hallelujahs and Amen's, following quick on my tracks.

"God might have found me that day, but he'd have to sure haul me down by the seat of my pants to do it! I thought I might run all the way to the edge of town and maybe even more, if I had too. I'm not really sure why I ran. I just did.

"People respected song and praising of the Lord in their lives, but somehow seeing the child that I was, sing like that undid them some-how. They didn't know what to make of it. I kept seeing their faces. My brothers and sisters, their mouths hangin' open, father looking at me with those eyes, Lily smilin', but not my mother. The others, who just sat there, waving their fans, watching me as strangely as they might to some new invention unfolding in front of them. So I ran, but only as far as the farm, where I hid myself in the barn till nightfall.

"By the time my sisters and brothers had me alone later, I had cre-ated quite a stir around town. It was the attention, I think, that made my family turn on me, all except Lily. Her smile pulled up to both cheeks and stayed there for days. At first the others tried to ignore me. They'd talk about me as though I weren't there, about the way I seemed to always get what I want, that people around were always bringing me the best hand-me-downs, how the chores I did, seemed to happen all their own, without me liftin' hardly a finger.

"Later, when the family would go into town, and a person would ask about me, Lily would go right up and say, 'Yes. That's my Annie.

I hear her sing all the time. She has a voice like angels do. When she sings, I feel lifted right off the ground...'. Father and the others just walk on past. Then he would turn back and say, 'Lily you comin—', and she'd look down, smile at me, and we'd follow on too.

"She seemed happy to have me then.

"But it weren't long till the smile was stole from her face. She had been sick for a long time. But now, the cough was so bad she couldn't keep down food, or find the strength to stand up. She went to bed and did not get up again for the three months that I cared for her. She didn't want to see her own children. All she wanted was me. Her husband never once asked how she was. And none of her children once offered to get her anything. I think they were glad to be away from her, and me.

"Then one day he came in, and said this had gone on long enough. That the two of us had been walled up in here well enough time now. He wanted me back to work. But Lily, even in her weakness stood up to him, something she rarely did.

"'I'm a dying woman.' she said to him. 'But I ain't dried up and dead yet!' She took a swing at him too. 'You taken just about everything out of me I could give, but you're not gettin' Annie. She stays here! You got all them other children to help you. Get one of them. If I want to hear her sing in my last days, I will— now get! All of ya!'

"She reached out a swing to them as far as she could, though none of them was in reach. And each of her children, her own flesh and blood, though you'd never have thought it, not one looking back, went out and left her. And her husband went out too, slamming the door shut after him, closing them out and us in. I stayed in my chair, too afraid to move. Death had reached up and given her power over that house. Such that she never had before. Like a hammer, she wielded it. Nailing them in as hard as she could."

"'Sing for me Annie.' she said to me. 'Come, sit here and sing, so I could hear you. It would make me feel better.' And I did as I was told. And as I sang, she would hold her chest to her, rocking just slightly, eyes closed. The old quilt, that had pieces from my dress in it, was pulled up under her arms. She seemed almost as small as me. Her wrists were thin, like two dark saplings coming out of an old trunk, only she wasn't old, she just looked old.

"Lily had raised five children, plus me, and had married just three years older, than I was then. Before I'd even crossed her doorstep ten years before, she'd grown old."

Annie stopped speaking, looked away, then back. The light reflected somewhere between Magenta and Burnt Sienna across her face. A hint of Cadmium Yellow, that I imagined sewn into Lily's quilt, I added to her dress front.

Her face again took on a subtle sheen of emotion and memory. She took several deep breaths, reached up to touch her cheek once, then replaced the hand exactly where it had rested on the chair arm. "Whenever—" she sounded out the word. "Whenever the coughing would shoot through her, I would wait for it to pass. But then she'd try to say in-between each cough, for me to keep going. I was a choir of one and she was a congregation of one. There was no preacher. And no sermon. Just singing. Sometimes she'd ask for certain ones, or for me to do one again. She never seemed too tired of hearing me. She would just hold herself and listen, until my voice would give out, then she'd send me out to cook some dinner for the others, or fetch some water for her, and then we'd just sit. This would be our silent prayer. I could never tell whether she was praying to get better, or to die quicker. Seemed to me, she wanted both. This made me afraid, but I didn't say it. It was not my place to question older folk's decisions.

"When the others would come back to the house, Lily took no notice of them. Unless they took after me, then her voice could be heard all the way to the road in front of the house. If they were in, when I was out of her sight, she'd talk real loud to me, until I came back. 'Annie, bring me some cool water. Annie, don't be long. Annie, I need you to bring me another towel...' Her voice was like a rope thrown out to pull me back. I was tied to her, and kept alive by her presence.

"'Better run along Annie, your *ma's* callin' you.' Father would say to me real low, so she couldn't hear. I'd get what I needed and hurry back past them. 'She won't be around much now.' He'd say. And I'd keep going. 'Go sing for your supper Annie.'

"Each day the coughing became worst. Some hours she could hardly have heard me over it, but she wouldn't let me stop. 'It's the only thing that makes me better.' she'd say. But I couldn't see how.

64

"'Sing Amazing Grace.' she asked me towards the end. 'It's my favorite. I always liked it. Sing that one. But sing it slow, so I can remember.' So I sang. Slow, like she wanted. And tired, like I felt. We were alone in the house then. The hot air made me dizzy and my legs were numb from sitting so long. But I knew it would make her better. She had said it would. So I sang.

"When I finished she opened her eyes. They were rimmed with tears and red. I waited to see what she would want next. With her hand, she motioned me closer still, so I could hear what she had to say. 'Annie, you will make me a promise.' she said. '*Promise,* you hear. I want you to tell me, that when I die, you will sing that for me. Sing it, so I will hear all the way up in heaven.'

"I curled up beside her, listening to the way her breath came out in little puffs between each word. 'I will.' I said. 'I'll sing it for you.' But I could hardly say the words. Promising it, meant she was also promising to leave. To die. But I kept the fear of what her words meant in, like the way I was twisted all up inside at the thought of her going. Leaving me.

"The voice that came out of me, she said it made her think of wanderin' just over to the other side, to see what it was like. So we laid there together, under that quilt, pieced together in song. Her, about to be sewn up in heaven and me, inside. But in her last days and mine, there was singing about the promised land. About mountains, and good souls. About miracles and things of which were not of my world, or hers.

"'Sing—' she whispered, held herself close. 'I'll just have myself a look. Just a little one.'

"Don't stay long." I said. And as I pulled the quilt up to cover her, her eyes closed and she was gone. She wasn't comin' back. That thread had come loose and slipped away. But it was with a smile, when it did."

"Some things just put together, come out all right, even for a while." Annie said slowly. Her eyes lowered, the light in them becoming dark and liquid shadowed. "It wasn't the best thing, but it's what we had on hand." she said, eyes closed tight. "So again, I sang like a *mountain.* Because I had promised. Because I owed her. And because that last little piece was what I had loved."

11

I dialed the number and waited for John to answer. When he did, I said, "It's me." paused, hand shaking.

"When are you coming home?" he asked. He knew this already from the note on the kitchen table, where I had left it.

"I don't know." I said. "Soon. When I'm done."

"Are we?" he asked.

Several seconds passed, throat tightened. A phone book was open, crammed underneath the phone. Yellow pages. Lists of ads. Tall black letters that said, 'Yes, You Are...'

"No." I said.

"Can I see you?"

Strained, half-laugh, I said, "Close your eyes."

"It's not enough." he said.

"It's all I can give right now."

"I miss you." he said. His breathing loud, tears pushed at the sound of it.

I caressed the edge of the receiver, to touch him. It smelled of hot metal and rubbed onions. Closed eyes to see him.

"I know." I said. It was all I could give.

Section Two

So fragile the lives, we crush so easily—

12

"The only good thing out of that marriage, was it got me out of their house..." My mother said this many times. She said it with a flair of triumph at the end, as though it had been a success, and she the better for it.

I think my mother was moving from man to man, like the way they moved from city to city, when she was a child. She'd stay awhile, then leave, and everything would be different. Maybe she was gathering hope for herself— hoping things would turn out better at the next stop, or that things would be nice the next time? She kept making worst and worst choices, continuing to take wrong turns, getting lost, and ending up back where she started, *alone*.

My father was the first man she would love, and her first mistake for believing in that love. The marriage lasted only a year. When I was born at the county hospital eight months later, the name, Franklin was attached at the end of my name, making me a legal, fatherless child. My first name, Katherine, was a last moment decision to honor the mother of my father, or maybe even a plea for him to return to what was his? And then my middle name, Eve. The broken syllable of Evelyne, my mother's name, stuck in the middle, a link between who she had been and what was left to remind her. It was a rare thing for her to say my name. Katherine Eve Franklin, became 'Hey you!'

Karen's father was little different. With his quick moves and quick words, she married him thinking he had truly loved her. He called every night, begging first for love, and then later, for forgiveness. On his forth second chance she gave him, Karen was conceived. But he soon forgot his promises, and quick-dance stepped his way out the door, and left her for another, less pregnant woman in another town.

Third times are supposed to be the charm, but not in marriage. It was just plain bad luck. How could she have seen below that sun-tanned and golden-expression, that his father had beat his mother, and he would her too, once she was married to him? It took three years and another baby to get out of that marriage. She held onto it the longest. Maybe again, she was hoping? For what— I could never guess. And she would never say. She gave no explanations. Maybe she didn't even know?

Burnt Umber.

"Woman— you are *fat*." He put down his beer on the edge of his chair. He is in the living room, she in the kitchen. "Look at you." He sounds like he has just noticed this about her. "How in the world did you get so fat?" He sounds drunk and his words are tilting and humorous sounding. She remains quiet. Makes dish washing noises at the sink.

"I'm going to have to keep food away from you before you get any bigger." He laughs to himself. "You look like my mama. She was fat— fat as a house. My daddy told her not to eat one more thing, and she still got fat. Do you hear what I'm sayn' to you?" She rattles the plates, turns on the water full blast to rinse. She keeps her back to him.

Between them both, I am eating my lunch at the table. I wish there was a door. Then maybe it would have been closed and he wouldn't be looking at her from behind, like he is now. "If I see you put one more thing in that mouth—" He drops the half empty bottle to the floor. It takes him a long time to lean over and pick it up. When he does, I can see the top of his head where the hair is gone. It is shiny the way new coins look. When he sits back up, he raises the empty bottle to his mouth to take a drink. He finds nothing coming out, so he lets it fall back down to the floor. He looks at her again. "*Fat!* My God, just look at it..."

She is hunched over the sink as far as she can go. Water is running down the sink, falling in little puddles on the floor. He goes on, talking about rolls of fat, pig fat, lard fat, big as a house— ugly, good-god-huge, how can you fit through the doorway kind of fat. He ties these words around her to keep her still. I listen, imagining that she cannot say anything, because she is so full of what he says she is.

Jessie runs in, holding her hand out to her daddy, for him to see. Her sandals make tiny slapping sounds across the wooden floor. "Daddy look what I found. It's mine." she says first, then opens her hand.

"A whole quarter!" he says. "You've struck it rich. What you goin' to do with all that money?"

"I dunno-" She leans happily over the chair arm, one foot balanced on the empty bottle.

"Don't you go spending it on no candy. I don't want you turnin' into your mama. See how fat she is? Don't you turn into her. No man wants a fat woman like your mama. Gimmy a kiss—" She kisses him on the cheek. "How 'bout getting daddy a cold beer, pumpkin? Will you do that for your old daddy?"

She giggles, hands him the quarter.

"No, I don't think this will buy it. But I know there's one in the 'fridge. Why don't you keep this and go look in there?"

"O.K.—" She takes back the coin, runs through the room, echoing sound follows her away.

At the sink, mother is still scrubbing a pot with a brush. She makes, slow circles, grinding the metal, and staring into the water. It seems to me, like she has never moved from that sink. She has been draining away, little by little with the dirty water and food pieces. She went down when no one was looking.

The sound of his voice is grinding too, wearing thin the rest of us. Her face turns beet red, burning from the look of it, then flushes pale. Sometimes between her eyes small hills rose up. Her chin quivers, then falls still. The edge of the sink disappears under her she leans so far over. Soft elbows have disappeared under the water. Her fleshy forearms are dripping with soapy dishwater. He throws his second empty bottle at her and it crashes against the cabinet. She jumps, but doesn't move away, or turn and look at him, instead I hear something like glass breaking underwater. Her hand goes round and round, scrubbing. When she takes it out to put in the rack, there is only half a plate left. He laughs out-loud and slurred, opens another bottle.

She makes herself an easy target. A large presence impossible to hide, it should protect her, but doesn't. She is still pushed around easily by him.

. . .

When I remember her, I see her from behind, large, against a white tile kitchen. Splashes of water across the wooden floor.

I believe that putting on weight, like with animals, is instinctual. It is meant to protect us from the cold and hunger, wrapping around the body in layers, like tree rings, or winter blankets. To keep us safe inside, tucked away inside ourselves, hidden. She *was* huge. But not in the way he described her. She had been disappearing inside herself over years, her body wrapping round and round, folding and tucking her in like a child put to bed with fever. She had been sick— sick to death of him, her last man. Her last chance man.

Some weight can also be invisible. It can be felt, but not seen. It can grow heavier over time and reach out to others like two hands. This is the weight my mother gave to me. It continuously pushes me down, even today. It has slowed me. Everything around me seems to be going fast. People, cars, lives, words, even time goes fast now. I'm left behind by everything.

I feel like I haven't moved in years.

13

"He's only let me do this the past year." Annie said. She had Amos seated on a low stool in front of her. Wrapped around his front and shoulders, a white towel. His head stuck out through the middle, an aged apple with goose down hair, pinched cheeks. She picked up a large comb in one hand and undid his braid with the other. "Now hold still, less you want me to lop off an ear." she said.

"I am holding still. You shouldn't be anywhere near my ears. All I want is a snip off the bottom. No more than that."

She pulled her fingers through the strands to make them straight, then combed them. "Only off by a hair maybe." she said.

"Don't you crew cut me either." he warned. "Katherine here'll be my witness."

"Oh now, I know what I'm doin'. Don't worry." She reached over to the small table and picked up the coffee pot. With one quick motion she poured it in his hair.

"Ohh- that's cold!" Amos yelled, wobbling a little in his seat.

"If you'll just hold it. I'll have it rubbed in before you know it."

"Coffee?" I asked.

"Best thing in the world—" she said, giving Amos's head a good rub down with the towel. "Brings out the shine. You ought to try it. It would go real nice with your hair. Almost as long as Amos's here. Ain't that right Amos?"

"Humph—" he sounded beneath the towel.

When she pulled the towel away, his hair mashed in circles was sticking out every which way. "My goodness." she said. "Could be rats hiding in here."

"They'll be no rats in there." Amos said, "Just a family of snakes."

"Snakes?" Annie picked up the comb again and began trying to untangle the strands. "If I find a snake, Katherine and I will push you off this dock and make a run for it."

"Ouch— that hurts!"

"It's supposed to hurt."

"Why do I let you talk me into these things? Don't you have a gentle bone in your body?"

She ignored him, smiling at his complaints. I pulled one of the rocking chairs over beside Amos and sat down. "Much painting yet?" she asked me.

"No. Not much." I said. "The feeling comes and goes. Mostly goes. I would like to work on yours again, when you have time."

"Just say when."

I squinted to see her through the morning glare. Surrounding her face, a halo of blue sky. Cerulean Blue mixed with a little Ultramarine, titanium white blended in where the clouds had gathered, softening the blue to a much paler hue. In this light, my hair had visible red highlights. Inside a room, or dark place, it appeared black. Here, the red flushed out through an ordinary brown, a farmland soil brown. Grandma's hair was once deep red, flame red, when she was young. Now it was brown, turned this way over years, as though the fire had gone out of it. Strands of seashell white were taking over the brown now. We shared this. Dead hairs, no life left. When I pulled them out, they grew back. They were frustrating evidence of things that could not be changed, once in place.

Annie had finally managed to comb all Amos's hair and had parted it down the middle, each side straight and flat. She picked up the scissors, then stood back to study the length before she made the cut. "OK Medusa, now don't move an inch. I'll scalp you for sure if you do."

"It'll be me you have to live with if you do. You remember that."

The clippings fell along his shoulders and the planks below. She made each cut precise and sure. As she cut his hair, she hummed quietly. Amos closed his eyes. I had noticed the way their words often took playful stabs at each other without any real hurt intended. It was a contest sometimes, who could back talk the most. John was a humorous person who knew many jokes, but he said he wasted his jokes on me, because I never laughed. It wasn't because I didn't think the joke wasn't funny, just not right then, when I was feeling serious. His jokes made light of things I found dark.

Annie and Amos's words were like little shovels digging into the other to get closer. John's words did not make me feel lighter. But I wasn't made of warm sand. I was cement. "Lighten up." he was always saying to me. "It was just a joke." Only his shovel scrapped across me leaving a long invisible gash of raised stone.

"All finished." Annie said.

He patted the top of his head to see what was left. "About time." he said.

"Oh hush up." she said back. "It could be worst."

He eased himself up, bits of hair falling into the wind. "I feel like my head's been plucked clean."

"That's the way it goes for chickens like you."

"I'm not a chicken." he said. "Never in my whole life was I a chicken."

"Well then, come on. Let's get you inside. Come on."

"Don't rush me. I'm movin'..."

"You want to come in for some tea?" Annie asked me.

"No. I better get back. I have some sketches to look at."

"Keep up the good work." she said.

"Well, I wouldn't call it that."

"All artists say that. Isn't that right, Amos?"

"What?"

"They can't see their own work. That it's good."

"I suppose. Right." He turned and looked back at me. "Can't see the good." His eyes lit up and he waved, following Annie back to her house.

. . .

I spent a lot of time looking at the faces of people, at the mall, the supermarket, the office, stoplights. I would pick out one face, study the shape and color of it. Imagine how I would paint such a face and expression? For a painting to have interest, it must reveal something other than surface alone. The smoothing and folding of the face will lead me to conclude about the underside they keep to themselves. Angry people are tight-lipped and narrow eyed, a crease on the forehead pulling their thoughts to a point. Happy faces flow backwards, revealing, opening like a flower to the sun. The emotions are never the same for long, but change constantly, even in the few moments I might be watching.

If I walk slow through a store, the waves of people will rush around and past me. I pick out another face and imagine the histories behind it. An ocean of lives follows the one face, back through time, generations, immigrations, migrations, and distant places. The face does not reflect the weight of this history. It is oblivious and small. It does not remember those who built up layer by layer the straight nose and far set eyes, the subtle shades of color on the skin. The line stretches back, until I imagine a bent looking figure crossing a hill with furs draped across a waist, a first human. Then sometimes for fun I take into account past lives. If this one person had fifty other lives and each of these followed a line back to a beginning, then of course a lot of lines get crossed and I end up unable to follow what has now become a tangled web from the belly of a spider. Pretty soon everyone is related by blood, and life, and history, one way or another.

But the face passes and all I really see is the look of the moment. Hurried, frustrated, laughs too loud, and too easy. Probably worried about something else. Loneliness in the crossed arms, hands tucked in under the elbows to hide what the heart would like to offer, but cannot.

I could never tell someone the whole story of my life. By it's nature, it would take a lifetime. But I can offer parts— even to myself. Much escapes me— reasons, moments that happen too quickly, things that seemed unimportant at the time, I've lost forever.

When I walk past store windows slowly, but won't go in to look, John would often get mad at me. I tell him I'd rather have a glimpse of what I couldn't have, than a feel of it. To touch the thing I want would make me want it more. "We can't afford it." I will say. He will look at me with that odd expression. "It doesn't hurt to look." he says.

"But it does." I say back to the reflection in the glass. I smile, but it doesn't help him understand.

"Do you want to go in or not?" His patience will slip.

"No." I say. He takes my hand and we go on past the window. He is mad and shows this by walking faster. I try to look in less windows.

Shopping is not something we do well together. He doesn't understand my feeling— that if I can't have something, I'd rather not know what it feels like. Looking through the glass is safe. It lets the store clerk know I'm not really interested. There are no hands to reach out and grab at me, asking me what I want, tempting me with good prices and pretty colors. Choices.

The feel of his hand over mine is rough and warm. I choose this hand in marriage. It was something I wanted. But the touch of it did little to comfort me. It did not ease my loneliness or make him understand my feelings. He could not see all the faces that stretched back from mine and created the reasons I didn't like to go into stores just to look. And I did not know how to open up like the petals of a flower, and show him the reasons that lie inside.

14

There are so many arms, legs, soft cheeks, tender hands, faces leaned toward one another, that I feel smothered by embraces.

Mary Cassatt paints these impressionist images of mother and child. The room is filled with them. Before her, a child sits half perched in a chair, one foot on the floor, ready to move. She captures only the necessary— an expanse of red hair, armrest in solid blue, highlights. The brush moves quickly, each stroke precise, thickly spread. The sound of the paint going onto the canvas, would be like a woman's hands putting on lotion. The colors are smoothed out, with brushes that imitate the palm of the hand, deft finger tips. With faint slapping sounds, she works it in quick to obscure fine lines and wrinkles,

How could I be afraid of soft places? I ask myself, then am flooded with the overwhelming sensation of being small. Mary's brush shows these things, small bodies leaning into someone bigger, stronger, trusting. Loving. All of the things I saw missing in me. For the moment I let my eyes feel what it is like. Freshly washed soap and water hands, scented powder smell, cotton shirts with tiny hemmed sleeves, milk smells, kitchen places, baby curls brushed with baby combs. Here, I can know all these things, safely, and from a distance.

. . .

Resistance was losing it's foothold. I felt it slipping. Turning in my chair, I could see that Annie still watched me. All that was left of her, were two dark eyes lit in the glow of Amos's pipe. She wanted me to talk about it. The will not to, was vanishing like the sun. Each day something would float to the surface, words I would almost say, but didn't. In my face was something she recognized, some strand of familiar history.

She was about to try another direction. I could tell that by the mischievous look the red glow had, watching me still. I felt I was slipping even before she began. *Why not?* A part of me whispered. What could it hurt?

"No child on earth can resist a game." she said finally.

I leaned further back in the rocking chair. Part of me, slipping out on the wisps of smoke and falling back in the rocking motion, started forming words to give her. This time, I let it. "What is the game?" I asked.

"Hide and seek" the pinpoints of light said. "Just hoping the right person will come along and find us."

"I know some that could hide pretty good."

"How are they at seeking? There are lots of good things to find if a person looks."

"The best hiding places, are those right in the open." I said. "The obvious places, like a ditch, or up over a shed. Right in plain sight. As long as you stayed still, you wouldn't be caught."

"We're still children at heart. No one grows up on the inside."

"I have no choice then."

"Well, going against it is a good fight. Maybe you'll win. If that's what you want?"

"I don't want to go back, even for pretend. There's nothing I'd want to go back too."

"There's only one difference between now and then." Annie said slowly. "Now, we're supposed to know certain things. Like don't stick your hand in the fire or you'll get burned. Don't step in front of a bus or you'll get hit. Look both ways before crossing the street. Though Amos here, is still working on that one. He never looks where he is going. Just plunges right in."

"Always a surprise that way." he said.

Her voice drifted on in the darkness. "We know what our name is by now, but we still don't know much about who we are. Our parents can't tell us what to do anymore, but a great deal of things like them can."

"That's a damn fact." Amos said, blew out a long plume of smoke. The smell of the tobacco was strong and soothing.

"Children's games are the simplest of greater necessities." she said. "We are in school everyday, learning, falling, picking ourselves up, and trying again and again. We're still afraid of the dark, and the bully, and the things we think are hiding from us. It takes the equal part of our days on this earth to learn how to walk, talk, see, hear, smell— and to figure out what it all means and what to do with it. All this time, all these lives and families and years of learning— and we still, every one of us, still get burned and hit. We do not look both ways at something before running to conclusions, and still don't know who we are other than the name we learned our first year of life."

I said to this, "But there is also the feelings from all that hearing, seeing, knowing. There's the people around that child doing all these things too. When I think of six years old, I think I wasn't a child, even then." My body had disappeared. Only my voice was left. It said things I didn't want to say, but wrapped in invisibility, I felt beside myself and the words. "I don't know who in hell I am? Or, who I was."

Amos's voice echoed somewhere to the right. "Katherine don't like jumping rope and pigtails. No sir-*ry*, she don't..."

Around us, the wind picked up, then fell away. Several seagulls flew overhead calling out to each other, flying away where we couldn't see. Then only the sound of dry, wood rocking. Each moving to its own rhythm, but the same.

15

Every spring I did the raking for my grandparents. As I moved around the Azaleas and Monkey Grass hedges, I found the thoughts of my childhood. Each one was like a shiny quarter on a sidewalk. I would rake and think, pick up each coin as I came to it— *Here in this spot I remember this. In this place I see this, and hear these words...* Each pull of the rake across the brown layer revealed the new green underneath. What was removed was more than leaves and damp pine straw. The ground was alive with movement. There were worms and bugs, spiders that ran over my feet. I got down on my knees and peered close to smell the wet earth and roots, to see what I had disturbed. Living things scurried for new places to hide, down in holes, under leaves. I'm not sorry that I did this. What was theirs, would be theirs again, long after I was gone.

Raking is something that is done over and over, always with the knowing that it will have to be done again. The effort is somewhat worthless in this way. It is not something that can ever be finished, or done away with.

Each spring, I pulled back my family like a dry wound. They are old coins from previous winter pockets. Their words, I still hear, are the leaves crushing underfoot. Their faces stick through with needle sharp points of pine straw. They are clinging and dirty and wear the skin of my fingers into blisters. Not everything is bad though. The good earthy smell is there. I pat this lovingly, as a gardener would. This is the blackness smell of deep things, holes where things are hidden. Sometimes I see myself reaching down far enough, to break through the other side of them. The look on their faces is full of shock, to discover that they are so thin and easily penetrated. They hurry to pull themselves closed again, but it is too late. I have already seen through their collapsing ant hill sides.

Viridian.

"Please let us stay!" we cry together. "We'll be good!" Grandma's face looking down at us, she wipes her hands on her apron, then touches our pleading faces. "Oh babies, you know you can't. You have to go home."

"We don't want to go. Please grandma, let us stay with you! Please— *Please!*"

"No honey. You know your mother won't let you."

Behind us the front door slams open. Nathan's boot holds it open, his arms full of diaper bags and toys he is carrying to the car. "What's all this hollerin'? Didn't I tell you two to get in that car? Why aren't you moving?" He struggles to keep a cigarette in his mouth and talk at the same time. "Let's go. I mean it."

"They want to spend the night." grandma says to him.

"No." His voice is sharp. "Get your stuff now and get in the car. I've already called you three times. I'm not telling you again—" The door bangs shut and baby Jessie starts crying.

Grandma leads us, still holding onto her, to the center of the room to pick up our color books and crayons. "Come on now. Let's get everything together." She tries to bend over, but we are still huddled under her arms, standing on her feet. "You don't want to forget anything. Help grandma now." But then the door slams open again. Nathan stomps toward the playpen to pick Jessie up. Ashes from the cigarette trail the air beside him. For one second it is still a flame, then goes out before reaching the floor.

Karen and I, hold on to grandma's skirt. In whispered voices we try to change her mind. "Can we stay grandma? Make him let us stay!"

"Babies... Babies..." she keeps saying, the sound of her words going down at the end, in defeat. She cannot do much more than that, it says. "Quit crying now. Grandma doesn't want to see you crying. Be good girls."

"Look." His voice rises beyond us. He has put Jessie over his shoulder like a sack. Eyes wide, she looks around, hands clinging to the fabric of his shirt. "How many times am I going to have to tell you? Get out here, *now.*" He picks up another bag, then goes back outside. We don't look at him. Our faces are turned up at grandma's.

"I don't want to go..." Karen's cries.

"You have to." grandma says.

"I'm afraid."

"Afraid? There's nothing to be afraid of. What's the matter?"

"Ghosts." Karen says and I feel the same, though I would not have said it. "There are ghosts there."

"There are no such things as ghosts."

"I've heard them. I don't want to go."

"It's your imagination."

"It's not—"

The front door opens again. Mother's face sticks in. "Get-in-this-car!" Her face is red. She looks like she is about to cry.

"They're afraid of ghosts." grandma tells her.

"I don't have time for this!" Her whole body emerges. She goes straight for our clinging arms, pulls us away.

"They can stay." grandma says weakly.

"They're going!" She pushes us out the door.

"You could stay..." Grandma says, but the door is closed hard on her words.

Grandma's brightly lit house pulls away. The truck lunges, jolting our small bodies against each other. Each street takes us farther into darkness. In the truck there is only the wind coming through the open windows. No one speaks. Jessie nods her head into sleep. If I look to the side, I can see Karen's chin occasionally quiver, but it looks like the bouncing of the seat doing it. The wind blows my hair around my face till my face cannot be seen. With my eyes closed, I let the sound take me into the darkness and waiting. I push myself down in the seat, so that no one will see the quiver of my lips, hidden in the whipping hair and wind.

. . .

Remembering always made me pull the rake more strongly, so I would get done faster. The ground I opened, shows the tender new shoots of grass that had been trying to get through. I want to heal the wounds, but it is a slightly worthless effort. It will have to be done again and again. I don't know how long I can keep it up. There are so many dead leaves still falling on the rising spring. *So many.*

16

"The day Lily died, was the last day I would know peace for a long time." Annie said this, lifted away bit after bit of the breakfast crumbs that had fallen to the table. Then she shook out the dish towel, wiped down the cutting board and put it away. "After that—" she continued, "I remember each day, as kind of a long, solid piece, hard, like wood. The grains ran deep in three things— fear, pain, and unforgiveness." I handed her the last of the mornings dishes, washed and dried. The coffee cups she set along the window ledge. She put the plates, stacked, on a shelf over the sink, draped a checkered cloth over the top of them. "And all for being wanted by a dying woman." she said.

"For comin' into a life, I hadn't even asked to be in, I was punished. Just being alive, or standing still. For a look I couldn't have explained crossing over my face. For not knowin' my place— judgment was passed on me, and I was found guilty. But what they asked of me! Of such a sentence I was given... It should not have been *that*." She stepped through the screen door, with me following her, went over to her chair beside the outside window, sat down. I didn't have to tell her how to pose. She placed each hand down carefully on the arm rests, head turned exactly as it had been days earlier, and as I looked, I thought, *maybe years too...* There was a firm set to the chin, strength of neck, straight look-you-in-the-eye gaze, as though that neck had bore the weight of more than a hard life. It also carried with it, something close to fierceness. A wild beauty.

As I watched her, angled the canvas for the right light, thought, the wood wasn't long and flat anymore. It had been made into a sculpted form. The grain sanded, polished— it shown back a reflection now. I could just catch a glimpse of myself in it. "I'm ready." I said. Already a Magenta had leap to the brush, waiting to bring out the grain of her skin.

Her voice low, she said, "The need to sing, was in me every minute, of every day. It's like I needed it to live. Only now, no one wanted me to do it. Holding me down, I was forced by those people, who I called brothers and sisters, by a father who never showed me anything but the back of his hand. They put before me a Bible and made me swear before God, that I would never, as long as I live, *sing again.* If they could not break my spirit, they would break my heart instead!"

I deepened the shadows around her face with the Magenta. In the hair, wisps of highlight, Raw Sienna. A touch of blue reflection on cheek bones, but this was too much. It made her face seem almost carved into the surface. I hunted for a fan brush, found it, brushed the blue to soften the edges.

"After Lilly was gone, I thought I knew what loss felt like. But when I lost the one special thing that had been given to me...that had taken away more than 'singing'. It took away my right to feel any good thing. Without it, I could not think of my mother, or Lilly, or God— or making bad things easier... Everything was left dry and hard. Course, this was then, not now. I found goodness in other things later. Tom was good. Amos a good friend. This place was a good place to live."

"But you never sang?" I asked.

"Once more. The last time." she said.

"The day of the funeral, I was made to sit in back of the church, since I was not a member of the family, they said. So I sat in the back row watching people come in and pay their respects. There were glances to me, and I'm sure they wondered why I sat alone in the back, but it was not their place to ask and they didn't.

"No one knew of my promise to Lily. A promise I had made first. It might be the last thing I ever did, and I thought that I could possibly be dead by morning. She hadn't been my real mother, but she was all I'd known. When the Reverend had finished with his words over her, I stood up, walked all ten rows to the front. Turned around. Opened my mouth and disappeared in the sound that came out. *'Amazing Grace, how sweet the sound— '*, I sang. I sang that song to reach all the way to heaven. I was dying with it. I knew it. It would be the last song I would ever sing.

"When I started, they had looked at me, their eyes so close to hate, I nearly fainted. I was hoping that as I sang, God would throw a rope out to me and pull me in.

"And maybe he did. I did survive them. That day. The life I had with them after that. For five years more, till I would marry Tom and leave them.

"The Reverend did ask me to sing again after that day. I just shook my head no. When he asked why, I said, 'That it was just best.' He asked, 'Don't you want to share your gift with God?' And I said, "God could hear it just fine in my head...'

"And that's how it's been ever since. We left that town and it's people. I never went back or wrote. And they never did either. I guess they got what they wanted. I went away and never came back. God sent me here, to this place."

Annie was silent for several minutes. I moved my brush lightly, not to disturb her. A breeze moved over us, sand pelting the wood steps, the shadows of tree limbs, burnished her skin. "I never sang for Tom." she said softly. "He did like my humming though. Said it made everything around calm." she smiled. "Said I could probably even calm a storm to sea if I wanted. But I never sang for him. I kept my promise. He wouldn't have looked kindly on breaking a promise to God. He didn't know. I thought that best. We were husband and wife. We worked hard, made a family, kept our credit and our name good. We did what we were supposed to. We never were much more than that. He was a good man, kind, but he had his world and he expected me to stay in mine. Our lives were full with things to do, and we did them. We didn't waste too much time finding out about each other. I was always sad about this. I would have liked to have known my husband."

I laid my brush and palate aside. "You may have tried to keep the song in Annie." I said. "But it came out, in your words. When you talk it's like music. It's poetry."

She laughed. "I have been called many things in my day, but never a poet!"

"You paint pictures with your words."

"An *artist* too now—" she said incredibly.

"Artists I understand. I could talk to them. Maybe I'll tell you my story, when I know what it is. I'm not really sure what it is. I have to find out first. That's why I'm here."

"Take your time. Listening takes no effort or energy. I'll be here anytime." She smiled her warmest smile. "How's that painting coming along?"

17

My face pressed forward with only my eyes moving to see where she went. The palms of waxy leaves hit against the sides of my face. It smelled of flower pollen, dirt and wet bark, and dog hair— hot on a sun-warmed porch. Mother didn't call me for dinner or because she was worried, most likely, it was to watch Jessie or to run up to the store. When she looked for me, I became so still, she didn't notice I was there, hidden among the leaves and branches. Only her shoes could see me.

The leaves formed a canopy around the outside of the tree where I hid, but left the inside clear, the branches pale and smooth, like bones. I still have the impression of crawling around the inside of some creature, sitting against a rib cage, taking hold of a hip bone, leg bone, to pull myself along. I would have become easily the giant red heart of this creature pulsing secretly with my own life. I moved around freely, drifting to the surface to watch closely the outside world when I wanted, or settling deep in the center to sleep in a cradle of ribs when it was too hot.

On one side, where the tree over hung the edge of the porch, I would lay down on the cool dirt and rest my chin on the end of a wood plank. I could view the back door and watch her feet as they passed from this angle. I noticed how the heel of her left shoe was coming apart, a sliver of skin showing. The shoe leather flopped open with each step, made a sucking sound, then turned, heel and toe making sandpaper marks, went back in the house where the door screen slammed shut. Dog hair lifted, then settled. The smell of sunlight was there again, made from the things in that tree and the porch's view, and even the shoes, I think, the open shoe spaces showing the yellow skin underneath.

We had moved to our first house, two years after Jessie was born. Outside, the house appeared to be square. Inside it was a circle. All of the rooms were connected by a long hallway that went from door to door. In some places the hallway opened up and became a room, like the living room or the kitchen. Everything else it passed by, doorway to doorway, two bedrooms, one bathroom, storage room at the back. If you started at one room, you could make your way past every room in the house, until you ended up back where you started.

It was an old house. It smelled of damp wood and rotten places. The floors were wooden and the walls were white painted boards. Nail holes and rusty wires stuck out of various places along the walls and were strung together by long webs of dust. Each time a light was turned on, the strands would move, shimmer in the air over our heads.

When it rained, the house smelled of metal pots and rain water, large plopping sounds as the roof leaked the outside in, next to our beds, every ten steps in the hall. It washed away the dust, but made the damp wood damper, soaked in everything like a sponge. The open windows each had a stretched out circle of water in front of them, blown in from the wind. When we opened the closets, our clothes smelled of outside things, wet earth, mildew, and crushed green. I can remember rolling over at night, to press my face into rough, line-dried sheets that smelled like this, and it's like I was sleeping outside against the trees.

It was always very hot, or very cold. My skin toughened through the seasons, like the bark I imagined I lived in. Getting thicker, coarse, raised-up from bug bites and scratching. Karen's and Jessie's skin were like mine too, colored in summer tans, fall-down bruises, scratches that went down too deep and drew blood, redder skin. Our appearances were roughened and heeled over at the same time. Old skin, raw and chafed, grew next to newer pink places that were tender and thin, shiny like fingernails, only soft. Our faces blurred from the hair that hung down over it, shielding our eyes and expressions. To other people it would have seemed we were made only of limbs, arms and legs, fast moving hands and dirty fingers. No one could imagine what we were thinking, or what motivated us to spring suddenly to run from a room. In supermarkets and laundry mats voices whispered, 'wild children—'. But it was only because of our thick skins, enclosing us like our very own made walls.

At the front of the house, my thick-skinned sisters and I shared one room. Our mother and newest father slept at the back. There was some comfort at being at opposite ends, and at having wooden floors. Whenever our mother approached we were forewarned. The wood, forced suddenly to withstand so much weight, made each step a piercing cry of squeaks and groans. The rate of such sounds also told us what possible mood she approached in. Anger played out in pounding, fast sounds, heavy footfalls that would make us scatter quickly for hiding places, or in stillness to wait, breath held, hoping the sound would pass us by unnoticed, scratching bites quietly, making ourselves thicker, redder. Less like ourselves, and more like trees.

Indian Red.

"The next time I tell you something you'll do it. Do you hear me." A sound squeezes out of her. "Yesss— " He must be very close to her, in her face. She is whimpering like a baby. "What did I tell you? Huh! You think you're better than to listen to me? How about, I make you listen?" I imagine his hand on her throat, squeezing the life out of her.

When I see her again, she is alone, standing in the bathroom. She is talking in whispers to herself and the mirror. It is frantic words, angry. Hissing sounds, she is trying to keep quiet. Her hands are moving so fast she is knocking things over. She does not see me. Then she does. *"What!"*

"I have to go to the bathroom." I say.

She slams the bottle of makeup down and turns to me. I see the other side of her face now. The picture of it, slices into me. For the first time, I am frightened by what I see. The shock of the long bruise, stretching down the side and into the neck, the color of bruised plums and flesh. She pushes past me, muttering something I can't hear, and I go in and close the bathroom door. I stand trembling for a second, feeling the loss of my tougher self. That's how cut through I feel, skinned by a look and a color. I pinch the middle of my stomach to make it stop the feeling it is getting, sick wanting to come up, metal taste. I breath in the Ivory soap to feel better, hold it's coolness to my face.

In the sink pale drops of makeup are sprinkled across the white porcelain. A piece of toilet paper with blood is crumpled up on the edge. I pick it up by the corner, wonder where the blood is from? Pull the step bench over to look into the mirror, the cabinet behind the mirror, then the toilet, the bathtub, the stove pan full to the top with rain water. I pick up the bottle of makeup she left open, put on it's cap, twist it closed, put it carefully back on the shelf behind the mirror.

Always her hand is across the neck. Fingers cover the side of her face that she doesn't want seen, elbow in the other hand, supporting her own neck, chin, head. She walks the hall if he is gone, sits by the kitchen window if he isn't. For a long time afterwards they are both quiet, which makes everything else seem loud. He calls us 'noisemakers'. Our slapping feet, slamming doors, unwilling to be still hands. We are always swinging like door hinges around him and her.

Towards evening the silence we don't make, gets to be too much for him. He makes his own trail of sound to her, boot steps she must know are moving in her direction. "Come here woman—" his voice tells her. He pulls her head to him with the crock of his arm. His voice is low and slurred and his movements slow, trying to imitate gentleness. "You know I need you." Drapes an arm over her like a hook. "Don't I love you?" Her chin drops, barely a nod. "Sure I do." he says. Her hand goes away from her face to between her knees. "Look at your kids." he tells her. "They want to see their mama smile." A half swollen smile, eyes lifted to look at him, child-like. He pats the top of her head, tells her to get up now, go make us all some dinner. He says he doesn't want us all to starve, then follows her around with his hands on her wide back.

. . .

That house, I know now, was haunted by the living. My mother was the ghost. When he stopped pretending and turned back to what he really was, she wasn't always still, sometimes she ran. I would hear it. It was her running I heard across wooden floors at night, fast, pounding, thunder sounds, closer and closer, then moving away. She was trying to get away. She followed the rooms, the circle inside the square, but failed to get out. She was running nowhere. He always knew where she was. In a shaking voice, ready to fall apart, but doesn't, she tells our grandmother, "I am afraid to leave him." She says he'll find her no matter where she goes.

. . .

In our room at the front of the house, Karen buries herself under the covers. Jessie sleeps with her blanket over just her head, her legs and feet sticking out. She turns restless in sleep, every night talking out loud with her eyes closed, sometimes crying without waking up. I listen through the darkness, through walls. My mind pressing out at each sound, trying to draw together a picture of what I was hearing, fearful things, breaking sounds, half-said words cut off. I strain to hear until my body becomes tense and hard with fear and not knowing, shaking so bad, that I squeeze my hands to my ears so I can't hear anymore. Only breathing sounds, heartbeats beating fast. I listen to the blood in my head, roaring with it's ocean sound, flooding the darkness inside me, till I fall asleep.

The next night she tells us to sleep in our clothes. Around midnight, after he has gone out, she wakes us. We escape quickly under the cover of darkness and silence. She doesn't take us far. Only to our grandparent's house to sleep. Where grandfather will sit all night in the front room with a World War II gun across his lap that has no bullets. Grandma will tuck us into bed and tell us he isn't going to shoot anybody. "It's just for show." she tells us.

It is from these days I begin to take the pieces of my mother and bury them under the tree by the porch. In the hole are tissues of blood, though I did not know where the blood was from, torn photographs, a ripped shirt that she had thrown away, pieces of glass from a dish I'd seen her break on purpose. I buried them and smoothed the dirt flat over the top, then patted it down so no one would know. I stand guard over the spot. Keeping it secret. Passing back and forth as a soldier would, carrying my stick as a gun, but just for show.

I used to imagine the world as a very small place like our house, a place where everyone knows what is going on, but no one does anything about it, a circle, inside a square. There is a hole beside it filled with dirt, and pieces buried inside that nobody else knows about. Nobody, but me.

Grandma tells us to pretend nothing's happening and to go to sleep. I close my eyes, but I can still see. I push my hands to my ears, but I can still hear.

The ocean is still screaming.

18

"These taste like forty years ago." Annie said. "Lily loved blackberries spread thick on a piece of bread."

Amos looked at her in amazement. "On bread? That's no way to eat blackberries. You have to hold them in your hand, warm them up by rolling them around your fingers, then pop 'em in your mouth hot!" He rolled some in his hands like dice, ate the whole handful. She went on eating hers her, own way, one at a time, purple juice staining the ends of her fingers, savoring each plump bite. Around us, the clearing was a blanket of blackberries. So many, so huge and ripe, that the ground at a glance, cast a black sheen like marble, run through with it's dark green leaves.

"Maple syrup sounds a better thing to roll them around in. Not a sweaty ol' hand." she said.

He made a loud show of eating his. Warming them first, blowing hot breath onto them, then taking another handful in one bite. He reached over to Annie to steal some of hers. "Get your hand out of my bucket." she said.

"Let's see what you got over there?"

"Get your own."

"Mine's empty."

"Well then, don't you think you should be picking some more, instead of steal'n from an old woman? Didn't I say it, 'bout a wolf in man's clothes—" She pulled her bowl away. "You, who did not want to come along to begin with...have eaten your own weight in berries."

"Fine." he said. "Be that way then." He crossed his arms and sat back against the tree. He looked like a mismatched chief from another time. Brown, faded corduroy pants, too short for his legs. His ankles were uncovered and scratched from picking berries. His striped shirt, dotted with purple juice and crushed green streaks was wrinkled, the cuffs unbuttoned and hanging open. He stuck out a purple tongue and licked each purple finger.

Taking a slow bite of my last berry, I let the juice sit on my tongue. The wild berry flavor, something found, not bought. Forest food. I had heard of Acorn bread. I wondered what it would taste like? Or teas made of strange leaves, flowers, cool spring waters. All natural ingredients. So much of things were artificial, man-made, I thought. Five percent real orange juice. But what made up the rest? What was I made up of? How much of me was all natural and how much artificial? *Five percent real me.* Low in self-esteem and no confidence. Only a hundred and thirty self destructive thoughts per serving... I laughed. The sound of it is strange to me, sweet and warm.

Then I imagined Lily eating blackberries on a thick piece of home-made bread and a young Amos filling his pockets with stolen berries. Annie started talking about recipes and king-size berries, as big as two fingers pressed together. It used to be a well known berry picking place. No one had been here for years as far as she knew.

Behind closed eyes, I let myself dissolve, followed the tide out of myself, focused on the exact feel of deep water. How much pressure it created on the skin's surface, the chill or warmth that soon disappeared, once totally immersed within it? I could feel young fingers pulling through it's underside, little waves streaming between. Then reaching bottom, struggling to stay below, blurred colors, gray fish, endless expanse of darkness. How nice it seemed in my head. How peaceful.

Then strangely, I remembered, that my desk at that job I last had, was the exact color of those fish. Steel gray. Fake wood pattern along the sides. It was peeled up on the edges, plastic underneath. The darkness of ocean waters became the feeling of long, dark days, going down halls, mental darkness. I could remember thinking, that it was hard to believe beautiful places existed at the exact moment I sat at my desk, staring at a calendar with pictures of such places, wondering how some people never get to leave and go to them? Like living underground, no windows, no release, no breeze, no feeling that they deserve, or are allowed to know such things. Only work. Only oppressing heat, pushing down, down, down.

In the distance, there was the sound of waves, surf breaking, the mad cries of gulls. I opened my eyes, imagined myself rushing towards the ocean. It was that close now.

"Over at the point is where the view is best." Amos said, watching me. "You have a better chance of see'n your whale there."

The look on my face was startled. "The whale?"

"Might be too far out in the Gulf to see from here." he said.

"Did I say something about a whale?"

"You mentioned it."

I think back to remember. When had I said something? What did I say? Now things were slipping out that I couldn't even remember saying?

"The one you saw when you were little." Annie said.

"Oh." I said.

"You'll have to walk it." He pointed to where the sound of the gulls was coming from. "Water's too rough to take the boat round that way. You'll have to cut a path further on. But out there's the best place to catch a whale pass'n."

Annie smacking her lips, wiped her hands on the end of her dress, said, "I went there when I was younger. I used to sit and watch the waves come in across those white sands. Won't be there much longer. Some builders bound to come along and take it. But as far as I know, it's still just a spot with a real nice view. You should go, at least once before you leave. It's real nice."

"I'll think about it."

"Good, good." she said, fanned herself. "Goodness! It is hot out here. I think I've lost ten pounds just sitt'n here."

Amos smiled. "It'll do you good."

"Don't mess with me, Amos. Your ol' brain cells probably fried up by now with all this sun."

"Good with a few eggs and a slice of bacon! How 'bout you and me head on over for some real food?"

"Don't your red blood think of anything else? All you think of is food."

"Not in the presence of a real good cook. Katherine, how 'bout it?"

"I think I'll stay here awhile. Take a walk. See how hard it would be to go around."

"Storm's come'n." he said, nose to the wind. "You sure?"

"I'll be fine."

"Stay out from under those trees then." Annie warned me. She pulled herself up to go, her dress strung with leaves and branches. A wild woman. "I've known many a fool who danced with lightning under a tree!" she said, looked at Amos.

"Nothing like a dose of it now and then." he said.

"No wonder you're crazy! Probably did it hundreds of times out here in these woods. Don't listen to him Kath-honey." The remaining berries in a sack, hung from a cord at her neck. "Come on you old fool." He picked up the empty bowls, stacking them, red, blue and yellow, on top of his head, rainbow crown. She took his arm, placed it in hers, said, "I'd like some of these in some blackberry pancakes."

"Ummm UMMM!" His voice growled in hungry sounds. "Sounds good to me."

"Now who says I was fix'n you any? You got two hands."

"And you got all the berries."

"You don't know how to pick your own?"

"Who do you think cleared out this place for them berries to grow here?"

"And just who let you live here in the first place?"

"Woman don't mess with this warrior. I'll have to put you in your place!"

"I'd hate for you to have to try. You know what will happen if you do." Laughter, spilled warmth.

"Vile woman."

"Old koot."

"Hen pecker."

"Old dog— *come on.*"

Their voices disappeared down the path where I could not see. I heard Annie say, "When you ever goin' to learn to be civilized?"

"When you learn to show your warm, southern hospitality on the less fortunate."

"That is true." she was saying. "What is?"

"That you're unfortunate."

"Them unfair words—"

"You can never beat a woman. She'll always come out one step ahead. "

"Tar-*nation!*"

"Oh, come on..." Then only wind.

And the memory of a whale.

19

Fingers of light cut sharply into every corner of the room.

  When I had taken the lamp shade off, the entire room became white with light, crisp shadows. I moved a few steps to the left, then to the right, viewing the painting from different angles. But no matter what angle I stood at, the glare was still there, so I leaned it against the back wall, stood back to look at it from a distance. Then turned it upside-down. For an hour, I did nothing but look at it this way. It was an entirely different painting upside-down. Every fault in perspective or form, became suddenly visible. Already I could see where a hand was too small, a tree that was awkward in shape, things I could not see at all while working right-side-up.

  Most of the time spent on a painting, was spent in this silent looking. Every inch of color followed by eye, till I could see down to the crosshatched fibers of the canvas, or notice where each hair from the paintbrush had come out and dried in with the paint. Just looking, until my eyes would get heavy and burn from having stared too long without blinking.

  Bare light sliced into me, revealed my faults. Flushed out my imperfections, and showed in it's light, a whole trail of things gone wrong...failed artist, ungrateful daughter, a wife who had left a note on the kitchen table, walked out.

Cadmium Red Light.

On the table sit the unfired ceramic figures that my mother is working on. Beside her is a lamp, the shade removed, the same bare bulb so she can see by. I am sitting at the end of the table doing my homework, but really I am watching her.

Crowded around her are bunches of crushed wrapping paper, old newspapers, paints, cleaning liquids, rags, jars with brushes and the painted and unpainted figures lined in a row in front of her. Dipping her brush into a color, she paints the faces and body of each piece. It is a nativity scene. She chooses a red for an angel's robe, holds it by the wing.

Passing between us there is just silence and light and the smell of paint. I wonder what she is thinking? Her face is smoothed out, no wrinkles of frustration, nothing tense or angry in any part of her face. The light washes out the shadows of her skin and she appears white, like the pieces she is working on. She has two shepherds, a cow, and the baby's manger done. The brush she holds, makes soft scraping sounds against the ceramic. Little puffs of white dust comes off on her hands as she pushes the paint down into each fold and crevice.

Every year since I can remember, she has said she will finish the whole set. But there are many pieces. She puts them all up on top of the TV every Christmas anyway, some painted, some not. It is as though the color showed up in slow motion over long periods of time, so slow the eye could not see it take place. Each year a new face appeared, black outlines around the eyes, a dot of blue or brown inside, red lips, one color for the clothes. The figures stand in a semi circle over the static filled picture of the TV. When someone slaps the side of the TV to fix it, the figures jump, move dangerously close to the edge.

As she finishes the angel, a chair is shoved into the table's side. Nathan has been passing through the room for over an hour. Their voices though close, I barely hear. She drops the angel, the red paint smearing across her hand and the angel's face. The spilt jar of mineral spirits spreads across the table, soaking into cloth and paper, forms a pool around the figure the baby in it's yellow painted manger.

The color is pouring out of me too. I am becoming unpainted. There is no feeling, no movement. Only my pencil vibrating against the table, moves. I stare intently, eyes wide open. In my head, subtracting numbers, columns of mathematical figures that become less and less, lead to the lowest number. Zero minus zero equals zero— zero plus zero equals zero— zero times zero equals zero. The circle it makes stretches outward, surrounds me, then tightens around my forehead so I cannot move. The light is blinding, stark. Everything on the table is outlined in light and the smell of mineral spirits. I concentrate on the vision before me, so that I can see nothing else. Watching as the dust from the naked light pours down onto liquid pools, falling softly, like rain, or snow.

20

Every morning and evening I spent with Annie and Amos. In between I painted. Sometimes, I'd take a break from painting and wander down to the beach. If one of them was out, we'd sip ice tea in tall glasses, sit in the shade and talk for a while.

Their voices had formed a safe place around me. Little by little, I was tempted out of the silence I had made my home and join in their easy laughter. I was becoming a child again. I didn't feel like the child I was, but the free child I could be. Making brush strokes of color like finger painting, blowing dish washing liquid bubbles into the morning air to catch Amos's sun, saying the first thing that came to mind, as Annie would. Laughing at silly things.

Slowly, I found myself, hidden in the stretched out shadows of hand shapes, the feeling of driftwood, sand, in the comfort of nice things, like rocking chairs, the feel of old quilts, warm, strong coffee steaming out of a mug. I saw things I'd forgotten. I felt them emerging, and rising in the heat of the sun. Warmed up and thawing from the coolness that lie inside me. Images were coming back now. Coming closer from a not so distant past. Tracking me down by scent alone.

Cobalt Violet Deep.

Orange-sugar-syrup-flavor smelling, Jessie's breakfast. The orange popsicle is yellow where she has sucked the juice out, and is melting down her hand. She sits, inches from the front of the TV screen. Cartoons are coming out of her head in a halo of bright colors and happy sounds. Karen is on the floor tearing pages of a magazine into strips. Between her knees is an old doll of Jessie's. The heavy plastic head is lying backwards over her knees, the eyes rolled up to look at it's own forehead. Yellow matted hair is standing straight up in clumps that end in frayed points and the body, made of cloth, is shapeless. Two plastic hands dangle over the head, in surrender.

One of the dogs had chewed up the doll and eaten all the cotton stuffing. The naked doll skin was open in the middle, and Karen is balling up the strips of paper and stuffing it inside. Since Karen doesn't play with dolls, I wonder why she is doing this? It makes a terrible sound when she stuffs the paper into the doll's neck.

At the window beside me, flies are bumping against the screen, probably smelling Jessie's popsicle. They know that inside there is sticky, perfect fly food waiting. Jessie sucks loudly.

The cartoons charge into a delightfully loud how-do-you-dos. Karen stuffs, rips, tears, crumples, stuffs again. I wonder if she will give the doll back to Jessie when she's done? I look at her to see if I can tell what she is planning to do. She flips roughly through another magazine, chooses pages to tear out. I can't tell what she will do.

Jessie turns and says, "I want another one."

"No more." I tell her. "You didn't finish that one."

"I did."

"You just sucked the juice out is all. You have to eat it too."

"I don't want it."

"You can't have another one."

She turns back to the TV. The ice left on the stick she lays on the floor, wipes her hands on her shirt.

"Couldn't you pick a better time to tell me!" —comes from the other room. "I forgot." mother's voice answers.

"You don't just forget something like that unless you want to."

"I had to pick up the kids."

"You can't do two things at the same time? *Kids, beer.* How simple does it have to be?"

"I'll go right now—"

"You got money?" he asks her.

There is a silence.

"How the hell are you going to buy it without money?" More silence. "What happened to the money I gave you?"

"I bought groceries."

"You pick up kids. You buy food. There is a beer department in the same place. You go out *without the beer.* You come home. You forget to tell me this. Saturday, I look in there and I don't find any. How many times have I said, I don't want any beer. Don't pick up any while you're out? Not once. Now, how come?"

He puts that word, 'now' with almost everything he says. He sounds like a baby always crying, now, now, now— 'Come on now. Come here now. I want it right now...' He can't seem to understand why he doesn't get what he wants, when he wants it.

"I don't know." The sound of her voice jumps at his every word. He seems to confuse her by asking so many questions.

"I don't know—? If that isn't the stupidest thing I have ever heard."

They are both in the room with us now. She is trying to make her way to the living room and the front door. Karen has stopped tearing paper and is watching them. Jessie has moved to the couch to sit beside me, but is still watching the TV. I watch mother trying to make it to the door, forgetting the money she needs, him lining up his words and adding them up to mean only one thing— that he got out of bed, went to the refrigerator and found that there was no *bloodsucking, maggot tasting, stink filled, fly food,* to put his nasty mouth around! —I add those words up in my head and make him drink it.

Forgetting the money he holds in his hand, he waves his arm violently in her direction. She ducks and moves backwards towards us. "I don't think you're going anywhere!" booming voice.

"Not without this—" Makes a grab at her, misses. Makes another grab. Then gets really mad at having to make so much effort, takes a swing. His fist closed around the bills, makes contact with the wall next to the TV. When his hand comes away from the wall, the bills are gone, and in the wall, a huge, dark hole the size of his fist. She is gone before he can cover his surprise.

Karen picks up the doll by a leg and throws it as hard as she can across the room. Little pieces of crumpled up pieces of paper go flying everywhere. The doll lands in the corner on its head. He doesn't notice, disappears into the back.

Jessie says in the silence that follows, "That's mine."

. . .

The three of us sat on the dock picking through the left over chicken bones. When Amos was finished, he pulled himself up out of his rocker, stretched back loudly with his arms, yawned, stomped his shoes without socks, skin slapping ankles, hard soles loud against the wood. Yawned again. He cracked his fingers to sound like firecrackers, then eased himself back down.

"Sack of bones." Annie called him.

"Sack of somethin'..." he says. "Getting tired before the sun goes down. Soon as I eat. I want to go to bed. That was a good dinner."

"Hold up those hands." Annie ordered him. He did. "Just look at the grease. Here, hold 'em out." She tries to wipe them off but he won't hold still. "Hold *still.*"

"They just too slippery."

"Feisty."

"Cool." he said. "Fast hands are a sign of coolness. You ever seen people talk with their hands?" He wiped his hands flat against his shirt front. His fingers moved fast, twitching. He grabbed hold of the grease stained shirt, said, "Here's the church." Hit against his chest, pointed to his head. "Here's the steeple." Arms wide, draped back over his chair, rip-roaring laughter. "Open the door— and here's all the people!" Pointed grease stained, finger people at me. *"All the people!"*

"Quiet—" Annie said. "We aren't but two feet away."

"Hand talking is for the deaf. Can't hear—"

"We hear just fine. You don't need to shout."

"Preachers shout The Word. They stand up there, yelling down the souls like drain pipes! Want to hear it echo!" Annie managed to grab the fingers of one hand, ran a dish towel over it before it got away.

"You know some of them preachers won't let their flock go to dancing?" Amos said. "Why, how do you suppose they live then? If I couldn't dance— I'd sooner die." He stood up, tried to take Annie about the waist, ends with just moving her arms in a pretend waltz. Around them, the light closed in with a softness, candle light.

Putting my fingers together, I closed the thumb doors, put up the pinkies for a steeple. Opened the doors, "All the people." I said back, turned the palms up, showed him mine.

He was shaking his head and laughing. He did a feet-stomping dance in his shoes without socks. "All the god-damn-people!" Pointed at me with his and Annie's intertwined, wiggles his. "There they are, all right. Right there..."

There they were. The people— knuckle backs, hard fingernail heads, fingerprint faces. Inside people. I turned mine up and out again. Unlinked the chain of bodies, to become two hands again.

"Whao— Amos! It's *time*." Annie said.

"So it is." He let go of Annie, picked up the dish towel, carefully cleaned both hands off, folded it three times, handed it back to her.

"Mother!" Amos said in a loud, strong voice. It sent a tiny jolt through me, something I felt in my bones.

To his long dead mother, Amos talked. He told her how good Annie was to him. And how especially good was the fried chicken she'd made for dinner— just the right amount of pepper and batter. He even told how he'd managed to do a two-step, unwilling though, his partner had been...

As I watched, I couldn't help but wonder why he talked to someone who wasn't there for him? Telling of his day like a school child, recounting his life to a make-believe parent, to a sun who left and arrived each day and night...waking him, tucking him in. He did get something from it. What, I couldn't exactly say? But something changed in him. Something like relief, a sigh afterwards. He gave something away and something came back from another direction, unexpected, grateful. Surprised, I think. I wondered how long ago he started doing this? Had he done it since a child? Or only the last few years? Was there just a time when suddenly he needed her? Amos had no mother and never would. But everyday he called out to the sky where he said she lived, called her name— and she never answered. And it didn't matter.

A thought slipped through as I watched him. *It was time.* Time to face the darkness. And the people who lived there.

21

I prefer to see in the dark, to look at things in almost no light. A dim view. Only it's very difficult to paint in the dark. I've tried. Mistakes are easy to over look, but all the detail is washed away. It becomes abstract.

"Do you think the sun has a soul?" I asked the next evening. Each of us looked at the glowing waters, another setting sun.

"For all that light, it would have to…" Annie said.

"It will die one day." Amos said. "Move on to another life some-place else. Leave us in the dark then." We all look at the colors the sun has left behind in the sky.

"Do you think it's death would be easeful, or sudden and violent—an explosion of fire?"

"I don't want to know." Amos said.

"I don't think it's something I'd want to see either." Annie said.

"It would be the last thing. Nothing would matter after that." I told them. "Same as us dying. Won't matter."

"Oh now, that's a different story completely."

"We won't explode." Amos cut in.

"No, I mean death is very important." she went on. "It is because we will die— that our bodies will not carry us on— that our spirits want to know life, before it's gone to us. To know the taste of apples, or the feel of pie dough molded around a pie pan, the smell of pinecones, wild onions, honey and butter. We should live knowing we will die, *because* we will, like a condition of agreement. God gives me so many years, I accept it— do the most I can in that time."

"Why do you think we don't?" I asked.

"Well, everyone is different, and there are so many choices. It's hard to decide for some. And there's always those who forget, or don't want to, or want to do things the hard way. We struggle around a lot of opinions on how living is to be done. There are hills, steep valleys— and more ideas on how to live, than either. It's not a question of *why*, but, *how*. How have we prevented ourselves from having the one thing we want most? I know what it is that keeps me back. Do you?"

I smiled like I was guilty of hiding some fact. "I wouldn't even know where to start."

"Figuring out how is easier than why. How has a remedy."

"What's your reason?"

"By making a promise I shouldn't have. By keeping it. By allowing myself to be tied to the reasons behind it."

I imagined having to tell a child what it means to be dead. Always they get this look on their faces. Trying to figure it out. If I look at people just right, I'll see that same look underneath. No matter what they're thinking about. Only it's not about death, it's about life, trying to figure it out, and not being able to. They pretend they do of course. They don't want to look stupid. They don't want to look like they have no idea how they got this far, without the slightest idea or notion— how they did. "How can you fix it?" I asked.

"By changing my mind."

"Oh Lord..." Amos said.

"Will you?" I asked.

"In time, I will."

Some faces know. Answers. But it doesn't make it any easier for them. Annie's looked as though, she'd thought about changing things in her life a long time. She may not have done it yet, but she knew she could. Possibilities floated in space, waited to be plucked like an apple, waiting for it to ripen, just the right color, shape and size. Then without warning, seizing it to take a bite.

Payne's Gray.

She is naked underneath. I can just see the curves of shadow that make up her body. As she passes under the street light, wearing only a nightgown, barefoot, she looks back, then slips between the trees. From the bedroom window, I can see my mother.

She is standing just inside the trees watching the house, holding her arms like she is cold. I wonder if this is a hiding place she has used before, and if she is afraid of the bugs that could crawl up her feet and legs from the ground? In my mind I fashion methods for her to conceal herself from him. Feet together, held out arms for branches, she would be a tree in a wall of trees, a massive oak. If he were to look, he would walk past her and never know she was there.

In the living room, where he had put his hand in the wall and made the hole, I had discovered something I didn't know before. I did not know that walls had insides. There's a space there that I could put my hand in and feel around. There were wood beams and spider webs. Roach eggs were glued in the cracks in rows, and old wallpaper pieces and numbers written in wide lead pencil marks too. There were things I didn't know about in this wall. Good hiding places that stayed good for a long time.

The hole was not fixed. It deteriorated, grew larger from little fingers peeling back the plaster skin, picking at the edge, an open wound that drew our eyes always upward. This was how strong he was, strong enough to punch right through a wall, and not break a finger, or scrap a knuckle. This was what he could do, it said. His accomplishment. His mark.

The sound of his boots crossing the wooden floors, tells me he is searching for her. He is making his rounds. I could just barely make out her face in the dark wood shapes. It was a good hiding place she had. Until light came. Then he'd easily see her for what she was, not a tree any more.

At some point while watching her out there, I remember wondering if he could punch a hole right through her face, like he did the wall? And if I reached in, what would I find?

. . .

Each time I came back to the present, it was like coming up for air, only to forget how to breath. So I practice this, breathing. Deeply, down in the stomach and held it there. Letting out slowly, slower still. Outside. Inside. Solid, sure breaths. In the dark, my breath sounded exactly like waves washing over the shore. The air surged, flooded over my body, dissipated, drew back in. Expanded the places inside me.

I reached out, laid a hand on the window sill next to the bed, tried to feel it like a solid place that would never change. The grain was rough and weathered. It had lasted a long time. It was here now. I tried to feel some comfort in that.

I knew there were things in me, I had yet to discover. I was afraid of reaching in.

22

Leonardo da Vinci is an earthbound man, who feels greatly the weight of age and time and place. By day, he stands on the top of the hill that overlooks a valley, looking over the backs of birds. For hours he watches them, wings rising and turning on invisible drifts of air. He tries to imagine how it feels.

By his hand, drawn lines imitated the flight of birds. Circling back and forth across an object put to paper, lightly at first, darker as the lines become more sure of it's shape. A sketch is as near to being like a nest as it was a drawing. He follows the paths of moving things, storm clouds, rivers, even summer bees darting over his pen. Listening to the sounds of movement, humming sounds, wings tickling past his thoughts.

Sometimes Leonardo felt even the weight of knowledge. The more he learned, the more people wanted of him, the more he carried, like his notebooks and tools. He envied birds. Their daring leap from branches, the miraculous weight perfectly balanced, wing tip to wing tip, so that it is never too much to bring them down. Never too much to keep them tied to the earth.

At night, I know what Leonardo da Vinci dreams. He dreams of flying. Arms stretched out, wind in his beard, robes flapping, for a few brief moments in the night, he does.

Cobalt Blue.

Nathan marches, face crowding in on itself. "You trying to make her like you? Look at her. Always holdin' on like you, like she can't do without. She's not a baby anymore!" He is yelling at the top of his voice. "I don't want her suckin' on no bottle— take it away from her!" He pounds each word into the floor boards with his boots. His voice is past being fed-up. It has reached the end-of-the-line, right-this-minute tone. Disgust. Somebody-would-have-to-pay-for-this. Everyone scatters to get out of the way.

Karen makes her retreat to the furthest corner. I grab an armful of dishes and make for the sink, with no more reason than to get out of the way. Jessie, too young to know what to do, stands with bottle in mouth, juice trailing down her chin, eyes big, head turning each way, watching everyone move at once. Mother, knows she's cornered no matter what she does, stands wringing her hands.

"I don't want to see any more bottles in this house!"

He walks over and pulls the bottle straight out of Jessie's mouth. She stands there, mouth still open after it is gone. He slams it down on the table. Jessie makes a move for it. He picks it up again, this time going all the way to the garbage can under the sink. A cry sound comes out of her. "Ba-ba..."

"No more bottle." he says to her. "You're a big girl now." She moves toward the garbage. "Now, I said no. I mean it. Go and get yourself a cup." She doesn't move. "Mama get her a cup. No more pumpkin." He slams the cabinet door shut and stomps his way back out of the kitchen. I have to take Jessie by the hand to pull her away. I manage to get her outside before she starts screaming.

For three days they put a cup in front of her. She cries and throws it away from her. She cries for hours straight, until she is hoarse and all that comes out of her are tears. He pretends like he can't hear her.

While she lay in bed one night, coughing tears and kicking the wall, I sneak out of bed and steal back one of the hidden bottles. I put some juice in it and take it to her, telling her she can't let the others know. She has to keep it hidden. "Keep it in here Jessie, or he'll take it away again." She nods her head, big tears rolling down her cheeks, making grateful sucking sounds. I pull the covers over the bottle and tuck it in around her. "Remember, it has to stay in here." Her eyes are already beginning to close.

The next morning she comes into the kitchen, blanket in one hand, bottle in the other. He walks up to her, yanks it out, and asks in a disbelieving voice, "What is this?" My stomach feels as though it has folded in half, fists of air trapped in my throat.

"Didn't I tell you to get rid of this?" He doesn't say this to Jessie. He turns on our mother. She jumps up, but doesn't answer. He makes straight for her. Jessie is crying again. Karen sitting at the table does too. I get up and move back from the table, pulling Jessie with me. "How many times do I have to say something before it gets done around here?" Every question asked meant a wrong answer was already made and done.

As he passes me, I hate him. I feel this deeply, from the very inside of me. I hate his bony walk and the way he holds his hand tight, in a fist, whenever he says anything. His black, specked chin— his red, sharp lips. I will this hatred at him, hitting him with my stares, till my eyes feel bruised. Words are coming out of me before I know it. Words I think will stop him. "I did it! *I gave it to her!*" I plant my feet down firmly and loudly as I can. But he still grabs for her shirt and slaps her hard across the face. "I did it stupid!" I scream again. "I gave it to her!"

He looks back at me only once. "You can't even teach your kids to do like they're told. They're just like you. Don't do nothin' they're told—" The wall meets the back of her head again and again, walnut cracking sound.

I run to his chair and grab his beer. "How 'bout your bottle, stupid!" I scream to his back. "You're still suckin' on your mama's teat— here it is!" Behind me, Karen and Jessie are crying hysterical. The glass comes down and smashes across the table.

"Why you—" He moves towards me.

"Come on you big idiot! I broke your bottle. You going to cry now?" The smell of the beer is rising around me. The feel of it on my skin is cool. The glass slips from my hand and I run. Over furniture, around tables. I am fast and out of reach. I'm out of control, his control. I'm laughing, but I don't know why. Maybe seeing him trying to catch me? It is funny how he stumbles over everything. He's so mad. He doesn't see that I tricked him. That I made him stop.

He is so stupid... I think, laughing inside. He falls over and I get away under a coffee table. I turn and run back towards the kitchen. Just as I think I'm safe, two giant hands reach out and grab me. Mother. I feel the hit before I know what happened. I don't try to get away from her. I only look at her. My face stinging, the laughter gone in an instant. His voice, still yelling, I can barely hear.

She is all I hear. Her face is low, close to mine. Her breath comes out in fast, rapid sounds. It is cool, like the beer. She says, hardly controlling the sound of her voice, "Don't you *ever* do that again." The words turn me warm inside. Blood stopping under her hands, fingers pinching hard, I know my arm is red underneath. *"I'll kill you..."* she says, burning me.

I cannot get the sound of it out of my head.

It is faded from time, like the way old records do, with scratched over noises on top of the music. The words are still understandable. And the way it feels is the same as when the record was new, played over and over until it was locked in the head, in memory. People have a way of hearing past the wear of scratched out time, to the feeling, to the words, to remember it as though it had just happened.

My mother had a way with words.

23

Nothing cleans as well as I want. This may have something to do with my impulsive habit of buying cleaning products— grease penetrating, no streak, guaranteed stain removal, or deep cleaning soaps, facials, sprays, powders. I am always looking for new products to try, unsatisfied with the old ones. I think I'm trying to scrub away more than surface dirt or dead skin. This is easy to figure out. But still, under every cabinet, I have stashed soaps, bottles, colorful promising ingredients, that I tell myself will one day turn out to be exactly what I am looking for. Technology is always improving.

I'm stained and dirty. My house is this way. The minute my back is turned something will be out of place. It gives me something to yell about and feel miserable over. John will always agree, "Yes, it's not like you left it. Yes, I should have cleaned it up myself." He agrees, but doesn't change. He doesn't feel about dirt, the way I do. He can't see how it gets embedded in things, works it's way further and further in. I think he knows it's just something I like to gripe about, as if dirt were a person I was always talking about, someone I like to treat badly and push around— even get rid of, if I could. It's a fight. Me against a house full of awful smells only I can detect, seeping from cracks between walls, rolled into the furniture seams and under cushions. I chase it down like a dog, and still it gets away, running loose like it does. It always turns up again.

Mars Violet.

The back seat rattles and jumps like a rocket ship blasting off across asphalt and concrete, following along a flight path that never leaves ground. Karen in the front seat, rolls down the window and hangs her head out. Her face is scrunched up, lips forming O's, swallowing mouthfuls of hot air. The fumes of gasoline and oil make me sick and my eyes water. Jessie beside me, is sniffing back tears, and trying to drink from her plastic cup. "I want my daddy..." she cries.

"I don't want to hear another word!" mother yells. "We're going over there to pick up some clothes. Then we're leaving. He's not there." Outside the window the houses, cars, and trees are speeding by. The sick feeling is racing through me too. I feel sick all over. With my head pressed against the window, I can see one hand clenched to the stirring wheel, the other motioning furiously to the side of her. She is doing it again.

In the driver's seat, talking and motioning to the invisible person. She is having an argument.

Sometimes she looked as though she were in pain, or crying. Then she'd frown, her brows turning downward, her mouth a thin line and all the motions would start over. The fingers point, stab the air, then the hand opens, pleading with an invisible other, a silent picture show figure only she can see. The expressions change constantly. It isn't always silent. Stopped at a light, I might catch a word or two spoken out loud. She only stops when she pulls up into the driveway of our old house.

No one moves to get out of the car. We just sit there, staring at the house. Everything looks the same as when we left it. Same bare front porch. Same sloping roof, that appeared to be caving in slightly along one side. Same pulled-up and grass-bare yard. She parks beside the sagging chain link fence. The dogs are standing against it, barking at us as if we are strangers. The driveway is flooded, so the dogs are mud covered and wet. They look as though they have been rolling in the puddles, or sleeping in it, or both. "We're only going to get what we need. Nothing else." mother says. "I don't have room for anything else."

The dogs, hesitant now, but still barking, half wag their tails, then stop, then bark. Mother yells at them and unlocks the gate. The backyard is littered with puddles. In a line, we snake-walk around as many as

126

possible. The dogs splash through the middle. "Go away dog..." Jessie says, mean-eyed down at the dogs, safe on my hip.

"I don't believe it!" mother says suddenly. Just off the back porch, surrounded by a lake of rain water, is a huge mound. The dogs run to it, one jumping up to the top, looking down at us. "I cannot believe this." she says again.

"What is it?" Karen asks.

"It's everything—" I say, disbelieving my own eyes.

Jessie is squirming to get down. "I want to see too. Down..." I let her down. She stands in front of me, unsure of the dogs. The one on top of the muddy hill starts barking at us again. "Shut up!" she screams at him.

Karen walks up to it and Jessie runs after her. "Mine!" Jessie yells, reaches toward the pile.

"No, Jessie— don't touch it!"

Halfway sticking out is something that resembles a toy phone. She pulls it out, mud sliding off the red plastic, a brown leaf stuck to the top. A sock wrapped around the cord dangled, black and gray. The dog barks again, and Jessie jumps back, dropping the phone.

I watch them all now circle the mound, of what was once our possessions. The dogs circle it too, sniffing at various objects. Mother doesn't pull anything out, but she keeps looking at it. I wrap my arms around my stomach, hugging tight. I feel sick again. Jessie squeals at some discovery. For one moment mother looks up, in my direction. The thin line of her mouth pulls tighter, her eyes deeper, shadows instead of eyes. They look too small, the eyes do. Two black acorns pushed in deep, like a mud pie face, a piece of grass as her mouth, and a stubby, hard rock for her nose. But the face is really blank. Someone has smoothed away the words and expression. It does not know how to speak.

"Come on Jessie." I say out loud. "You can't have it. Leave it. Let's go back to the car." I break away from looking at anything but the ground. I go to Jessie, who is trying to pull on a jump rope. It is wrapped around her hand like a checkered snake that refused to let loose from it's hole.

"I want to stay." she cries, trying to pull away from me. Something else has caught her eye. "I want my stove..."

"Jess, come on. It's no good. Nothin's any good now. You have to leave it." She starts to cry again. I pick her up and start back to the car.

"I want my daddy." Cries into my shoulder. "I want to go with my daddy."

"I know Jessie. I know."

The overcast sky begins to break up. Puddles, lit suddenly with reflections of blue and lesser grays, move across the yard. From the car, I dare look at my mother again. She is still standing out there. Looking at the remains of our life, now drying with the sun's light, mud-caked, colors softening with earth tones of browns and muddy whites. Nothing worth saving. She begins motioning with her hands again, speaking feverishly in the mouthed only conversation. The hands close, then open, brushing the air with invisible words. She motions at the ground, at the house, at the air again. Nothing is different because of it. Nothing changes. She has no power.

"Daddy..." Jessie says again, this time without emotion. I look down at her sitting beside me, streaks of dirt covering her face. She is staring out toward the yard too.

"It's all his fault. Your daddy did this!" Karen says.

"Don't talk about my daddy!"

"It's his fault. I hate him."

"Shut up..." Jessie cries. "I hate you! "

"Don't be a jerk, Karen—" I say back.

"You can't make me..."

I give Jessie her cup to quiet her and look out the window. She still hasn't moved. I hate you too..., I mouth back to her. But she can't see me. She is looking away.

This is his way of showing us what he thinks of us. Our insides turned out, like my stomach wanted to do. Everything that was inside, was now outside, from the house, massive heap of stuff. We were all staring at it, marveling maybe, at the sight of it— to see everything from a life piled up in one place. Everything we were, now one big dump pile, mud-covered, and ruined. There was no place more to sit, or clothes to wear, or toys to play with. Even our school books and papers littered the yard. It looked like the last day of school had arrived, as if we were let out for the summer. We were free, it seemed to say. We were, *nothing left.*

24

We left our mother's body not only hungry and struggling for air, kicking for life— we left her as three forces of will, determined to survive anyway we could. Primary forces. Primary colors. Karen is red. Jessie is yellow. I am blue. A deep, dark blue, almost black. Navy blue, like the sweater my grandmother made me for my sixth birthday, and mother would not let me wear until I outgrew it, and it just hung in my closet till the blue had faded to gray.

I hate to look in the mirror. Blue veins have snaked their way around my legs, making spider web lines that stand out against pale skin. I'm fatter too. John says I am not. But I can feel it, pushing out the veins, stretching the skin, boiling under my anger as grease would bubble over a fire. There is nothing I like about me. Nothing I want to look at. *I am a mess.* If I could, I would turn off, like a faucet. But I keep on thinking and feeling, running on and on. Same as time, because I don't stop— wearing down, changing into something else, something chipped and scarred and worn down completely. Dead tired, but still going. This is all reflected outward, in the way I look at things. A haze of depreciating value settles on everything.

There are some things that don't give me any trouble, like laundry. I do it well, with no fuss. Just me and dirty clothes, detergent smell, bleach clean. The heavy, wet towels I carry by the arm load to the dryer. I love the tumbling sound it makes, and how warm the room gets after it's been on awhile. I fold and hang everything as I take it out, to keep the wrinkles out. Tall, perfect stack of towels, washcloths, matched socks, work clothes hung on hangers. My order is imposed on the life of dirt, made into warm shirts that I press often to my face.

But by the time I carry the basket to the bedroom, or linen closet, the warmth has faded, and the clean smell cannot be found. It no longer matters that the towels are all folded in the same direction, or that the socks are all matched. I find myself getting angry, shoving the clothes into the overstuffed closet, cramming underwear into drawers that barely shut. *And worst,* I always put the clothes up on Sunday, day before Monday. The job I hate, hanging like a wrinkled shirt, one that I cannot shove far enough back in the closet. Waiting, the warm, clean smell of Saturday gone already.

Seconds start ticking down, taking me back to the week's beginning. I start to hate the hand's of clocks. Stealing the moments, speeding up on purpose, blank, white face, pointed metal hands, numbers counting down, ticking and ticking, until I am ready to explode, or fall into bed, saying nothing to John, who I know is wondering, what's the matter with me now? I turn away from him so he won't ask. Fuming at the bedside clock instead.

Cobalt Green Deep.

"Things aren't worth shit around here." Karen says.

Grandma swings around on one foot like a dancer. A look of impossible horror make the lines of her face fall into a heap. "What did you say!" She snatches at Karen's arm, pulling her back quick. "What did you say?"

"I didn't say nothin'."

"You did. I heard you—"

Karen pulls away, hip thrown out to the side, cross-armed, standing with one leg stuck out as if to trip someone. "Then why did you ask what I said?"

Grandma hisses between her teeth. "You stop that this minute!"

"I'll do anything I want. You can't stop me."

"Oh no, you won't."

130

"*Shit,* I will."

"Stop it! Stop it!" Grandma wrings her hand on Karen's arm, pulling her towards the front door. "Why are you such a terrible child? You stay outside until you know better. I don't want to hear such language in my house." Jessie and I follow them outside. We take the porch swing for ourselves. "You stay out here!" Grandma tells her. She sounds like she will cry, as though Karen has hurt her in some way. When she stands back, looking her up and down, Karen is unmoved. She stares out across the yard instead. "You just stay out here till your mother gets home. She can deal with you."

"Ha— make me laugh!" Karen yells.

Grandma only stares at the back of Karen's head, then turns to go in, letting the screen door slam shut behind her. Inside, there is the sound of sink water and dishes moving around under the water.

Jessie and I keep watch over Karen. We keep our mouths closed and our eyes open to watch every move she makes. She knows we are doing this and tries to ignore us, but she is weak when it comes to anyone staring at her. She'll break under the pressure. In a matter of minutes, she is yelling through the door. "Grandma, she's staring at me! Tell her to stop it!"

I kick against the porch to make us swing. The chain on both sides, squeaks painfully.

"Stop it!" Karen yells back at us.

"No." I say.

"Stop it—"

"No."

She yells through the screen door. "Jessie's starin' at me too!"

A voice answers back, "Jessie honey, stop staring at your sister."

"No." Jessie says.

"She's still doing it..." No answer. Karen then starts screaming as loud as she can, her hands pressed to her ears. Her face is scrunched up like a knot.

"What's all that racket?" Granddad yells out the door. "What do you want now?"

"She don't want anything." Jessie tells him. "She's just screaming, cause she's mad."

"What are you screaming like that for?" he asks Karen. She can hear us talk even with her hands to her ears. She says without turning around. "I want to!"

"Cut it out, before I come out there."

"Make me!"

He opens the screen and steps out on the porch. "Look here—" he says. "I expect some manners when you're in this house."

"I'm not in the house. I'm on the porch."

"Don't you smart mouth me young lady."

"I ain't no lady."

He pauses, regarding the stubborn, pout-lipped look she is giving him. "Might be so, but that's what your mama gave birth too."

"She's not my mama."

"Get on out of here then—" He waves his hands at her. "I don't want no stranger's kid in my yard. Go away. Get on out of here!"

Karen stands up to face him. Hand on hip, foot thrust out like a doorstop. "I'll tell her you kicked me out. I'll tell the police you did. They'll come and take you to jail."

"I'll tell them some good for nothing kid's in my yard making trouble."

"I'm not making any trouble."

"You are trouble." He tries to look mean. "Shut up that yelling, or I'll send you home."

"I don't got no home."

"Well, wherever it is you live then."

"She's livin' here." Jessie says to him. "We all are."

He looks at her, hands deep in his pockets. One hand comes out with a coin. He looks at it, studying it. With his thumb he flips it over. "What a shame." he says. "What a shame." He puts the coin back in, then turns and goes back in the house.

Karen says when the door is shut, "He better watch his mouth. I'll tell mama on him."

"How much good you think that will do?" I ask.

"Yeh." Jessie says imitating my tone.

"Better watch it Jessie."

"No—"

"Grandma says she can't do nothing about the way mama is. Says, mama's got to live her own life."

"Isn't that what she's doing?"

"I guess she must be livin' someone else's."

"I wish she'd die." Karen says.

"You don't die before you're supposed too. You can't wish for her to die today, if she isn't supposed too."

"I wish it was today. I'd throw a party and invite all my friends. I'd even invite my daddy."

"He's dead."

"Is not."

"Grandma says he's got no more life in him than a dead dog by the road, run over by a truck."

"Aren't you a walkin', talkin' grandma. She didn't say that. Your's is in prison."

"That's nothin'."

"Killed a hundred people first."

"At least he's not dead. He writes me a letter once a week."

"Nuh uh. Let me see."

"She won't let me see them."

"I know where's she's got them at. I read the whole bunch. He don't say one nice thing about you in a single one. He says you are the most god-forsaken-brat he'd ever laid eyes on, and he doesn't ever want to see your sorry face again. That's what he wrote."

"Sure."

"He did."

"You haven't read anything."

"You callin' me a liar?"

"Jessie don't spit."

"You callin' me a liar?"

"I said stop it, Jessie." Jessie leans over the porch edge, wets the grass again. She is practicing this method of spitting that her father does. "I'm watching you." I warn her again.

"I'll take you out right here." Karen says without moving. The summer heat has melted even her intentions. "That's a good one." she says to Jessie. "I bet you can't spit over there and hit where she's at?"

Jessie eyes the distance to where I am. "Jessie Marie, if you do I'll spank you for sure."

"Go ahead. Do it." Karen grins. Jessie leans back over the porch edge and sprays the grass. "Chicken." Karen says under the crock of her arm. "Chicken *shit.*"

25

"Do you believe in angels, Annie?" I asked.

"We will all be angels one day."

"Do you believe they appear to people— here?"

"It would only be natural. How else would we know they exist?"

I thought about this. Picked up several shells, dropped them into the water, watched them settle to the bottom. "My mother claims two angels appeared to her as a child."

"Children can see them easiest." Annie said. She was sewing a button on one of Amos's shirts. One eye was squinted. Fingers gathered together, the needle held close to her face. The thread was aimed carefully at the eye, then pushed through in the space of a breath. "Their eyes can still see the Holy Light without prejudice."

"Would angels appear to someone, who was their entire life, *cruel?*"

Long pulls of green thread, pulled, up, then in and down. "You can never say someone's been a certain way their whole life." she said. "You cannot get under their skin and ride along with them. You can only know pieces of them." She held the button till two tiny arches of thread were formed in the middle, turned it over, made a knot. "There are reasons for the way a person is. She was a child once. Not always a mother. Not always old." Cut the thread free. "Maybe she was not always the way you see her?"

"Her mother says she was always mean." I said. "Even as a child." I tried to picture my mother as a child. Couldn't.

"Still, she has to have some reason." She smoothed the shirt out, folded it gently. Wrapped the used thread around a piece of cardboard, tucked the needle in. "Angels always have reasons for visitin' a person."

26

I am afraid of Paul Gauguin. He cuts out the hearts of people and fills them with pieces of his own. I imagine that when I look at his work. Soft-fleshed paintings, that can be peeled back like a banana, or oranges, yellow ripe, juice reds. In his hand, a brush plunges into the canvas, cuts a slice first for taste, then for arrangement. A flood of color that always seems to run down the hand and mouth.

I had never seen a yellow sky, until I saw his. Not ordinary yellow, like the surface of some things. More like how the sun is described as being yellow, yellow and light being mixed together. It is a color he has chewed awhile before making it into a woman's thigh, the edges turned brown and curling up from the tropical sun. Only one bite, I tell myself. I am afraid of the fruits he offers. But always, I reach anyway, and go over every page, till I have seen all there is to see, hungrily eyeing the leftover pieces of color and shape. Till I have seen behind every stroke, the flame and heart he has hidden. Behind every expression, even in the brightest blues, I see it. Even in the darkest darks, there rests the coal-black wick.

. . .

From our separate points in space, we watched our mother. Growing quick like weeds, trying to get a hold in anywhere. Our young limbs turned restless in dirty pockets. We moved. We ran. Without knowing why, or where— instinctively.

We were always on the lookout for places to conceal ourselves, suspicious of every sound and movement. Hugging ourselves to the sides of walls, forced to move quickly. Since there were no set patterns for us to be wary of, we were wary of everything. We would learn to be dangerously unpredictable in order to survive. To throw the predator off our known tracks. We would prove unapproachable, undetectable, and unlovable. Even to ourselves.

Alizarian Crimson.

A smell like burning macaroni, is coming from the stove. "Awh-hh!..." Jessie is crying.

"Hold still!" mother says, yanks the hairbrush. Her face is red and splotchy. She looks like a red crayon, with sick, flesh colored spots showing through.

Jessie is squirming in the chair. Strands of hair fall as her hair is brushed straight up, into one big ponytail, that will stick out the top of her head when it was done. I could remember how it made my own hair feel. Painfully tight. As if it were pulling the skin away from my skull, leaving empty pockets of air around my brain. It always gave me a headache.

Jessie moves and mother loses hold of the mass of hair she was ready to clasp in the rubber band. The heavy hairbrush slams into the side of Jessie's head. Her mouth goes wide and lets out a terrible scream. "Now look what you did!" She pinches her fingers into Jessie's arm to hold her still. Mother's breath draws in like a vacuum cleaner. Then suddenly stops, something caught inside, making the red of her face redder, spreading down into her neck, disappearing under the apron collar. "Look—" she says. Her voice breaking up, keeps time with the hairbrush. "I said- hold- still- right- now!"

I will my mother to stop. I stare at her, hoping some thought will jump out of my head and knock her down, draw her attention away from my sister.

"What are you staring at!" she yells at me.

It's working. But not enough.

"Look what you made me do!" Jessie is trying to get out of the chair, but she can't reach the floor.

The sounds in the trailer become a vacuum too, and are sucked in through my ears. I can hear the overhead fan on full power, the TV screaming out something about a sale at K-Mart, a dog barking by the back window of my mother's bedroom, the frying chicken on the stove, popping and spitting of hot grease... and the sound of the hairbrush hitting such a small head. It seems strange, dizzying for a moment, as if it were a game, and someone has said to me, 'Pick which of these things doesn't belong?'.

"Get out of here!" Mother shoves Jessie off the chair, knocking it over. Her hair is tangled and wet. She runs past me, a small blur of pajamas and running feet. "What the hell are you looking at!" a voice screams from someplace else. A smoke fume is rising from one of the pans on the burner. The macaroni. I keep hearing over and over shout-loud words, pots and pans crashing into each other, silverware scraping against the counter as they're shoved out of the way— noises that pull away from me as I move down the hall. *Move now*— my body says. Walk into your room and shut the door. Safe now. Remember.

On the bed, the cat looks at me. For one second, his eyes regard me, pierce me with things I cannot comprehend, then close, and I am released. He prepares himself for another nap. Turning, I close the door softly, with only the click of the knob, telling me it is done.

. . .

Sometimes words have no meaning beyond the sound. The surf crashing into the shore beyond— fills the spaces we leave between us. Voices are speaking. I do not hear what they are saying. I am drawn up inside myself, holding myself.

From one point, the entire sky was pulled up, sewn together in one place, into one burning face without expression. Another sunrise. You were not supposed to look at the sun. But I did. I would go blind chancing a look at the thing that gave me life. Without a thought, without effort, just there, cradling the sky with long strands of pinks, soft oranges. The safe, morning gray. It has gathered up a new sky for us, I thought to myself. Or maybe, thrown one out, unfolding pillows of cloud shapes, drawn up to kiss, then tossing it away— spread out like arms. Almost reaching down to me it seemed. Almost a heart-felt gesture, such beauty. Almost a comfort.

27

I would move around the apartment in slippers, scrapping the floor with the bottom of my feet. I hated the sound it made. I thought of nameless, past relatives, who would talk in high-pitched voices, down at us as children, in a language that seemed foreign, but was only country. The same sound made me depressed and lazy. I felt old if I could hear my feet touching the floor when I moved. Saturday pacing, wondering what to do. Sunday stomping, thinking of what I had to do on Monday. Hating it already.

"I don't know what to do. I don't know—" I went from room to room saying this to myself. I did know, but didn't want to. Even the effort of trying to think about anything would make me tired. I took a lot of naps.

Eventually, I noticed I was shedding. The way a dog loses handfuls of hair in summer. I was losing things that kept me closed up and tight, like bras. I had become bra-less after only one year into marriage, on weekends anyway. I shed jewelry, make-up, socks, tight clothes, belts. I didn't want anything close to me. I lost myself in oversized clothes, dissolving the way rain dissolves crumpled paper by the roadside. The minute I was home from work, flannel over shirts and wide cotton shorts. Then to take up my feet slapping trek through rooms, back and forth, collecting dishes, dirty clothes, lost bills, bits and pieces, things. Who knows where they came from, pen tops, scraps of paper, a string with a pencil tied to one end. *Stuff.*

There were moments I wanted to just throw away everything in a room. Nothing spared. Start over completely. Or just have a room with nothing, empty. What a relief that would be?

As I move through the rooms, John might say something as I pass, and somehow I hear only what I have to. "Yes. No. I don't know. Maybe." one of those answers. The sound of my voice is strange to me. It creaks from lack of use, like an old staircase. Each word becomes more effort, putting one before the other, going there and back between us. "John, where did I put— Oh, never— Here..." He doesn't seem to notice the ends of my sentences have dropped off, like nails, or molding.

I don't think it was one thing. I think it was a lot of different things, work, John, family— especially the way I felt, or didn't feel is a better word. I was numb. It seemed like all of the sudden, but I don't think it was. Over loaded till I couldn't feel anything on the outside. Inside I could. Inside I was restless, fighting, angry. I was afraid. She had been right about the future. I was losing everything. The sense of loss was everywhere.

Ultramarine Blue Deep.

I am staring at my feet under the water when John opens the door. The light slices through me, cold air rushing in over my skin. I don't answer when he asks why I am sitting in the dark with candles like I am.

"You know, you worry me when you act like this." he says. He stands in the doorway, leans against the side. "Is it me? Did I do something?" I don't say anything. There are dark specks of mold growing in the tile grooves. Under the faucet, a line of rust stain. "If you want I can fix you something. You want a drink? Something to eat?" Old soap remains stuck to the wall, its tracks, like hard snow. He starts to turn on the light, then doesn't. He waits for me to say something, anything, but I cannot open my mouth. The bath water is cold and I can feel that my skin has gone slack, wrinkled along the bottom. I imagine it sliding off as a snake's skin would, if I move. No reasons form in my head for my behavior. I simply cannot think of anything to tell him.

142

"I'll leave you alone." he says finally and shuts the door. Two of the candles are blown out. I reach out to the nearest one, tilt it over into the bath water. The wax makes perfect circle drops. I touch the wick to the surface, extinguishing. I imagine the water as stronger than flame. It overcomes it, till all the light is gone out. With each one, I do this.

Slowly, the shadows eat up all the tile mold, rust circles from shaving cans, grime around the handles, soap film. The last one held over the water, its flame bent over the candle's neck, I say very quietly, "This is why."

I am in darkness again, floating in a pool of frozen tears. As I lean back, my body creaks, an iceberg it sounds like. Darkness covers everything. There is nothing left.

I go under, holding my breath.

28

Daylight was giving way in one last wash of color, before the night pulled across it's cool blackness. It was the same sky that I looked to, so long ago, high above a trailer park, where I would watch the sky change the color of my world to something less distinct, and more beautiful, where obtrusive details of reality disappeared with the light. Hard structures softened. Pine trees, once spiny and awkward, became deep, lush, and taller than they might have once been. Where voices, disembodied, called out for lost and hungry children to come home. These were spirit voices, echoing down tin walls and cement paths. That twisted in and among themselves through the evening mist, looking for what was theirs, and calling it home. My own two hands, as I looked at them, glowed red with fire and curved shadow. Held up to the dying light— these were not my hands. They were something changed and wonderfully apart from this every-day-place.

Venetian Red.

I hold them up and watch as my fingers ignite long, dark shadows across the pavement. "Jesss...sie!" I yell in the direction of the ten or so-trailers beside ours. "Come home—It's getting dark!" Other voices were calling out and being answered. Somewhere my sister would be trying to pretend she didn't hear me, holding to a few minutes more of play as long as she could. She would be the last to walk back in darkness, covered in mosquito bites, dived at by bats flying through the power lines, running barefoot through the sticker bushes and stubbed-toe sidewalks.

I straddle the edge of the trailer roof with my toes, fearlessly looking over the side, not worrying about falling, or how to get back down from here. It was like lying on the bottom of the pool and looking up, only opposite.

Out over the trailer park the other dark shapes with lighted sides are spread out in groups or single file. I could see as far as the main road to the other side, by the way the shapes converged, or left open the space around them. One main road moved around the park and connected all the smaller roads. Yards were a patch of space ten feet wide, some with grass, others only dirt. These were yards most likely with two or more children, as the dirt would show if it were light, the little hand prints, sneaker shoe-dents of heel and toe, a litter of toys, mostly broken, an unraveled garden hose, a single tire ringed at the top with mud pies— where little girls played, and fortress holds for toy cars where little boys drew stick roads and obstacle courses.

Each trailer had it's own concrete slab beside it to park a car, a mail box, a thirty or forty-foot wide trailer, of which every child referred to, as their own 'tin-can house on wheels'. Each claimed with certainty, that theirs would one day roll loose, or lose the cement blocks holding it in place, and would start on it's way to someplace else of choice, like Disney World, sometimes to lesser known places, like Okefenoki Swamp or Batonrouge. Every hurricane season held the promise and bets—on who would end up where, and in how good of condition? Our own trailer was set at the end of a road at the farthest edge of the trailer park. It did not have any grass, and only one leafless tree. It's wheels were not likely to ever roll, but the metal sides did rattle in a strong wind. It smelled hot like a stove in summer and steamed whenever it rained.

The trailer park centered around a playground and swimming pool, and a small pool house with it's two doors, one side for girls, the other for boys. A large sign in the middle was hand painted with all the rules to swim in the pool. Every sentence began with the words, 'No-', or 'Not allowed-'.

Overhead, a completely dark sky, a few stars. Still no Jessie. I breath in the night-edge smell of cooking food, gasoline, the cut grass and sprinkler water smell from the neighborhood behind us, chlorine from the pool. I watched and observed without moving, hung on the edge. No longer the world from a trailer roof, with it's streetlight edges and black ground below— but hovering, floating whaleback in a sea of other whales.

I knew about whales from school. About how they followed invisible lines of migration they kept in their heads. They followed the same routes every year, every season. One whale didn't. The news reports said it was an accident, that this whale had swam off it's natural course and paid our city a visit before going on it's way. Had somehow made it's way into the Gulf of Mexico, traveling all the way up past places like Key West, Miami, Tallahassee— all the way to our little port side city, to the very day and place, and perfect made spot for viewing the ocean, where all four of us had been that day. A winter day too, one in which we had all been too cold, and too miserable, to enjoy.

Later, I had cut out a picture of a whale, pasted all around it other pictures of fish, that became whale babies, and hung it deep in the closet to look at when I was alone. I liked to recreate it up here, on rooftop, the whale back, drifting serenely across the water. It was so much nicer to look at and feel, not warm, like a warm blooded mammal should feel, it felt cold, slick like metal.

. . .

For years I dreamed about the whale, changing it's course to go a different way. I wanted to follow in the dream, but was afraid of swimming so far out. I was afraid of the dark water. But I wondered about it. That's what the whale did for me. Made me wonder if I could so easily change the course of my life— instead of following the path my family knew so well.

. . .

Between the three of us, we were able to keep from stumbling, as we walked back up the path to the rentals. The ground was difficult to remember in pitch black darkness. Our steps were slow.

"Night all—" Annie's voice called out.

We each answered in return, went our separate ways up the sandy path. But before I went in for the night, I turned on the rental steps, towards the bay, took a deep breath, said out loud, *"Come home."*

29

On close observation, the colors of objects, placed around the figure, are reflected on the skin. The body is not simply skin colored, but blue-dress tinted, red-rug shadowed, golden cast from the yellow paint of the wall behind. This is a subtlety of reflection that an artist tries to capture. The eye picks up the color and follows it around, until the painting seems filled with movement, and action, or feeling of some sort. It's like being inside out and walking around, seeing everything up close first, instead of far away where we would have a chance to get used to it. The feelings and thoughts don't have time to react before the paint is already put to the canvas. Instinctual movement.

Ivory Black.

Karen's face was greasy, her mouth wet around the edges. A smirk was pinned up by the corners of that wet mouth. When she spoke it was through spit, with rolly smirk words of a powerful child, especially over a year older sister who she saw as weaker than herself. "Where you think you're going?" she asks.

"None of your business." I say.

"Oh yea? Well I'll follow you and find where."

"I don't care. "

"Sure you will." she says, slapping her feet down as she walks. "I'll follow you around until you get mad. Then I'll tell."

"So."

"So... " she rolls. "So..."

Karen could puff up like a blowfish, to seem more than what she was, when no grown-ups were around. It was mostly harmless as long as no one touched her. A touch could send her into a crazed frenzy, then she became more like a shark at the scent of blood. Or, if she had others to impress, children like herself, who like to seem more than they were, adult-like and in control. Near them, she was likely to become dangerous too. The face puffed up now. "I like telling on you." she says. She turns her head away, then back. "You make me sick." she says. "I'm bigger than you. I bet I could whip your butt no problem. I'd say you hit me first. What would you do then? Would you cry— I bet you would." Her sandals dig down into the dirt and kick it at me. "You're crazy." she says. "I heard mama tell grandma that. She said you're a loony." She smiles at this.

"No matter what I do, I would get away with it. You're crazy. I'm not."

"Hey Karen— What you doing?" Several heads poke out a trailer door as we pass.

"Nothin'." Karen yells back. "Just walkin'."

The heads became four bodies and they come out and make a half circle around Karen. "What ya doing?" They ask again.

"I'm not doing anything. Just following along." The heads glance at me. "She's crazy." she tells them. "Don't pay her no attention. You can do anything to her and she won't say a word." To prove this she kicks my leg, but draws the foot back in one quick motion. They walk along silently. "We're going to the pool." Karen says. "I need some sun. I'm *so* pale..." She looks at her arms.

"Yes." They agree, looking at their own, holding them out. They can feel the power of Karen and follow along safely behind it. She beams like a sun to them. Each look, warms them.

"I might stay out all day and night, if the weathers nice." Karen says, hands in back pockets, looking up at the sky. "See, my mama knows I can do that. She let's me do whatever I want. I bet your mama's don't let you do that, does she?"

"No." they say.

"Of course not."

One of the girls is sucking loudly on a lolly-pop. Karen looks at her and says, "Don't you know sugar rots your teeth?"

The girl glances at the others, then pulls the red sweet out of her mouth. "I brush." she says.

"I wouldn't put nothin' like that in my mouth. Brushing won't be enough. Teeth rot through to the brain. Why do you think she's crazy? Brain rot." The girl takes another lick then tosses it over her shoulder. They each put their hands in their back pockets and walk closer to Karen. Karen's wet face circles theirs, admiring their weakness.

My voice is drawn tight when I speak, like a metal spring suddenly released. "Why don't you go play in the sandbox with the other babies?" I say. It freezes them. I move away while they stand there, trying to figure out this new meaning.

"She don't sound crazy." The girl with the red tongue says.

"Well, of course not." Karen says back. "They don't sound that way. They just are. You have to live with them to know it."

"Yeah." the others agree.

The pool gate squeaks open. On the wet pavement, a splatter of bare feet follow behind me. Heads bob upwards with seal-like faces, cling to the pool edge. Others run along the sides, noses held, fly into the air— legs and arms awkward and posed, airborne seconds, splash and disappear. The high pitched screams are spaced between the leering voice of Karen's. "So..." her voice rolls around the girls. "She isn't all she pretends to be."

I stand at the pool edge, stare down to the eight-foot bottom. Bodies dart back and forth below the surface. Around me, others dive, turn head over heals, touch bottom, burst into the chlorine filled air.

"Miss Know-it-all. Miss Can't-you-see-I'm-a-good-for nothin'-Janey-baby...Ain't nothin'! Ain't nothin'!!"

Two hands shove into the center of my back. I fly forward, hit face first the cold water. Sink fast. My body goes down to the bottom, eyes wide open. I let my arms float upwards, limp. Bubbles escape, trail behind my ears, till I bump against the cement bottom. Float weightless. Play dead. I do this so well that screams erupt from overhead. Rough hands reach out to me, pull me back to the surface.

Karen's voice washes over the concerns of other's. "So...what of it?" Denial. Her face grows round and red. Fingers are pointing at her. Then, at the top of her lungs, shrieking voice, "She's just plain *crazy!*"

30

"Bones grow just as plants do." Georgia O'Keefe says this. She is holding a cow's skull. Moving her fingers over each ridge and crack, she explores the deep cavities where the eyes used to be. "They go by the same design. From a single grain or seed, to a living organism that sustains and makes beautiful the life around it." Her voice has a rough edge, and a smoothness where the edge fades, rounds out like a river stone. It does this when she talks about the things she has painted, cow skulls, hills, desert views, places made only of color. Her hands lift the skull away from her, hold it so I may look at it. "Everything fights to get beneath our skin, to make us feel it inside—the sun, the sand, the jutting rocks, the dry, hot wind. We might as well be naked." she says. "It all gets through. In your eyes, your hair, under fingernails."

Her face has the worn look of ancient pottery, thick, tough skin that seems handcrafted with finger-groove places, molded curves. From the roof top, where we both sit, the view is hazy from the desert heat rising above it. Sand and rock have the sun-baked colors of brown and orange, simmered off-white colors. She sees it with her hands. Fingers are raised up to the wind, hot light. The way she sees, molds itself around her, the landscape, her face pressed up to it. She knows everything by touch. Georgia O'Keefe cannot see. She is blind.

· · ·

"Creating something is easy." Annie said. "Learning to live with it is the hard part."

"I'd like to have children one day. I just don't think I'm ready right now. I wouldn't know what I was doing."

"You never know that."

"But shouldn't there be a...feeling? An instinct or something? Nearly everyone I know already has a kid or two by now. I can't imagine myself as a mother, a year from now, or even five years."

"Maybe you're just trying to understand better what that means first?"

"I knew what it felt like once."

"When a mother loses a child, it can be hard for her to take to another one. She can be afraid of losing it all over again."

"I took care of her." I turned to face her. The struggle to control the words was unbearable. "She just gave her away. Threw some stuff in a bag— handed her over, and said, 'Here, you take her. I don't want her any more." Annie nodded her head, without saying anything. "They talk now. About things in ways that are wrong. They're making it up, pretending like nothing's wrong."

"Some people need to do that." she said.

"They couldn't have forgotten. What's real and not real, split down the middle— they take one side, me on the other."

"You can live awfully close on either side, so close, you believe that's all there is." She patted my hand with hers. "You'll make a fine mother one day. You just wait and see."

I try to imagine holding a baby. There is an overwhelming sense of loss. It seems, that if I looked close enough there wouldn't be anything wrapped in the blanket, only air, something missing. "I remember a lady once, in the trailer park. Her little boy had fallen into the pool. He'd been dragged out and laid out in the grass, lifeless." I said. "She was standing in the middle of the road, screaming. People went running to help. But she just stood there, screaming, her hands at the sides of her face. One long scream, that just kept coming out of her. She was frozen there. Standing in a doorway watching, I couldn't move either. We just looked at each other. Seemed like forever, locked in the sound of her scream. Like she'd lost herself, and was holding onto me somehow— with her eyes. Until somebody was yelling, 'He's breathing!" and she broke free suddenly and was running away. I still couldn't move for the longest time afterwards, even after she was gone. It seemed like I was waiting for permission to move again. He was breathing. I wasn't. The first words my mother said, when grandma told her Karen had tried to kill herself, were, 'Oh, *shit.*'

"Somehow it's just not the same." I said.

Annie's eyes, followed the horizon, searching it seemed. "Some mothers don't know how to let go." she said. "Others, don't know how to hold on. It's that way with some animals. Some feed and care for their babies to a certain age. Others drop em' and leave. They have to learn to survive on their own from the minute they're born."

"Some kill and eat their young." I said.

"That too's the way of nature, sometimes."

Primary Yellow.
Primary Red.
Primary Blue.

"No." I say, then a rush of words. "You can't do this." I tell her. "You're takin' her, cause you don't want her. You don't want any of us! You going to give us away? Our dads out there somewhere, waiting to take care of us? They can't, can they?"

"Shut your mouth—"

"Why? Why are you throwing Jessie away? She didn't do anything to you."

"Shut up!"

All that's me, centered inside, heavy like a rock. A child's words that tumble out, "I won't let you *do it.*"

Mother's face is smoothed over, hard. "I'll do, whatever the hell I want."

"No."

"You just watch me."

"I won't let you." I will my face to show the rock inside me, betray nothing.

Teeth clenched together, she presses me against the door, out of her way. "You get in that car right now." I don't move and she hasn't let go.

I think she might throw me down the steps to make me move, but she doesn't. "Jessie—" she looks away, "get in the car." I keep looking at her face, even though she no longer is looking at me. "Karen! The car—now." We are all three dripping wet from the pool. Jessie is still in her bathing suit, sucking the tangled ends of her hair. She drops her towel, squeals out, "daddy!", runs to get in the car. The events are sudden and without warning.

Mother releases her grip. Goes straight to the driver's side, gets in, slams the door. Even after the car pulls out of the driveway, I don't move. I feel like she is holding me still, the pressure of where her fingers were. The car is down the street before I can move. Then I think, *Jessie*.

Inside me something, sick.

Jessie.

I go down one step, then stop. What it said was true, my mother's voice. Then take another step back up, look in through the door. I go in the living room. You can't stop me... In the middle of the room, staring at the walls, as though I don't recognize them. I don't know this place. I hate this place! Then I am running. Out the back door, round the corner, the tree, rooftop. Look towards the road over the tops of trailers. The car is nearly out of sight. Tears are flowing out, but I slap them away, choking. I feel like I can't breath. *Jessie!*

They are gone.

I follow the shaking of my knees, down to the metal roof. My body, drawing up into a tight ball over leaves and dry branches. Eyes close in the howling sounds of wind. It washes over me, rip tides pulling— and I am washed out to sea, and under, below the angry water. There is a deafening sound of muffled surf and bubbles, of blood rushing, and the hard, painful pull of the current.

I can feel the water getting deeper. The pressure folds around me, wrapping tighter and tighter, condensing on my heart. The walls of my insides try to resist, fail gradually, till my body is like a bobbin, feet facing downward, arms floating out, head lifeless.

The whale.

I call out for the whale.

"I am a fish." I say. "I am not a person anymore. I am a fish— a whale-baby." There is a great clanking of metal, and crunching steel, and walls. I am lying on the back of a whale. He is breaking free from some place. "I am a whale baby." I say again. A trailer from another world, is pulled up from it's foundation, and submerges in a great splash. "I want to go all the way down. Till there's nothing. Nothing left...".

Wings extend.

Diving downward, flying forward. No more light. No more shadow. Only blue, blue, blacker. Unfeeling now. Cold, colder, coldest. No air to breath. Nothing. Nothing. Nothing. Slipping into darkness now. Two heartbeats thundering, rolling, diving, downward through depths, through layers, through time, denseness Down to nothing. Down to bottom.

Cold.

Dead.

And blind.

. . .

"One day I'll face her." I say this to Annie, knowing it is true.

"I'll see her eye to eye, across a room, or on a road. But I'll see her, and have to say something. I wonder now, what it will be? Maybe I'll say, 'Hello mama, how are you?' She'll say fine. I could then say, 'That's good. I'm glad things are fine for you.' Then I'll stop, let the moment pass over a bit. Then go on slow-like, the tone plain and drawn, like a straight line. 'I'm real glad it's fine for you. Cause it's been hell for me. It's not one bit fine. I want you to know that. I want to be *sure* you know, that you don't misunderstand my meaning. I'll stop again, look straight into her, hold her with my eyes, so she cannot turn away. There will be no emotion in my voice, only words. Plain words. No colors. 'Well, bye now mama. Maybe next time we meet, it'll be different. Things change. Maybe you and I will have a longer chat then. Smile now. Anything's possible.' Then I'll step off the curb and move away from her, before she gets the nerve to say anything, ruin the moment.

"If she were to open her mouth it would be a lie that fell out. It would be to please. The words change for every person. Please this one, that one, all of them with any lie that would fit. She can pretend to be the hurt mother and tell me I am the terrible daughter. She could cry, telling me how unfair this is. How it wasn't her fault. But, if she doesn't say anything, just listen. My foot will be jammed in the door of her eyes.

I'll creep back inside her, only for a moment, throw in what I have to say and be back out before she'd even know I was there. Then, in her head, after the door is shut again, where no one else hears, where it's just her. Maybe there is truth in there? Before things come out as lies, where she *has* to know. Where everything is as it was! I didn't forget. The mind doesn't lose one bit of anything. Not one scrap. Just her in there. Deciding who she will be in that moment. I'll walk away, before she can forget how she knows what I'm talking about."

Thoughtfully, Annie said, "Tom believed that all men were good at heart."

"Maybe some." I said.

"He wanted to see it in everyone. Sometimes, when he met a downright mean person, he'd try and coax the good out. Not always a good thing, makes matters worst on some poor souls. Like they were afraid of being any other way. Me and Amos had to rescue him more than once. One fella even had a gun. Said Tom had no right messin' in matters that didn't concern him or God none, and if he didn't clear out, he'd put a bullet between the both of them. He was ready to kill Tom over having to look where he didn't want.

"That fella could have easily been what killed him off. And Tom, just might have let him too." She lifted out her skirt, smoothed it down. Her eyes were looking at the patterns there, as though each shape had just appeared. Finally she said, "I would like to say it was old age that killed him." Smoothing out the folds again. "But it wasn't. It was something inside that wasn't right. It gave him pain that he tried to hide." She looked at me. "I think he was trying to forget his own pain by looking into others. The words cured some and left others untouched. It was more the effort of trying, that gave him any happiness. That's all that mattered to him. His pain didn't go away, but in his heart, it was filled."

"He died."

"That he did."

After a while I said, "Men who preach only goodness, find their end by angry hands. One way or another."

"Don't you believe in good words?"

"I am *surprised,* only by goodness."

"I cannot imagine a life without saying a good word now and then." she said.

"No, I don't think you could. You are a surprise Annie. A wonderful surprise." I smiled. "But it won't change anything. Nothing I say will matter to them."

"Your cure may not be what they need."

"I know."

"Maybe you should stop trying to give it to them."

"When the bottles empty, I won't have a choice. Do you think I'm like Tom when I keep trying? I'm looking down the barrel of a pretty big gun. I haven't been able to get out of the way yet."

"Give me your hand." she said. I do this. She pulled it to her, me with it. "There." she said. "The way is clear. *The is clear.*"

"I hope so." I said.

"Believe it."

"I'm trying." looked in her eyes. "I really am trying."

Section Three

How sweat these words of love
How bitter their echo—

31

"I believe it is possible to call out at fate, or such forces as those, and pull them off some other course, towards your direction." Annie said. I thought about this, watching the light move across the water. I imagined a rope tied to a mountain, tied to a boat, to me, trying to move the impossible— and doing it. "It is also important to hear the signal, to know what to watch for in order to recognize it when it's arrived. As a child, when you saw that whale, you knew it was your sign."

"I did, I guess." I said. The whale was a mountain, the impossible happening.

"Change does not happen by itself. It has to be made aware that you need it, want it, that the time is right and you're ready to listen. You have to *call* it."

"How do I know when the time is right?" I asked. Amos was laughing softly.

"Ah...when?" Annie said. "The heart knows when. But you got to know how to listen to the heart. It's voice is not loud. The brain is loud. When the heart speaks, it's almost a whisper, an angel-feather lightness. It takes work to know the silence of a whisper." she said this, then smiled brightly. "But you've already done that. You followed that whisper here."

Amos leaned forward to throw his bread crumbs in the water, said, "Calling a whale— changing the future. Now, that's a real trick. Don't hear many claim to that.

"The future's not a made thing, Amos. Doesn't take much to change what hasn't been done yet."

"It makes no difference what it is you're callin' after." he said. "How it's done, is the thing."

"Do you think a person could call angels?" I asked.

"There—" Annie said after me. "Katherine's mother called angels. Katherine's just doing things a little differently."

"Coincidence." Amos said.

"There is no such thing as coincidence. Angels do not appear for no reason."

Amos stood up before us and proudly announced, "A ceremony!" We looked at him wondering what he meant. "That's what we got to do to call a whale. We got to do us a ceremony!"

Annie let out a roaring laugh. "Old koot—" she says, rolled back in her chair. "You couldn't call a buzzard to dead meat!"

"Well missy—" He flapped his arms like a bird. "Why don't you just use some Voodo-Hoodo magic, and conjure up a dead whale for us!"

"Amos Harold! You watch what you say—"

He settled down. "I was only kidding... You couldn't anyway."

"I'll have you know, I can do anything I set my mind on doin'."

"I'm sure you can." his tone implying. "Sure'e dog, you could."

"Don't you back talk me—"

"What you gettin' all hoffy about? You started this."

"I most certainly did not."

"Katherine did, or did not, this woman here, start this to begin with?"

I said, "If you two were my kids, you'd drive me *clear up a wall.*"

Turquoise.

"I couldn't convince her it was a dream." Grandma says. "The more I said, the more she cried." Grandma is drying the silverware. She polishes each one with the dish towel, then places the spoons, forks, knives, each in neat stacks in the drawer. When she is done she carefully

166

lifts and slides the drawer closed, not with a knee, or the side of a hip, she uses both hands. It goes in without a sound, smoothly.

"What did she say, exactly?" I ask.

"Well, at first, I couldn't make out what she was saying. She was just all tears and hysterical. Then she started screaming, 'They've come for me! They've come for me!' She absolutely refused to get out of bed and go to school. 'I'm going to *die!*' she kept saying.

"'Who's coming for you?' I asked her. She held the covers over her head and said finally, 'The angels.'

"I didn't know where she'd come up with that. I asked her what she was talking about? She said, 'Last night I prayed. When I opened my eyes, there they were.'

"'Well why would angels want to kill you?'

"'I was praying to God.' your mother said, 'For us not to move again.' She cried and cried, 'He's gonna take me away!'. I simply could not convince her it wasn't real. She said they were there. Described them in detail. I almost believed she'd seen something the way she went on about them, standing there, two of them, looking down at her, the looks on their faces. She said they never spoke a word, only looked at her, 'Smiling, like children do, but partly grown-up like, too.' she said. And they had no wings. Imagine that?"

"How did she know they were angels then?" I ask.

"Well I suppose you'd know if it was an angel or not, if it was standing right in front of you. She refused to go out for a whole week. But she had to go eventually. We were moving. He'd been re-stationed. And the whole way there, she was convinced she was going to die. Plain silliness. Making such a big deal out of nothing. She knew we had to move. She was just trying to make matters worst. I put her in the back seat and told her, "That's not you I hear.' But she'd only cry louder."

Grandma picks up the dish-towel carefully folds and lays it over the sink edge. Her hands are thin, finely lined. I admire the way the fingers move, quick, but delicate, strong but graceful. She reaches across to the window ledge where she had placed her wedding ring. She always removed it to do the dishes. It goes on easily, the fit somewhat loose.

"I just didn't know what to do with her. Why do you want to know?" she asks me.

"Do you think she saw anything?"

"Since when would I believe anything a child says?" She moves away, straightening things as she goes. "Moving was what we had to do. It wasn't a choice." Her voice sounds pulled in, like the words aren't moving out towards me, but going back, into her. "It's just the facts she had to live with."

32

My grandmother is a farmer.
  She has raised people her whole life.

From the dry soil around her she dug in with her hands. Up to her wrists, she pushed through a Depression's dust. Up to her elbows, she pulled apart failed ambitions and threw out the broken promises that had taken root. She had reached in past wishful thinking and things that were never meant to be. Clearing out the soil as best she could, she tucked in each seed lovingly with store bought fertilizer and the miracle grow of her silent prayers. She had high hopes for us all. But even the best of intentions and care, can still produce a bad crop.

She is a great grandmother now, by my sister's child. Before that, she was grandmother to my sisters and I. And, before that, the mother of my mother. And, as the oldest daughter of her mother, was the second mother to her seven brothers and sisters.

I think it was running after all those children for so long that caused her to grow old, not time.

There are more worries pressed in-between her eyes and words each time I see her. She's looking for the remaining thread that will finish up what she has to do. She is always looking around her, with a hint of surprise, the curve of her mouth just beginning to form a frown, as if seeing for the first time, how much has escaped her, and how much still has to be done. I was one of those who needed so much of her. I helped pull on the rope that bound her to us.

From the beginning, when our mother dropped us off at her house, we started yelling for her. From the tops of our lungs, and the top of the cold, metal playground slides, we called out from closet corners where we would hide, or across crowded school yards where we would run. Any place we were, we called for her to save us. We called and called, until she slid right past some other life that could have been hers.

With our screams, we surrounded her. From nightmares that pursued us out of our nights and into our days, we called her through the bent up eye of her sewing needle, begging her to come find us, until she did, and then became lost herself, and could no longer look back to things she might have wanted to do. Twisting and pulling on her, till we had gathered up all the little folds of skin along her face and hands, changing her into something other than she used to be. Making her into something full of lines, hidden patches of darkness, rough dry places, something much like her garden, just after winter.

Seems like her whole life ought to be sewn up by now. But I see her, still looking around, still running, still giving, still trying to fix what needs to be fixed. Time has helped me look back when it comes to my grandmother, and, if I could, I would smooth out her face with my hands. I'd press it to me, give back to it, all the warmth and time, and patience she gave to me. If I could, I would give all the years back. I would set her free.

Van Dyke Brown.

"You can't punish a child for being like her mother. Three-year-olds don't know what they're saying." Grandma's voice is tired. I imagine her leaning her head into the phone like a pillow. She says, "I tell her that isn't nice to call people names. She doesn't understand what I'm talking about. Her mother calls her that. She thinks it's like a name or something."

"Children understand a lot more than you give them credit for."

She goes on as if she hasn't heard me. "Could you imagine the look people would have if she yelled out something like that in church? I'd never be able to show my face again. When she's older she'll understand it's not nice to call people names. I'll keep on her."

"It shouldn't be your job. It should be her mother's."

"I know. I know. But someone has to help the child. She can't take care of herself."

"You've done too much, grandma."

She sighs heavily. I remember the way the wind sounds through a jacket hood, closed up tight to the ears, my hands ice cold and shivering. Grandma's do not feel as cold, closing over the top of mine.

"Jenny's a lot like you." she says.

"I never called you names."

"I mean her good qualities. She's smart, learns fast."

"It's taking too much out of you."

"I can't throw the child out on the street. She needs somewhere to go." she pauses. "I did it for you kids."

"I know."

"Someone has to be responsible."

"I know."

One day, I hope my grandmother will get to see my own children. I imagine them lined up in front of her. She holds each of their faces in her hands, and says their names in a row, like she is reading the inscriptions from tiny pieces of paper, planted over spring seeds. I want her to love my little flowers. I want them to love her.

But, each time I see my grandmother, I can find less and less of her left.

33

She is dead serious and means every word.

Grandma tells me, "You were such a precious baby, so sweet natured." Then asks, always following, "What happened to you?" She really has no idea, why I am the way I am now, that I no longer smile, or laugh, or say nice things. As if the child I was, had disappeared in a day, instead of piece by piece. I would like to say to her, that those smiles were worn down by-the back of a hand, and the laughter got knocked down my throat. But, I don't say anything, instead. To say the words would sound like a lie. That somehow, I made it up.

French Ultra Marine.

"Isn't she darling? She's so sweet. Look at that face. Here baby, look at me. Look at me—" Grandma is holding baby Jenny, rocking back and forth, talking to her, her grandma voice, soft and warm. On the couch, with pillows propped up around her, Karen is stretched out. She looks snug, like a cat on a window sill. She watches me with that same cat-look of seeing a bird out on the lawn. I force a weak smile at her. Behind her, mother is looking at all the things Karen has been given for the baby. An old crib is set up in the corner, piled with boxes of used baby clothes and toys. "Look at that—" grandma saying still. Every little movement the baby makes, made her say, 'Look at that', as though she were seeing all these things for the first time.

The baby is wrapped in a pale, blue blanket. Small, wrinkled face and reddish hands are peeking out of the hole where the blanket spills open. A tiny mouth yawns. "Look at that." grandma says again. "Can you see your aunt? Katherine's come to see you too. How 'bout that..." She makes it sound surprising, that I had. The baby just yawns.

"She needs a nap." Karen says.

"Oh not yet." grandma says without taking her eyes off the baby. "She's still awake. She wants to see what's going on. Don't you, Jenny?"

"I should give her a bottle." Karen says.

"A bottle—" grandma says happily. "I'll fix Jenny her bottle." Before I know it, I am holding the baby and grandma is off to the kitchen to get a bottle. The new eyes look at me now. If it were true that infants know their mother's face, then she must know me as a stranger. I wonder if she is trying to figure out who I am? Blue and dark eyes watch me, smiling expression.

"You plan on making me a grandmother next?" my mother asks. She has come up close, while my attention was on the baby.

"Why?" I say slowly, not looking at her. "Do you think it suits you?"

"I was only asking."

"I want a boy next." Karen says.

"One's enough." mother says back. "You won't want more than one."

"You did—"

"One's too much to handle as it is. I should know."

Karen's cat smile turns into a frown. "I'll have as many as I want."

"Well don't think I'll take care of them." Mother peers over my shoulder making elongated smiles at the baby. "What are you going to do with this one? That husband of yours going to take care of it?"

"Grandma's going to watch her while I'm at work."

"She isn't going to live forever you know."

"About used her up yourself..." I slip in.

174

"Don't you talk to me like *that.*" I feel the breath of her words on my face. Moving sideways, I make my way towards the table and away from her. "I wouldn't think it would make any difference how I talk to you." I say, laying the baby carefully down in it's carrier. I pull my head back just in time, as a line rakes across one cheek, stinging. Mother's hand is quick to pull away. With a slight turn of the head, to view her eye to eye, my words smooth and rolling. "Did that make you feel better?"

"Watch that baby—" Karen threatens, but doesn't move to do it herself.

"Stop that this instant!" grandma. She is looking at me. The baby cries, then everyone is looking at me. "I think you'd better go." grandma says to me.

"Hand me the baby." Karen's arms are outstretched.

"You're upsetting her." grandma says again to me.

Karen is smiling. Her new I'm-a-mother-now-and-you're-not tone already set in. "Hush. Hush now." she says over the baby's head, watching me. She has beaten me out by having a baby first, is more than me, and has gotten all the attention— her smile says, and is glad of it. The three of them are huddled around the baby. As it cries, they each put a hand to it. Grandma saying, "Don't cry. Don't cry." Mother towering behind them, the crooked half smile as she looks down at the baby, saying nonsense words that the baby will never understand. Karen holds the baby and jiggles one knee up and down. "Don't come back at all." she says low to me. "

I go to the door slowly, open it, and say loud enough for them all to hear, "I hope she doesn't turn out to be anything like you."

"Hush— don't say anything." grandma says to one of them.

I wonder which one she has said it to? But then, it doesn't matter. I shut the door on them all.

34

The soles of my feet remember if I've ever been to a place or not. I know when I've walked here before. I can tell by a feel, by the shape of the land, and the way the sand arches underfoot, making scrunch-scrunch sounds. I walk and I say, "I've been here before." I know this. Sometimes this happens when I hear certain words, or things happen, and I think, I know this too. I've been here before. It is like this when I'm with my family. Everything they say is like an echo. I know what it is before they say it. It's all been said before.

They always take them in. "For the baby's sake..." grandma will say. I give her that look of— 'Why do you put up with it?' She just shakes her head. She is always the first one to the door to let them in.

My sister swears she's never going back to him. Until the phone calls begin. Then the tears, and the arguments of, "If she goes back again, she's not welcome here anymore!" Granddad always had enough, always said no more, and always had to let her back. Grandma got her way when it came to men and children. Eventually, my sister would pack up and leave, carrying her screaming child to the car, starting over again and again, back to the man she said she loved.

In the corner grandad, arms crossed, shaking his head, "I told you. I *told* you." But no one listens.

Yellow Ochre.

Jenny is crying and runs straight for grandma when she comes in the door. Karen behind her, keys jangling, overnight bags overflowing and heavy, she drops everything in a pile to the floor. She then has to pry Jenny away from grandma to get her to bed. The child's cries become deafening screams. She digs her heels into the carpet, but Karen drags her, pulling her by the arm, down the hall to the spare bedroom. All the way, Karen is yelling too, "I don't want to hear it! I don't!" It seems she is saying this to everyone, the child, the silent looks, my looming face.

Everyone is drawn in, listening, the noise is disturbing in the background, coming through the walls, behind closed doors. She wants Jenny to go to sleep, but she won't. "Get out! Get out— out of here now!" I hear her yelling. The child cry's louder. She wants her grandma.

I find myself outside her door, standing quietly. I tell myself to wait. But what I am waiting for, I don't know. A small hand is trying to open the door, from the inside. It opens, slowly, and a small form in pajamas, without a sound comes into the hall. She closes the door carefully behind her, then goes past me as though I am not there. Down the hall, into the living room where my grandmother is sitting, she gets up into grandma's lap without a sound, and grandma folds her in with her arms, also without a word, begins rocking her, Jenny's small head buried in the fold of her arm. Grandma does not look at me, but stares off to the side.

I have the feeling, this has been played out many times before. I feel shoved backwards by this picture of them. It is from another time. It is as though, I am out of my body looking back, and it is I, who am rocked asleep.

I turn away from their silence.

I know what they are thinking.

. . .

"All pain is telling." Annie said. Inside me, my heart had a pulsing pain on one side, the size of a quarter. I did not let on that it hurt. I looked away, breathed slowly, imagined the quarter spent. Annie said, "It's a voice that tells us something's wrong."

178

With me? I wondered. Then said, "If it is a voice, it drowns out the whole world. I am deaf from it." I try to ignore the pain. It is sharp and stinging now. It will go away eventually. I tell it silently, to go away. "There's not enough words to tell me how I feel." Then I think, that's not true. There are *too many*. I see them inside, stuck. Without a way out, they fill me to the point of exploding. I might do that one day, explode, a volcanic eruption, a jabbering idiot, a woman gone over her own edge. For a moment, it seems an interesting prospect, but then the pain in me says, loosing all those words would be painful too. I might end up with nothing to say afterwards and nothing to hold on to.

"You think because you failed to help your sister, that you are a failure." Annie pointed a finger directly into my pain, told me what it said. "You were a *child*. What more could a child have done?" I didn't know. "She must go on her own way now. She's all grown now, just like you." She stood up, walked the few steps to the shore's edge, stared down at the water.

There was such compassion in her voice, and knowing. I felt ridiculously slow and pitiful, stupid even. A childish voice said, "I don't want to lose her."

"She is a thing of the wild." Annie said. "You can't keep her." She walked barefoot into the water, sunk up to her ankles in sand, looked back at me. I was holding my shoulder, hand concealing the spot of pain inside, knees pulled close together to lean on, shielding. I found it hard to sit still in the heat of the sun. It seemed to be boring down through me, pressing me down.

Annie waded back and forth through the water, the hem of her dress dark, trailing behind. "There is a friction between the land and the waves." she said. "A long, sliver of movement all along this coast. When a shell gets caught up, it can be broken down and made back into sand, or be polished up like a smooth apple skin. You get changed by every second you're here." The wind, in a powerful gust sent a spray of water over her. Her outstretched hand passed through it, shining. "Why do people come down from all over just to stare at the waves?" She looked back at me. "They see something, or wish they did." The heat was reflected from her, cool in the way she spoke, at ease with her surroundings. I pressed my hand firmly against my heart, ordered the pain to leave. "It's two grand, powerful forces coming together. It's what we are. Body and Soul. People sit and wonder about the part they have forgotten. The part that shapes the land. Moves things. Changes everything it touches. It's deep, and wide, and dangerous like the current. But it's the most important part of who we are." She looked up at the sky, smiled at the invisible.

"She's not what you're missing inside. Look at me. Look back into me, where my words are. One look, as a child, told me what I was missing. It's the same thing missing in you."

"What is it?"

"You're missing what you are afraid to feel. Love. You are loved. Let yourself open to it. It will fill up that hole in you."

"I don't think I can do that."

"It's not something you think about, just feel. Amos and I love you. John loves you. You must love *you* now. Being alone is a terrible thing forever. We need each other. You are a survivor. Teach your children to survive, to be smart, to love and find comfort in each other. This is what's left to you. Let love in. It is the greatest survivor of all!"

"You must think I'm the most hardheaded person alive."

"Second most, maybe."

"I feel so stupid talking about all this and not being able to *do* anything."

"Patience."

"I don't have much of that."

"Yes, you do."

"You have too much confidence in me."

"I have faith in you. You must find the confidence."

"Do you have faith in whales?"

"Why wouldn't I? Whales are whales."

"I shouldn't be so lucky twice."

"Why not?"

"I just shouldn't."

"They're free to go where they want. Why not here? Especially, if invited."

"That's the trick."

"That's the trick..." She mimicked the way Amos would say it. "Faith."

"Amos says, I have to trust what I believe."

"Same thing as faith almost. Both come and go from the same place."

"Faith and trust." I say the words like I am giving them a practice try. "If they were nails I could pound them in and that would be that. If they were rocks I could set them on the edge of the table cloth and life would be a picnic. Did they have to be wisps of air, invisible, hard to catch, impossible to hold, or prove I really have them?" Annie was laughing. "I mean it—" I said. "It's very hard to trust something you can't see, taste, touch, or smell."

"I know." she said.

"Annie," I asked, "—how did you get to know so much?" Her face was so clear in the sun's light. Every part of it was visible. Nothing was left hidden.

She said, "It comes from sitting on the edge of the world like I do. Things tend to spill my way. Eventually, you see and hear it all."

I don't know when Jessie stopped being the person I was trying to save and became me. Maybe when she was no longer a child, or when she'd moved too far away, or became the person she is now? It is still her face I see in dreams, but it is my voice I hear, an eight-year-old's back talking, demanding voice, that now runs up when I'm not looking, hits me in the arm and runs, yelling, "You're it!"

I've counted to a hundred before looking. I've counted all the days since. I've looked, but I still can't find her. Sometimes I say, "I give up— come out!" But then, I catch another glimpse, a bit of hair blowing in the wind, a flash of red, or blue, or yellow, and I follow, trying again. I just can't seem to help myself. It's as if a dare has been made I can't resist. I may not want to do it. I have too.

Annie's voice followed me as I made my way back to the rental. "Cast out your faith like a net." she said. "Over the air, down into the waters that run deep. After it has been out there for a time, pull and pull hard, till you can gather it in back up to you. It will be heavy with living things. Some good, some fine, or small, but all made by the hand of God. Take out what you need and give the rest back to it's element. You looking to catch a whale passing, you'll have to have faith. Cast it out over the water. Don't let go of the end. Pull! Remember, it will take your *strength* then. That's the most important part. If you let go, or aren't strong enough... there it will go, slip right through your hands, and that whale will swim right on past. It may take some practice. Fisherman don't always catch what he's looking for. Have to try many times. But each time you pull in that net, your muscles get stronger. Frustration doesn't help the fisherman, patience does. Faith and trust will lead him to the right spot! Faith and trust! *Listen!*"

If only I would.

34

The ceremony.

Amos offered his pipe to the four directions. He breathed in the rich, tobacco smoke from the end, then passed it to Annie, then to me. To us, he said, "We got to know how the whale walks." He turned and his heron feather headdress, rustling blue-gray feathers, fell like a single large wing down his back. To the direction of the ocean, he said, "We present ourselves to the Great Spirit. To this place." His voice, loud, for effect and presence, he tells us, "Listen to the voices of the crickets. Move with the cricket sounds." He moved his hand through the air in a motion matching their rhythm in an up and down wave. "They are teaching us the walk of the whale. His heartbeat. His way."

Somewhere, out in the darkness, there was the sound of a heron taking flight. We could hear it's wings lifting up out of the bay water. Amos took hold of this new sound, made it a part of the motion of his hands. "That is the wind over the whale's back as he pierces our world to take breath." His hands were flying slowly back and forth in front of him, then dipping down and up like two jumping dolphins.

The boat rocked gently, as we drifted out from shore, into the night. The ceremony had begun. *To call the whale,* Amos said, we would have to go out and create something magical. It didn't matter what that might be, only that it be rhythmic and hold our attention. So, we went out in the boat with our magic making tools, a perfect night, the water calm, the moon full with light, a breeze just enough to move us along without help.

Amos put a small drum between his knees and began pounding it slowly with a mallet. "These are the sounds of your spirit steps. As you go out to meet the whale, you must show him the way back. He will follow the echo of your steps as you return. Now, take up your rattle Katherine, and follow my sound..." I held in my hands two large shell halves that had been tied together. Inside, were dried red beans. I followed his drum sound as best I could. Annie, beside me, was trying not to laugh. She began to shake a string of silver Christmas bells. On one end, an old, red bow dangled. It sounded like a Santa's sleigh, a flat tire turning on it's rim, and a pail full of nails all run together at the same time. If not harmonious, we were at least individually rhythmic. Our spirit steps were loud and clanging, echoing across the bay. If a whale was passing somewhere out there in those dark waters, he could follow our unmistakable sound, a hundred mile radius at the least.

At some point, Amos began to sing and if there had been more light to see by, Annie's face would have been bright red from holding her breath, trying not to laugh. He made sing-song sounds that may, or may not, have been words. We followed the sounds as best we could. But, when he suddenly drummed out in three strikes of the mallet, at the same time yelling, *ho-ho-ho-* it was in the very least, too much for us to take. Annie was stomping her feet in a fit of containment that was failing fast. I lost count to the beat I was following, fell out of tune with the drum, dropped the whole thing into the bottom of the boat, at which Annie burst out with a sound all her own, loosing one set of bells over the side of the boat. It made a definite plop as it hit the water and sank.

Amos turned slowly to look at Annie, then at me. Carefully, he placed his drum mallet into the bottom of the boat, set the drum over the top of it, then reached down and began to take off his shoes. "Now, everyone in." he said calmly.

"What?" Annie said.

"In the water."

"Why do we need to do that?" she asked in all seriousness.

"If you want a whale to hear you, you got to get in his element."

"I'll do no such thing."

"You'll have too sooner or later—"

"What do you mean?" Annie and I looked at each other.

"I mean, those oars are half way back to shore by now."

She peered over the side again, where the bells had disappeared. "You old goat." she said. "I can't believe you'd do such a thing."

"You can't expect Annie to just jump in and swim." I said.

"I'm not swimmin' back with them oars." he said, lifted off his headdress, put it across the drum.

"I'll sink like a rock." Annie said.

"You'll float."

"It's pitch black. No telling what's out there."

"Only what you imagine. Now, come on. The longer you wait, the further you swim—"

"I'll never forgive you for this, Amos."

"Yes, you will."

"Not in my whole life, have I set foot in the ocean at night. This is too much, Amos! We'll be three stuck pigs by morning!"

"Quit complaining." He dips a foot in the water. "You're scaring away all the sharks..." splashed in all the way.

"I should hope so!"

"You'd be smart to take off some of those clothes!" Amos yelled to us.

"OHHH— Take off my clothes! Amos, if I know you, you had this planned all along. I'll catch my death of cold."

"The water's perfect, come on. You don't got nothin' I haven't seen my whole life."

"Ladies do not skinny dip in the middle of the ocean!"

"This is not the ocean, and I did not say you had to take off all your clothes, just some of them. You never swam in your underwear before?"

"That's not for you to know or see. And, I won't be abandoning a perfectly good boat."

"It'll come ashore down a ways. If you want to come back through the swamp, go ahead. We're only 30 feet from shore here. But, if you'd rather walk back a mile in the dark, fine with me..."

"Just you turn your head, while Katherine and I get in. And don't think for one minute, that when I make it over there, that I won't drown your sorry head!"

"Come on then—" He kicked up his feet to the surface, white arms treading the surface.

Annie climbed over and I eased myself down in the black water after her. It was a strange feeling to not see what I was getting into. Immediately, I thought of a dozen things to be lurking just under the surface. I didn't want to let go of the boat. I wanted to hold on till the last minute. Annie dog paddled past, swearing she would get Amos back for this. He, delighting in keeping just out of reach, swam circles around her.

There was so little movement to the bay, the warm water was almost flat. Ripples trailed away on both sides of me. I could see nothing below the surface, even the moon's light could not penetrate it, and my legs, moving back and forth did not touch bottom. There was only the strong, overpowering smell of bay water.

"What do we do now?" I yelled over to Amos.

"What do you want to do?" he said back.

"It's your ceremony—"

"It's your whale."

I didn't know what to do. I felt silly. I was in the water, in the middle of the night, in my underwear. We could probably be arrested for something like this... And if we were asked— what we were doing out here? *Calling a whale.* I had to laugh. Annie and Amos were laughing too. The three of us, under our spot of moonlight, delirious as three old children could get, were splashing away in the darkness and imaginary, possibly real, fears surrounding us. The boat floated further away, but the shore was always in sight. The dock was there, reaching out like an arm if needed. "That's it!" Amos yelled. "Go for it!" For some reason, I thought of my grandfather, telling me the same thing.

I laughed and I didn't care if anyone heard, or what someone might think. It hurt to laugh so much. I turned over on my back and started to float. My ears drifted just below the surface, the water lapping against the sides of my face, the sound of water filling my ears. At first, I closed my eyes, then opened them again very quickly, head snapping up. The sensation was like being out of body. My skin was tingling from a thick fear. I concentrated on the feeling of laughter I had just felt before, then relaxed back again. This time I looked straight up into the black field of stars, the curved back sky with it's tiny points of light, the sound of water breathing, heartbeats. I let go into the moment, of losing myself totally. There was simply no visible edges to be seen. Nothing to hold onto. The sky and water were without end.

It was not as terrible as I had thought.

For one moment, Annie on one side, Amos on the other, the three of us reached out at the same time. Our hands held to the others. For one precious moment, we were as one body floating under the universe, as a leaf might drift across a puddle of rain. I pictured the whale in my head, jumping over the moon, each barnacle lit with a different star.

I knew then, I might go on from here, drifting as I always had, but with something good in that. Something more. Something *beautiful*.

36

John never could find a way to touch me, that I did not hurt, that I might not strike out at him. I did not know what I was feeling, and those feelings flung themselves outwards as a child's first steps would, fearfully and hopeful.

He had been slowly learning not to love me. For years, I had been begging not to be loved. Every morning I would get angry when he'd tell me he loved me. I would get angry if he wanted to hold my hand, or ask for a kiss. I would ask, "Why do I have to say, I love you— when you should know it?" I thought he was killing me with love.

Sometimes, I had wondered if he was weak? Had I married a man who couldn't fight back? Who gave up after only a matter of years? It had taken years for him to realize, he didn't know me at all. In the beginning, it was my silence and cool distance which had been his attraction to me. And, he had been like an undertow that had pulled me off my feet and taken me wonderfully under. But, he soon discovered that he had filled in the blanks with his own words, his own image, not mine, not the me beneath my skin. He could not understand why I no longer seemed like the same person?

The first morning I got up and he didn't say his familiar, "I love you", I felt it like a hit. As we went our separate ways for work, he said, "See ya—" and that was all he said. He doesn't look at me, when I answer back. It was only then did I wonder what I had done?

· · ·

"What would you say, if I told you I had killed my husband?" This was unexpected. I could tell that by the way her eyes quickly changed focus, that such a revelation about myself, that if I had said too loud, or too fast would have been a frightening thing to hear. But, it came out like a soft breeze, as though I were very tired, talking through a haze of sleep.

Annie's face shifted under the light, regarding me a piece at a time. "Well," she said slowly, "I'd think you must have had a really good reason."

"What if, I didn't have a reason?"

"Then, I'd think you didn't know what you were doing. Was it an accident?"

"No. I did it on purpose. I don't really know why."

"Was he a bad man?"

"Oh, no. He was a very good man."

"He must have done something?"

"He loved me."

"That is a strange reason to kill a person."

"He forgave me for it." I said. "He came back."

"That's good."

"Not really. He killed me too."

"Did you make-up?"

"No. We just went on back to living together."

"That's not a good thing."

"It got better."

"But still not right?" she asked.

"No." I said. I watched the way my hand began to dissolve at the fingertips, blurring upwards at the fingers, the wrist above water still in sharp focus. *It was still not right.* I reached in as far as I could without falling over the side, still couldn't reach bottom. "I just can't seem to get over it."

Burnt Sienna.

John is restless. He turns one way, then the other. The sheets pulled up, then kicked down. Five minutes on his stomach, then on his back.

A hand would reach out, caress my shoulder, then disappear beneath the covers. I lie quietly, trying to pretend that I am asleep. I try not to think, but my head is crowded with words and images. His restlessness is making it worst. I can't stop thinking about the things I don't want to think about.

He has hurt me so deeply, I cannot find the edge of it. I rock and pitch, tumble helplessly over the unknown bottom, surface briefly, pulled down again and again, choking up water and darkness, breathless, losing strength. I give up slowly after the fight. Finally, he says, "I can't sleep." He sits up and leans against the wooden bed frame. It resists his weight loudly. I can feel him looking down at me. He says, when I don't move or say anything, "I feel bad about this evening."

I should roll over, face him. Force him to say it to my face. I think about doing this, but don't. The bed frame squeaks every time he moves, accenting the words that pour out of him. His hands must be moving, motioning like a conductors, grabbing the words out of thin air. He sounds younger, or like he is getting younger, flowing backwards into adolescence, trying to convince someone, though I'm not really sure it's me. His presence is removed from the words, a missing part, "...having a good time without you...feel bad...should have told you...wasn't—" Then silence. He starts to add something. "Never mind." he says. He is back to his old self.

Quietly still, my fingers search across the surface of the bedspread to find a loose string. I wind it around my finger like a curl of hair. "I know." I say. He tenses. The string is tight and wound all the way around the finger, cutting off the blood. When I pull the string out it makes no sound. "I've known all week." I say calmly.

He doesn't say anything at first. He moves away from sitting up and gets back under the covers, stuffs his pillow hard under his head. "The guys—" he says, and the back of my neck cringes. Too confidently, too easily, too sure, he says, "They're married. They know how it is. They wanted to get me out awhile, take it easy. It was good to cool out over a beer with them. No harm in that. Did me good. It did. I'm glad I did it."

Under my hand, I feel for another string. Like bunched up mole hills, the trails ran loose on a field of yellow weave. It was an old bedspread full of snags and holes. All I had to do was give a slight pull, and another string came out. I couldn't help myself, destroying it further. What was halfway gone anyway— why not finish the job, till nothing was left? It was a span of time I contemplated nights. How many strings would it take? Was there one string, that if pulled, the whole thing would unravel? I picture us lying suddenly naked under a pile of strings come loose. He would certainly have a questioning, confused look, as to how such a thing could have happened.

"There's nothing wrong with having a good time with friends." he says.

"Really..." I say finally. The word is full of suggestion, a mothering, disbelieving tone.

"You're being childish." he says.

Again, "Oh, really?"

"You're being childish *and* jealous!"

"That must be it." I say. "I must be jealous."

For a moment more there is only silence. We both know what the other is thinking. Words weren't necessary. They are only bridges we occasionally threw out to meet in the middle. Occasionally there are surprises. Quietly, he says, "She wouldn't do this."

"You're right. *She* wouldn't." I say.

"We are only friends." He sounds like he is chewing on something. His tongue, I wonder? Then, in a rush, he says, "I think...I think you don't love me. And maybe, you never have! You want this relationship to end..."

Something like string snaps inside me. "I—" choosing each word carefully "—*am not* the one running off, to someone else's house!"

"If you were a little more loving, I wouldn't need too!" I bite down, hold back. His voice, a wave, is swallowing me whole, "All I get from you lately are blank stares." he says. "You don't want me near you. You pull away from me whenever I touch you—" Inside me, a voice is yelling, *I wanted you! I needed you!* "She doesn't have anything to do with this." he says. The voice inside me dissolves into an internal sound, raging blood, pounding heartbeats that feel as if my heart has become jarred between my ribs. Every word he says is like a hammer's blow. "It's you, Katherine. *You're* the one that's breaking us apart."

You and me? Or you and her!

"I've done everything I can." He says. "It's you who won't change. You, who won't give me love. I love you. I'll never stop loving you." He moves away, back to his side. "I never have."

For several long minutes I listen to the forced, slow breaths coming out of me. Then, I make each finger and the bones on each arm unclench. I am even more tired now than before, but still wide awake. He is staring up at the ceiling, eyes open, sheet pulled up to his chin. The red glow of the clock outlines his body faintly. He looks like an ambulance victim, bathed in red light and shadow. Was I supposed to revive him? Is that what he wanted? The eyes of his body close. I'm too late to bring him back to me. He is gone.

I turn on my back and look up at the ceiling. If only I could slip into darkness, escape from all this… I pull back the covers until I am completely free of them. The air is cold on my legs, stinging all along the tops. I imagine my face flying up to touch the ceiling, leaving my body, suspended in death. One should be able to will death to happen—like stepping outside, through a door, a walk away. Nothing was holding me in. Just slip out. It should be easy. Go! Go—

But, nothing happens. I wait. Nothing happens still.

Little puddles of tears form, stream down my neck. The feeling of this—the failure, the loss of something that had probably never even been mine, has left me worst than anything else. I know this heavily, pitying and angry all at the same time. I can't get away from this, this feeling. Failure is a hollow, empty place.

"I may be late coming home tomorrow." a voice from the dead tells me.

"I don't care..." I answer.

"I know you don't. That's the problem."

I close my eyes against the ocean.

"You are cruel." The ghost taunts.

Silently, softer still, another string is wound up in the dark. *So you tell me.*

37

K nowing, is the weight of things and people.

When I knew what was in John's heart, all the things he was not telling me, I grew so heavy I could see only what my feet saw. My eyes, lifted, would see into the vistas of ants and the crawl spaces of bugs. My view of the world was sinking and I was carried down with it. So far down, I went, that I began to doubt the existence of light. Down below, where things moved without the eyes to see with. One moves by touch, stretched out fingers, slowly, grasping into the earth, pulling, clawing the soil aside, tunneling across the pathways of others, far below the sound of heavy footsteps, or falling leaves.

As John carried all the things he had decided to keep to himself, he grew two belt sizes bigger. But, he sucked in his breath and tried not to notice. When he walked past, the air whistled through his nose. He was continuously pulling at his clothes, stretching the seams, loosing buttons.

And, even though these things happened a long time ago, I can still be buried by the memories. At odd moments, just something, anything, might suddenly make me remember, and I shoot straight down into the hole inside me. Angry, I look at him standing there, innocent now, but not then— and I want all over again to take him down with me.

Sepia.

"Please God," I say to the silent room, "don't let him be with her." A numbness is rising from my feet, up my legs, and arms. There is a sense of moving through water too deep to stand in. I feel like I am standing on tip toe, my body heavy. It should float, but it doesn't. It just sinks. Resisting one moment, dragging the next, there is no control. I am going under.

Coffee. Coffee would help.

I turn on the tap to fill the pot and pour it in to brew. I watch this process, as though it is very important, filling slowly to the desired level of darkness. Then, reaching into the cabinet, searching blindly for a mug. Lifesaving, I find one. The cup shakes in my hand as I try to drink it, the dark rings spinning out and back. One moment I can breath, the next I cannot. I force myself to concentrate. To remain calm. I will not yell or make accusations, I think to myself. No surprises today, *Please.*

"Maybe, he hasn't done anything?" I say to myself. The coffee is burning. I put it down, stare at my hands. The crisscrossed lines of skin seem cut and sewn together, the patterns and grooves running in all directions. The future was supposed to be held here. Written in flesh, unchangeable, unique. Looking at the tiny x's braiding along my fingers, they were rings of barbwire. "Am I cruel and heartless?" I ask the lines, turning the metal ring around my finger like a screw. "Maybe, it's nothing." I want to believe this. "He should have been here... Why aren't you here?" I ask the walls.

"Are you mad at me?" he asks. I shake my head no. He walks over to fix himself a cup of coffee. The silverware drawer's pulled open, gets stuck, and is yanked out. Knives and forks clash together, then are silent. "I'm going to fix this one of these days." he says. I take another drink of my own, push down the cold water inside me. "I was out thinking." he says, his back turned to me. "Some time apart might do us good. Give us a chance to figure out what we want."

"If that's what you want to do." Hurt curls up inside me like a fist, punches me hard from the inside. "If you don't know, what you want."

"We need to know— what we want out of this relationship. That's all." His words stumble. "If we want to continue, like this?"

"That should be easy to do. When we're *apart.*" I put my cup down very carefully." I stand up, want desperately to run, but walk towards the door. This wasn't going to get any worst. I wouldn't let it. He moves away, lets me go past.

"I mean nothing to you." he says. I stop, as he knew I would.

"What would you like me to do?" I say, not pleading, defensive.

"You're not the only person in the world."

"I know that."

"You don't even so much as look up when I come home."

"So, what is that supposed to mean?"

"That's what you do to me. You do it to everyone. I don't know what you want, but it's not me."

"That's not true."

"It is, and I can't take it any more." He won't look at me, stares into the black coffee, the floor, his shoes. "I don't know why I'm here..."

Moving through deep water, I turn away, wander aimlessly through rooms, musty corridors. I didn't know what I was supposed to do against love. I fought. I resisted. I kept it to myself. It was what I knew how to do. I hadn't known he could run out of giving it. That didn't seem fair somehow. He was about to make a decision that would change everything. What I thought our life together was—was something entirely different to him. Something, he believed, he could do without. Without him to push against, I was falling flat on my face.

When I return later, he hasn't moved from the kitchen. He sits at the table, holding his still full cup of coffee, tracing invisible patterns on the table. I decide to make dinner, put on some water to boil, set the table around him. Normal movements that help me appear normal.

When the dinner is finished cooking, I carry it steaming to the table. It obscures the water in my eyes, helps ease the words out of my throat. "Eat." I say without looking at him. "Before it gets cold." I sit down across from him, careful to keep my face from being seen fully, away from direct light, stray glances. I concentrate on eating. Stab a fork into the peas. They slide away, my distorted reflection in their clear green juice, mixed in with the macaroni. I hate peas. Why did I fix them?

When he gets up, I pretend not to care. His footsteps are loud on the tile floor, each step, distinct, not fast, but slow, uncertain, deciding something. He walks all around the space behind me, mapping out the square footage and distance. Then, at the sink, I hear him pouring out the coffee, rinses the cup. When he is suddenly behind me again, I hold my breath. He puts his arms around my shoulders. Bent down low, his face at my ear. "I just needed to be with someone..." he says. I bite down onto the peas, nearly choke. Blackness threatened to rage out of me, but he moves away. I am sinking fast. There is a roaring noise in my ears, pain at my chest. I'm drowning.

God help me, I thought.

I am truly dead.

Section Four

I wondered how it was, I was born so cruel—
Without the eyes to see it, nor the heart to know it?

38

Color falls like rain on Vincent's canvas. Sometimes, I see the swirling blues off pool walls. Underwater eyes— shimmering, moving, converging shapes, Irises waving long stems and leaves as if seaweed. Everything flows. Rolling shapes like water through a fissure, squeezed between a narrow view, such as in a moment, or place. I think, he may lay above, looking down at us, a drowned man. His eyes are open, seeing below, painting in a hurry before death comes, or his breath runs out. Showing us his broken sunrise, over the field that has just poured from his brush. Hurry, it says to me. The moment rushes into change, into something else. It won't be the same after this.

. . .

There are no straight lines in the human body. Everything curves. When I draw the figure, I start with loose circles. Each part flows, curving in and around the next. The figure emerges with darker, more defined lines, layered over the top of the pale, beginning attempts. I do not look at the paper, except briefly. I look at the figure, let the chalk move unseen, watch instead the curve-shaped muscles turning over bones and poses. Hand-eye coordination is essential. Each learns to trust the other over time, and to follow separately the same path.

When I conjure up my mother to paint, she is part fact, part fiction. These two things are layered like the chalk lines will look, emerging and receding one beneath the other. As the painting takes shape, it will sometimes be the truth concealing the lie that creates the profiled head and steel-pressed mouth. But mostly, it is the darker lie that surfaces, with the truth of what she really looks like, buried deep inside, so small and faint, there is almost nothing left of her to see. I fill in what I don't know or don't remember with things I associate with her. I find it easier to remember her from the side, indirect, than to face her head on. If I squint my eyes at the canvas, everything is darker and less defined. From images half there, I pull forth those that are not— letting loose the curves, trying not to look, circling and circling around her, until the smears of chalk dust turn my fingers black and gray.

Since I could not paint her as she was, I painted her through the eyes of her angels. It was the largest of the paintings I had done, three feet by four feet wide. I stayed up most of three nights working on it. Now it was leaning against the chair in the middle of the room, showing two figures emerge from a darkness and standing at the foot of a bed. They face forward, so the figure of my mother is upside-down, floating on the patch-squared bed beneath them. Their eyes are fixed on her sleeping face. She has not yet seen them. They are dark haired, with long faces and thin bodies. They are smiling secret, knowing smiles, Leonardo smiles, in a background of Rembrandt hues and colors. The room behind them is dark, with the outline of a window to the right showing a night sky beyond.

I moved the painting to the far side of the room to study it better. As I turned off the light, the evening glow from my own window illuminated the window of the painting. Now the figures were emerging into the darkness of my room, standing almost to the foot of my bed. My mother was falling into a larger space, spilling onto the floor in a heap. They watched silently, the corners of their smiling lips stretched wider in shadow, became wicked grins, laughing at my expense.

Green Gold.

Grandma's skin drew moisture over the cooking stove, over the boiling pot. She watches in silence, letting the steam rise around her, unflinching, no matter how hot, or how close the metal rim might brush her skin. She never once pulled away suddenly, or yelled out, that I had seen. She would reach in, stirring with a long handled spoon, the sounds of liquid bursting open. To me, her kitchen was a warfare of volcanic stews, hostile soups that tried to boil over, gravies that threatened to stick or clump, or burn on the bottom. She knew how to handle these disruptive forces— waiting patiently the hours, keen for dangerous sounds or smells that would signal a need for immediate attention. Organization was her key ingredient. Every problem had an easy remedy and well proven approach. New methods were frowned upon. Recipes were never invented or improved. They were passed down— ingredients, measured amounts, exact preparation included. She said, 'If I followed a recipe exactly, I would never eat a failure.' She knew I tried to change things when I cooked. And 'Failures', I knew, could be eaten with a smile and be relished all the same. So, always I watch her, a little perplexed, wondering how she does it all? She drew in the kitchen battles, gaining something by being in the middle of them, totally absorbed in each step, listening for the right moment to attend, or leave alone. Each time she stood over the stove, her face became the color of turned up sand, wet underneath, and much heavier, pulled down under her chin and around her eyes. Battle-worn.

Old skin does not yield easily. Each groove is fitted stubbornly into place. I notice this too, when she talks to me. That after the words cease to move at her mouth, her face falls back together in all the same places and shapes. "She is your mother." she says to me. The deepest two lines on either side of the mouth move quick like switches. "You should forgive her."

"Which part?" I say back. "You can't mean all of it?" She doesn't answer, pours coffee instead. "Would it make things better?"

"Who said anything about better? She's your mother. That should be the only reason."

"Did she forgive you?"

"Me? What did I do?" The dampness of her skin has a fine sheen like an oiled pan.

205

"She's been fighting you her whole life." I say. "I think she was trying to get away."

"From what?"

"From you."

"That's nonsense. She's been feeding you lies again."

"She always said you were the one telling lies."

"And you believed her? I thought you were smarter than that? Anything coming out of her— is a whole lot of nonsense. I don't want to hear it." The spoon hit against the side of her cup as she stirred it.

"She wanted something from you. What was it?"

"I gave her everything."

"Did you love her?"

"Of course, I did. She was my daughter. What kind of question is that?"

"Did she know you loved her?"

"Is this what I get after all I've done? *Looks,* like this— from you of all people? This is not you I hear. It's her. Wouldn't listen to anybody but herself." She looks at me over the rim of her cup. "Where did it get her?"

"I want to know why she hates you so much?"

"What?—"

"Everything she does, is against you, to get back at you in some way."

"That's just being a daughter. Look at you. What is it you show her? The way you live is your business. Don't tell me mine. *Your mother does not hate me.*"

"I'm just trying to figure out why things are, this way?"

"The way it is, is from back then." She points at me with her finger. "In those marriages of hers. That's enough to make anyone crazy. Crazy is a good word for all of this..." The finger cuts the air between us. "Did you know that when she was pregnant with Jessie, he put a gun up to her stomach. Said, 'It better not be someone elses.' He'd blow her away if he found out it was. Then, he pulled the trigger. Wasn't loaded. Said, next time, it would be. Did you know about that?"

"No."

"Probably has something to do with *why* things are... She left him for three days, then went back."

"He always seemed so happy to have Jessie?" I say.

"He knew she was his. He just liked terrorizing your mother. It gave him a perverse thrill or something." Her shoulders raise up, then drop weakly. "Who knows?" Lifting her coffee again, she takes a long drink. She says, "We could have taken her and you kids back in here. Don't let her fool you into believing she could never have left sooner. She had plenty of opportunities. She wanted to do it herself. Wouldn't listen to anybody. God knows what lies she told other people? Her unfortunate life... How hard it was for *her*. The stories she could come up with—" She shakes her head slowly, carefully puts the coffee cup back down on it's matching plate. Looks over at the stove, watches the steam rise up to the ceiling.

"Karen's the same way." I say.

"Karen..." She rolls her eyes. "That girl, had the nerve to sit there and tell me, she'll do *it* again. 'Fine—' she said to me. 'I'll just kill myself. Then everything will be better. Jenny will be better off without me!' What am I supposed to say, 'Yes, she will?' Sounded exactly like your mother, the way she said it." she sighed heavily. "But I guess, a sometime mother is better than none at all, and a pathetic attempt, better than nothing. Maybe, that's the way they see it, an attempt at being something they're not?"

She rubs the counter absently. Her eyes are red around the edges and her voice quivers occasionally. She looks back at the stove again, then gets up, goes to stir the boiling pot. The spoon is hit hard against the edge. When she turns back to me, her face is moist again, like rolled dough, light and powdered looking. She says then, an edge in her voice, her eyes suddenly hard, as though the sounds I have made are something a-miss and must be turned down, subdued. "You look, and *you listen*. I didn't have to do anything for you kids, but I did. Nobody asked me to do it. Why she brought three kids into this world is beyond me? Your mother failed at everything she tried to do. She couldn't take care of you or herself. I did. I don't need to look at anything. I've seen enough. I'm still seeing it! She brought you children to me, because she couldn't do it. It wasn't enough that she kept going back, dragging you kids— the tears, *god the tears*— I know what she did was stupid, but I couldn't make her stop. She had to learn on her own. She'd come to me whining and cry-ing, 'He had promised' she said. She wouldn't listen! Only them—every one of them. I don't think she wanted away, not really. I didn't *make* her that way. I didn't tell her she deserved it. I am her mother. All I could do was watch. All I could do was pick up the pieces—you kids, and try to put you back together. It wasn't enough. I couldn't make you not see, or hear, or know what was happening around you. I couldn't. You think that a day goes by and I don't try and figure out why things are this way? Every night, I lie in bed, worrying about everyone of you. I try and try to think of a way to fix everything. I try to figure it all out. But I can't. I don't *know* why... I will never know. Only God knows. Only she knows. I have been raising children my whole life. I'm old and I'm still taking care of children. I don't have the strength anymore. It's gone out of me. I can't fight it! So don't you sit there and tell me to look at anything like I don't know what's going on. There are no surprises left. I've seen all I need to. All I'm going to..."

She throws her hands down in frustration and turns away. "You're just like your mother." she says. I feel this like a hit.

She leaves the room, but I can't move. She has nailed me in with her words.

. . .

There are no straight lines into a person. No one way clear enough to see all the way back to their beginnings. Only a part can be visible at any one time, this rise, that valley, that curve around the eyes, just enough to show me what direction they're looking. But, I still don't know what it is they see. I still don't know why they look that way.

39

In a sense, I am going back to when life started.

On a shore where evolution stepped out across the land, a birth place, a beginning place. There are ghosts walking this shore, of possibilities, hopes, lost ideals of one's self— swelling in on the tide, making the slow, hermit crab walk through the waves, showing itself by the ghost light of the moon, or the penetrating, hot light of the sun, by stars even, darkness even, in the black nights when nothing outside can be seen and all that is left to see is what's inside. I could wade out into it, dive down, claw the silt bottom with my fingers, kick against it, still it was always there— a force to be reckoned with.

Mother never spoke, rarely turned away from it. When the rough, blue waves would roll up to touch her, she would not pull away. As it surrounded her, she would not resist. Gradually, the sand washed away, so that it appeared she was slowly sinking, buried in the foamy surf. Her weight shifted against the weight of the ocean's. She leaned into it, tilting like a sack of grain that had lost it's balance and was turning on it's side. And just as the water was about to slip her out and away, she would turn, pull herself up heavily, move to higher ground to lay down on the dry sand, and go to sleep— where maybe, was the thing she was looking for, there in her dreams? Or maybe, with me watching, she just went to sleep, to sleep.

Phthalo Blue.

"I want my daddy..." Jenny says.

I felt a cold hand move down me.

She wanted her daddy. The invisible, a potentially better god, a kinder word, who yet had a face, except the one she gave him. "Yes, I know you do honey, but he's not here." Her tiny, smooth forehead wrinkles itself between the eyes. She looks like a tiny adult standing there. The worries of a future pressing in on her. She stares out the window without moving. But, what does a three year old know about the future? Did she know what she was feeling, or only look that way— a mimicry of older people, she would later grow into?

I always wondered if my father would have been the better half? I imagined him with the nicer qualities my mother lacked. Truthfully, living with them both, probably would have meant twice the hell, twice the pain, and twice the fear. I know that now. But, as I child, I could at least feel hope, like she seems too, when she says that word, *daddy.* A longing for the missing part. He still could be someone who would love her, someone who'll say, 'I'll protect you, don't worry. I'm always there for you. The invisible guardian of, *what if things were different...* But, in reality, wishful thinking that will at least get her through several more years to come.

It hurts me to see her now, in her innocence. When she calls out 'Mommy' and she runs to my sister, because for the time, it is still all she has. She cannot survive on her own yet. Her fragile years of hope, that she will be able to please her mother, and find love, comfort, safety are still possible. She will try inexhaustible ways to try and find her way into her mother. It will take years before she can think of no more ways.

. . .

The shore and I watch each other. I remember my mother, my birth. I think, *She brought me into this— world. But, she could not take me out completely.* Sometimes, I know this with certainty. Other times, I start to forget, and have to be reminded. I memorize the words to convince myself of their meaningfulness. If said out loud, they would come out backwards and upside-down, so I say them inside, whispered. I cannot shout inside my head. It always sounds like something soft-spoken, a prayer. But I can say it fast and over and over. I am not my mother— *I am not my mother—I am nothing like her—I will never be her—Never-Never—Never—Never—Never.*

40

They are my eyes.
    Though the painting is small, they are my eyes. Blackberry vines have overgrown the body around them. A stone heart is painted just off center, held in by the nest of thorns, and has speckles of white and black that stones have. I have painted my own heart and body this way, so that I can look at it. But those blues, the eyes— those I did not put there. The pierced sky blue, black marble centers, the color of oil slicks on water.

Looking at the brushes, then the metal tubes of paint, I try to figure out how I have created such a color. Decide it is not the color, but shape. Then expression. Follow-you-around-the-room eyes. A painter's trick. I walk away to see if it still works. Still, in any direction the leaves are watching me.

They are my eyes.

But, then I stop and ask myself, is this really me? There is hardly anything left that I recognize. The blue has a sharpness, a look that could cut. I try to imagine the things John would see in them.

I'd hoped I could make him understand. When I called, I could hear it in his voice, when he asked, "What exactly are you trying to do here? Is it divorce? Is that what you want?"

"No."

"Then, why are you doing this?"

"You're going to judge me no matter what I say."

"I am capable of understanding."

"But, you're not listening. I don't want a divorce. I'm not seeing someone else. I just *need* this. I'm not trying to hurt you, but I can't do this with you."

"Why not here?" he asked.

I had waited... I wanted to say, but didn't. The silence must have cut at him, stabbing. I can hear his breathing. He waits for an answer I cannot give. "I'll see you when you get back." he said. He crushed me saying it like that. "Just remember you've got a husband here?"

"I haven't forgotten."

"Later then."

"John—" I said. "I'm coming back."

"We'll see." he said, hung up.

There they were. Those blues were staring back at me through phone booth glass.

"How could I have become you?" I said to the painting. "I try to find myself...and instead, I find you." Tangled, knotted, saw-toothed vines— I could smell the green earth it was made of. "Don't *look* at me like that!" They stare back angry, never blink, never miss anything by not looking. I grabbed it and threw it across the room. In two steps, the others, paper and canvas, are flying in a whirl-wind around me. "No-No- No!" I kept yelling at them. Everything was wrong. It all looked wrong, out of proportion, bad perspective, colors off. How could I have ever thought I could paint? I had not done one thing worth looking at. It was all trash!

"What are you doing?" Annie yelled.

"I'm getting rid of everything! It's all terrible."

She slapped her hands together, stomped her foot. "Stop that— right this minute!"

"John was right. I've been wasting my time— I have wasted my whole life..." *Such waste!* I thought. Such a waste!

"Stop right now—" Annie stepped between me and the paintings I'd yet to reach. Before I tore her down off the wall, she stopped me cold in my tracks. "Your babies." she said.

"Don't say that! I don't need that too." But it was too late. There they were, scattered around the room, face down, crooked, one scratched across the side. I could see them now, looking like rag dolls, or children... *My children*. "I'm just like her." I said. The taste of horror in my mouth, of wanting to spit, rising in me.

Annie grabbed hold of my arm. "No—" she said softly.

"I didn't even know I was doing it." A lie, I knew. "I did." I said, wanted to crawl out of myself.

"Look at me." she said. Shame at not acting my age was rushing through me. "Now I say, it is not Katherine's *mother*—" She moved, careful not to step on anything, "but Katherine here, throwing stuff around and acting strangely. Why? I don't know why. But, I see it is her doing it. She must have a reason, but maybe, I'll stop her and ask her— before she finishes the job."

"I'm sorry."

"What are you sorry for? You were doing a pretty good job, I'm just being a nosy, old woman, thought I might be nosy and ask why you were doing this... What's sorry in that? Maybe you want some matches? Start a fire out back and pile everything up maybe?"

"No."

"You sure?"

"I don't want to. I am being ridiculous."

"Ol' piece of canvas never hurt anybody."

"No. It didn't." Sitting on the floor, the eyes were still looking at me. I was flooding them now, tears that would not stop, even though I jammed both fists against them, trying. Annie sat down beside me and pulled me to her. This only made me worst. I tried to cover my face with my hands. Big, baby tears smeared all over my crumpled face. I couldn't make them stop. I had no choice but to let them fall where they may.

She told me soft words till I was finished, rocked back and forth. "It's about time." she said.

"For what?"

"For that rock to crack."

I sniffed loudly. "I saw her in the painting. I am her."

"You're still you. It's just memories you're seeing."

"I hate my mother."

"No you don't."

"Yes I do. I can't think about her without getting so mad..."

"That's anger. Not hate."

My hands were balled into fists, pressing into the sides of my head. "I don't know." I said. "I'm not so sure there is a difference. In me, they seem like the same thing. My mother is pressed between the two, making the thought of any part—being angry, hating her for it, or thinking of her, all the same." Deep in my chest, the pain has returned. I get angry at this too. Think of my mother, chisel in hand.

Against Annie there was a soft warmth, pillow soft sides. She held onto me as though I were about to fall. Inside me, the pain lunges again, but this time it was from something different, not the same as before. *Pain in me, where something else should be.* I looked at Annie. She had said that once. Words began to flow out of me. Things I'd always wanted to say but never found someone else who would listen. Someone it was safe to tell.

"Sometimes, when I'm thinking of her, my heart begins to jump and flutter, like a bird's wing, or something trying to get out. There is this pain and I think, 'She has given me a defective part—'. Then there are times it seems to stop. I can't find a pulse. Nothing to prove I am alive— I could be dead and not even notice. Ghosts don't know they're dead. Am I dead? Has my heart stopped working? Is it there at all? Or have I only imagined it?" I looked at Annie, my face a pitiful mess, said, "The thing that should give me life, that keeps me alive— *does not seem to work right.*

"Tell me," I said to her, "Everyone keeps telling me I don't have a heart." I hit against my chest. The pain inside, knocked back. "See that— I can feel that. It hurts. It makes me alive, proof that I'm not dead. That means I have a heart, doesn't it?"

She doesn't look at me. Her eyes are someplace else. "Oh, yes." she said.

"I don't want to be dead anymore, Annie. I have to find a way to paint, not like this, but for real. It's been so long, I'm afraid of it now. But, I need it. Even some of the fear it makes me feel, so close to going over the edge all the time, but I don't. It doesn't let me fall, just lean way over. I can look into myself without getting lost in the darkness. Light gets in—" I said, "sometimes." Though I didn't feel it then, only the pain, coming from the broken heart. The blackness I had locked around it was pouring out in a rush. I thought of John. He had no idea of the pain I kept to myself. He had no idea what I felt inside. "I have to go back sometime."

"Yes." she said.

"Soon. I need to see him."

"Maybe, he understands more than you think?"

"He makes me feel so guilty."

"Are you sure it's him that makes you feel that way?"

"Who else is there?"

"You maybe? He needs to know this person in here—" She pointed at me. "What you have shown me. Maybe, he needs to see too?"

"Where is there room for the past, the one before him, or the one after him? Put them together— and he couldn't possibly understand what loosing him would mean to me. My marriage is hanging by a thread. I then go and do the worst possible thing, I pull on it. I leave him. Give myself a preview of what it would feel like, before he leaves me. Forgive and *forget*. Isn't that what my grandmother would tell me to do? I have never been able to do either of those things. This time here has been wonderful. But it won't last. I have to leave sometime. I am afraid, terrified— that I'll just end up right back where I started, before I came here— that I'll slip out of it again, further over the edge than I intended to go. Nothing to hold on to. That's the difference. I had nothing to trust, that wouldn't let me down. It's harder to remember each time, what I can trust." I wiped my face with my hands, sniffed loudly. Took a deep breath to steady myself.

Annie smiled, said, "Bad habits are hard to break."

"I can't do it anymore."

"Then find another way."

"Painting seems a selfish thing to want to do."

"Not so much."

"He thinks I want to leave him."

"Does he love you?"

"Yes."

"Do you love him?"

"Not enough."

"You can't love someone all the time. Do you think I loved Tom every day I was married to him? We're imperfect creatures. We make mistakes. We get angry at each other, especially when we're married. We think we should be perfect for each other. But honey, no one's perfect. Marriage is a trial through time and patience. If you make it— it's because you've learned to not see the clock as in each minute, but each hour. You manage through the worst times, and remember the good ones."

"I don't want to lose him." I see my life without him. A self inflicted wound. "I just like the idea of waking up in the morning, stretching out completely without a thought as to what way the covers are going, or waking anybody up, or what time it is... He says, I steal the covers all night. He says, I talk in my sleep...That I toss my pillow out and take his, I kick him, poke him in the eye, push him off his side of the bed. 'Wouldn't it be easier to get my own bed then?' I tell him and he says, 'But I can't sleep without you...'."

Annie laughed.

"I want us to share what we each have... to feel like friends, who'll have kids together. Who'll have fun, and joke, and be serious too." The wishful sound left my voice. "But he tells me, I don't know how to have fun, or tell jokes, or to even know one when I hear it. It makes me feel so bad I want to cry, but I don't cause I don't want him to see me cry either. Not even at a sad movie. I won't let him. I find some excuse and get up and leave. Even that makes him mad." I reached down and held onto my toes, imagined the spaces inside them, blood and bone spaces I could feel, but not see. "What is it I have? I put two and two together just like them. Two thoughts together— I see something. I feel it. I *move* because of it...and when I do, there's a spark— a fire! And I say to myself, I can! I will! I did! *God damn,* somehow I did it! This is the fire in me. It burns me, kicks my ass up off the floor when I've laid there too long, feeling sorry for myself. I won't just lay there anymore— I won't. *FIRE!"*

The weight of questions that cannot be answered pushed down on me. "But, I'm just kidding myself really. I may have that spark. I may have, almost, might-have, made it. But look at me. Where am I? Run off from everything, a coward. I think I'm getting away and I end up back where I started, going in circles! Before morning I'll be back where I was, you watch. That's what all this feels like. There's a rope tied on me too, Annie. It's pulled straight, and as far as it can go, and here I am making a horse path round my mother. No wonder I can't breath.

I'm strangling myself trying to stand up, to stretch past what I've been given, and what I'm told, and how it is..."

Annie held up her hands, "I know it seems like this world don't make no sense at all." she said. "People do crazy things. But, one thing I know is, if they're walkin', their livin'. There's a fire in them. You may not be able to see it, but it's in there, as sure as you feel it in you. It may go down, till there's almost no light to see by at all, just a candle flame, or a wisp of smoke, but it burns somewhere in there. *Even a life of lies hides a truth somewhere.*" She pulled herself up from the floor. "Come on now, get up."

I took hold of her strong hand, let myself be helped up. Somehow, I was lighter, despite the doubts, and my mother's eyes. Even though I knew I had to go back, and that everything that was waiting for me, was still waiting for me. There were a lot of messes to clean up and things to fix. I would have to start somewhere. The rock had cracked. Under it, was a pile of stone fragments that needed to be swept away.

"Annie?"

"Humm?"

"Why—must life be so hard?"

She stepped out into the darkness. "Cause, it wouldn't do us any good—to be easy."

41

If I imagine the cord that went back of reasons— why things turned out this way or that? — if my mother hadn't married each of the men she said she loved, if she hadn't married to get out of the house, if my grandfather hadn't joined the military and moved his family around, if my grandmother hadn't married my grandfather at the insistence of her family, if her father hadn't abandoned his wife and seven children, a gambler who left town to escape debts he couldn't pay, if the country people had never wanted to become city people— looking for a better life... So many *choices*. Too many to comprehend the length of. Each person's added to the next, everyone hoping for the best, taking chances, weighing directions, taking the risk.

I want a better life.

Something more than what I've been given.

Warm Gray.

How electric our words become, when they're said with such control, such blackness. Our voices are calm, as in the center eye of a storm. Each pause is a vital chart, a pin-point on a map, telling which island the hurricane has struck and which one it is headed for next. "It's not any of your-god-damn-business." Karen says.

"It is, when I'm here." I say.

"Maybe, you shouldn't be here then?"

"I have every right to be."

"You don't have shit."

"When I'm here, I have plenty."

She turns the pages of the newspaper loudly. She has made herself very at home on grandma's couch. Her shoes kicked off, car keys thrown down on the coffee table. She is looking up and down the want ads, telling me it is none of my business through the crinkled section of personals. Smiling faces, showing their best sides, mashed together under my sister's fingers. I had told grandma earlier I didn't think she had any intention of leaving him. She was playing some sort of game. "If she had really wanted to leave, she wouldn't go only as far as your house." I told her. "She'd pack up and get out of the city, or state even. Leaving would have to be more than a ten mile radius." She and Jenny had been staying here a month now, the longest time yet. While Karen looked for work, grandma watched Jenny. She was a handful, so sometimes on my days off, I came over to watch her so grandma could go out. I had hoped she would get back before Karen did. I just couldn't be *civil,* as grandma begged me to be. Things always seemed to get out of hand.

Jenny goes past me with an armful of plastic bowls. She dumps them at the feet of her mother and begins stacking them, one after the other by size. Everything becomes quiet again, except for the sound of hollow plastic. Jenny is carefully building a tower with the bowls. Each time one falls, she starts again. The little red book she had wanted her mother to read to her was still on the ground, where it had been thrown. "Read to me, Momma. Will you read to me?" she had asked her mother. "Will you read this one?" She pushed the book into the newspaper. The paper crumpled in the center. "What!" Karen snapped. "Will you read?" Jenny's small voice asked her. Karen had grabbed the book out of her hand and thrown it to the floor. "Leave me alone!"

I look at my sister now, the paper in front of her again, and I want to snatch it away too. "She only wanted you to read to her." I say.

"Shut the hell up."

"Pathetic way to treat your own child—" Jenny runs to the window as a car goes by, looking to see if grandma has come back. The car keeps going. "She will remember." I say, watching her. Lightning seems ready to strike, the air, electric.

Karen springs up off the couch, surprisingly fast for her size. "Bitch— " she hisses. I prepare, brace myself. But she doesn't move beyond the first chair that borders the living room. She points her hand at me, motioning in the air violently. "Say one more word and I'll rip off your head for saying it!

"Go on! See if I won't—" Jenny, still at the window, starts to cry. "I don't give a damn what the hell you *think* I should do. Just shut up—*shut up!*" She can barely get the words to come out one at a time, explosive sounds, thunder that rolls up from her gut.

"It's you— it's always *you!*" she is screaming now. She is trembling in her own fury. I watch, fascinated at the storm that has come out of her, keeping a safe distance away. She goes on relentlessly, pounding out the words in a long torrential rain. "I hope you never have kids—I hope you can't! Cause you're nothing! Not a mother like me—My kid'll love me—She's mine! All mine!" Crumpled paper in one hand, fingers bent white, shaking her fist with the other. She stands, her face contorted to a bellowing child's face, ten years old again. Her own child watches from the corner, afraid to move, the curtains wrapped around her to hide her.

For the first time, I can really see my sister. I can see how much she hates me. I am stunned at the depth of her hatred, and of my own fear. Before that moment, I had never really wanted to know how she felt about me. Nothing concrete, as her saying it. I had been afraid to know. Afraid I already knew, and had never dared to look at it. She stood there, breathing hard, gripping the chair as if she dare not let go. Her weight, leaning towards me. Wishing— her whole body seemed to say, to just throw herself at me and kill the look of me, to get me out of her face, something, I imagine, she has always wanted.

I take my time to say anything. I choose a slow, drifting voice, deliberately calm. To her, it is cowardice. "You don't see it. You probably never will. But you are her." Her hand is releasing the chair. She hovers over it, ready to move. "In fact, you're better at being her, than she is, and worst, much worst. Instead of me— it'll be your daughter, standing here— telling you she doesn't care if you live or die."

Her mouth opens like an animal mouth, teeth showing. "I hate you!" Again, she moves fast. Her hand goes out, thrust towards my face, talons. She wants to kill me, but I move, inches out of reach. "Fucking bitch!" she screams. A chair falls. I'm backed into the kitchen. The sound of a ripping cloth and I know she has a hold of me. "I hate you! I hate you!" she is screaming. I grab her by the shirt and shove backwards till she is against the wall. I have to throw all of me into her to do it. Her weight tilts and moves away from me. Grandma's clock goes sliding off the wall. So quick it happens— that we have embraced each other like this, the animal motions that we are, locked in a territorial fight.

"Don't you *ever* touch me again!" I say, inches away from her face. Conviction squeezed out of me. So quick, it is, that I know— that I am just as deadly as her. I burn just as hot, and I am just as willing to hurt because of it! Grab hold feeling of sharp teeth and claws, of power over her, of being in the dirt, with not her laughing, but me. "Not *ever!*" Then I let go and move away. It is only by surprise, I have gotten away with it. I have stung her, by turning into her. By letting go the forces inside me.

As I leave the house, it is like I am flying, the wind in my face, the taste of hot, outside air filling me. When I look back for one second, I can still see the one, small face in the window, watching, learning, and remembering.

. . .

I must be pulled from this shell. Pulled hard out of an old skin, to emerge, new, raw, and tender, pink skinned and sensitive. New, so that I have all my senses, and am completely aware. The sound of the old shell breaking, is like bark being pulled away from a tree. It is a terrible breaking away sound. It should be painful, but it doesn't hurt.

42

"This is where God talks, and I listen." Amos said.

I turned my head to look at him. "I thought you didn't believe in God?"

"I don't believe in a *Christian* God." he said slowly, concentrating on a piece of wood he is carving. "My God came with the territory. He doesn't charge me to sit and listen."

I looked out over the bay, the shore. Not far from where we were, a heron walked out of the woods. It made it's way among the reeds, head tilted to the side, looking for fish. The trees moved lazily in a breeze, casting long shadows over the shore, the heron, the low slung dock where we sat. The little bit of ocean visible in the distance, crisscrossed itself with small slashes of light and color, raced to fill the mouth of the bay, in salty collisions. I couldn't help but think *Vincent* would have painted this view. "If this was a sermon," I said, "I'd go to church everyday."

"Has a way of doing that." he said, paused to blow some shavings from the wood.

I watched the curls of wood floating on the water where they fell. When the wind blew, they washed along the surface. I could see fish trying to nibble the pieces. I could also see the darker shapes of hermit crabs below the fish. Several moved in the shadow of the wooden post. The smell of the water was strong. I leaned back, took a deep breath, imagined it all as a giant, open cathedral. The dry, wooden pier, became the wooden pews, the pines, scented candles and the shapes glistening in the water, became the fragmented stained glass windows. The salt air and the salt that I rolled under my fingers along the planks were once the walls of the church, worn down now, ancient grains that were once great stones, now particles, faint remnants of a place that had once existed long before me.

Amos flicked the sharp knife against the wood. I could not tell what he was carving. He held it closed in his hand. A mysterious, graven image. Perhaps the face of his mother? I smiled to myself. "I like your God, Amos. He says nice things."

"Most of the time. Sometimes, says bad things too."

"Who doesn't?" I said. He continued carving. I looked out at the ocean beyond the bay. The water was more green than blue. Small waves, topped with white were moving at an angle through the opening. "Did you ever see your mother after she left?" I asked.

"Nope."

"Do you miss her?"

"I can't miss what I don't know."

"Would you have liked to?"

He stopped carving and looked out over the water before answering. "I never met the woman in person, I knew her in other ways. In her absence. I knew her through my father." He blew wood shavings from his piece, studied it, then went on. "My father used to say, 'She left us both son— but she left some of her there in you. I know you can't help that, but it makes me want to knock it clean off of your face every time I look at you.' I looked too much like her, for him to forget. My face was her mirror, watching him, even after she was gone. He would have liked to have smashed that mirror if he could. If I'd have let him." As he talked, it was as though waves pulled back from around him. I could see him more clearly, a little at a time, forming like the pearls out of the blue, green waters. "This is how I know my mother." he said. "From his words. He talked about her constantly. Hating her, cursing her, and loving her, all in the same way he'd throw his beer at the wall. It all crashed together in the moment she left him."

"He could barely remember his own name most of the time, much less a son. I knew only one thing about my mother." he said, "That she was Indian. The one, descriptive word of truth I could ever get out of him. Now, I know one other thing."

"What's that?"

"She's dead." He shook his head. "Long dead and buried along with all those ancestors before her. When I pass on, I'll meet her for the first time."

"How will you know it's her?"

"She'll know me." he said. "Every mother knows her child. No matter how much time goes past. Even after death. The link is never totally severed." He looked at me from the side. "We are all connected to the Great Spirit, and we are all connected to our mothers who brought us into this world. We come in the same. We go out the same too. She'll know me. She'll have been waiting my whole life just to meet me."

I tried to picture her in my mind. All I could see was Amos in front of the sun, as he did each morning, whispering her name. I wondered how he saw her? "Don't you even have a picture of her?"

"I don't even know what tribe she called herself. Nothing. I couldn't even begin to guess. I came around to figuring that they had to come from the same source at some point, so why not make them all my ancestors. They would all be my mother's people, all my sisters and brothers.

"What did your father think of that?"

"I didn't tell him. He wouldn't have understood. I made it my quest to find out as much as I could about my families as possible. I've picked up a lot, and met many. My father was a lonely man. I am not."

"What about Annie?"

"Annie is the first star of morning. She is the first thing I see, and I know where I am. She is the light on the horizon of my path. I am glad to know her." He says this with a smile. "I've known my father." he said, flicked a long curl of wood into the water. "He's not a very nice man. But when my mother left, she gave me the whole world to make up for it. Hit the road at 17 and traveled, mostly on foot, from one corner of the states to the other. Took 15 years, which just about equals a high school and college education. What an education!" He looked at me briefly, went back to carving. "I found this place last and haven't left. I followed Annie's cooking, you can bet too. Led me from three states away by the smell alone." He drew quiet again and I watched the waves pulled back in around him. He submerged back within himself just as quickly as he had come out, tucked back in his own shell.

Overhead, a group of seagulls went loudly past. I watched them head towards the ocean till they were out of sight. They seemed to be laughing as usual. "Amos, do you think the whale will come?"

"Have you asked him?"

"Yes."

"Then, he's already here. You just don't see him yet."

"Can you see him?"

He stopped, looked towards the ocean. "Yep."

"What does he say?"

He looked out over the water again. "He says— 'What took so long?'"

"I figured he'd say that."

"He figured so too."

"Amos?" I asked. "What does your God believe in?"

He made a few more flicks with the knife before answering. "Me." he said.

I liked that answer.

. . .

My hands lie against her rough skin. It is cracked with lines, and rough, dry places. Even the eyelashes beneath my fingers feel like the frayed end of branches. "I'm a blind, old woman. Why say such things to me? I can't see with these eyes anymore."

"I want you to. Your eyes are my eyes. I am not blind. Open your eyes, Georgia O'Keeffe." I take my hands away, place my face next to hers.

Two heavy lids begin to part. As they do, the scene changes, color spreads across the mesas as if in a sunrise. The lines in her face shift, an ancient ridge becomes a smile. Around her, gray hair undone, is flying outwards. "Just as I remember it." she says slowly, taking it all in. The warm desert colors growing across us, the rooftop, over the edge, and beyond, moving across the land in all directions. "Now," she says, "I can *show you.*"

43

She should have stayed in Oz.

    After all that dreaming of going over the rainbow— and making it there, Dorothy still ends up back where she started, and happy to be back, on the farm, going back to the same old way of life, farm chores, farm-hand people, country dirt roads, open tornado skies that could, at any moment, reach down and eat you, house and all. And after having known something so different, so wonderful— why would she want to go home? Not once, as a child, did I hope she made it back. I wanted her to stay in Oz, with Toto, Scarecrow, Tin man and Lion. It was an incomprehensible thing to me, *going back.*

    I had followed the yellow brick road. Only it was neither brick, nor yellow, and it didn't lead to Oz. It was a right-hand turn at Belview and Jackson that lead me out of town, down to the pine forests and the dark bay that could look like a mirror on overcast days. *Rentals,* the sign said. I had to be very careful not to fall asleep along the way. The roadside Black-eyed Susans and their deep, yellow petals, were tempting pillows that I might stop and rest my head awhile. If I had not been so shocked at their color I might have, but I drove on past their sun baked faces, watching them in the rearview mirror until the pines crowded them out, When I knocked on Annie's door asking for the wizard, she introduced me to Amos, who had refused to say my name until I said something magical. *When I was a child...* I said. That was the key that let me in.

Only as a child could I enter the kingdom of Heaven, and the garden of Eden, as a Florida coast could become in it's wild, untamed state. A place I could stay awhile. For a short time, I have lived in the magical woods where Annie wears the ruby slippers, tells me wonderful, fairy-like things, and where Amos is building a balloon made of feathers, so that he can fly up and touch the sun.

I walk around barefoot, touching leaves, and trees, and old pier stumps, as though I have never seen any of these things before. I'm taking my time, to make it last. I have not thought of a reason to go home yet, except that I have to. That's how it has to end, with me going back, just like it started.

Indigo.

"Dinner's almost ready." John says.

I kick off my shoes next to the kitchen table and put the mail next to the telephone. "Smells good. I'm starved."

He nods at the mail. "Anything interesting?"

"Just bills." I go to the cabinet, take down two plates, two glasses, start setting the table for dinner. "God, my feet hurt." I say. The center of each foot hurt terribly. I try moving the toes to ease the pain out. It doesn't help.

"Could you see if there's another egg left?" he says over his shoulder. "This isn't working."

I walk on the ends of my toes over to the refrigerator and look in. "One left."

"That should do it."

Walking on heels this time, I put the egg on the counter next to him. He is mashing hamburger together in little balls. A pot of spaghetti sauce is bubbling on the burner. The lid is off and the smell of the onion makes my eyes water. He takes the egg, breaks it over the remaining hamburger, mixes it in with his fingers. "Can you save some of the hamburger for the sauce?" I ask. He looks over at me but doesn't say anything. "I like it mixed in." I say leaning over the counter to take the weight off my feet. "You haven't used it all yet."

"You have always liked it this way." he says.

I stare down into the second pot of water that will be used for the noodles. I wonder if this is worth it? "I have not."

"Yes, you have."

"I know I have never even tried a meatball. I have never made them. My grandmother never made them. I do not care for meatballs."

He rolls another handful of meat into a ball, then says, "This is the way I make spaghetti. The last time I cooked it, I made it this way and you ate it."

"Not those. I probably ate around them."

"I don't remember anything left on your plate?"

"Maybe I put them back in the pot." Now my neck was beginning to hurt too. I twisted it from side to side, ran a hand over the back, held it tight. "It doesn't matter. It's just something I don't like."

"You do."

"I think I know better than you, what I like."

"You ate it last time."

"What difference does it make? Do both. Don't do both. I don't care."

"Who's cooking here?"

I look at him wearily. "Do what you want." I go and get the mail and sit down at the table to open it. I don't want to think about bills, but it was better than this argument.

After a while he asks, "Are you going to eat this?"

Without turning around I answer, "I'm not hungry." I hear a crash and the sound of a garbage bag. I turn and see that he has thrown the entire pot of spaghetti sauce in the garbage. "What are you doing?" I ask calmly.

"You're not going to eat it, why should I?"

"All I asked, was for a little difference. How is that unreasonable?"

"Is it unreasonable you eat with me for a change, after I go to all the trouble to cook it?"

"That should be easy now that you've gone and thrown it away."

He throws the pot holders into the garbage too and slams the pot of water into the sink. "I can't stand this!"

"You're the one who pitched it—" I say back. "I have never eaten those in my life. I don't see how you can tell me..."

"Because you do!"

"I do not!"

"Fine! Fix your own dinner—" He stomps out of the kitchen. The strong aroma of spices remains and it makes me hungry to smell it. I can't imagine what his problem is? Pushing the mail into a pile away from me, I lean my head against my hands. Now the pain has moved from my feet to my head. God, I hate this! I think about what I should do? The thought of eating anything makes me feel sick. I could fix him something, but I knew he probably won't eat it either? I could clean up the kitchen and erase this whole thing from sight? But I don't move to do this either. I feel more tired just thinking. I stare blankly at the wall for some time. Finally, I reach for my shoes and put them on. I have to get out of here. Maybe I'll pick something up for later. He'll be over it by then.

With no place in mind, I get in the car and just head in a direction. I don't even think about dinner or what restaurants are this way. I just drive. As I go through the town, I continue in a one sided argument, as though he were here listening to me. "I can't believe we're fighting about this. I have always hated them. How could you not know this? Have you seen me eat them— no. You haven't. You could have eaten the damn things..." Then, there was the Black-eyed Susans, waving under the heavy sky, the sign offering to rent a place of heaven, and a road that led me where I wanted to go.

"Hi."

"Hello."

"I was looking for a place..." "This likely to be it, as any other."

"A place to stay awhile."

"I've openings. Would you like to see them?"

"Sure."

She smiled warmly. "Just let me put my bread in the oven and I'll show you."

. . .

I'm twelve years old. I'm yelling at the TV, "Don't do it! It's a mistake. The witch is dead! *Stay in OZ Dorothy!*" After all, I knew how it ended. I'd seen the same story play, out six times already. She goes

232

back and no one believes her. They look at her like she's crazy. Back home, the real witch still lives.

"It's just a bad dream, Dorothy... We dream lots of silly things—" Aunt Em tells her. *Close your eyes and forget now.*

I can't forget. Why do you keep telling me too? I can't ever forget. I don't want to go home, grandma. Don't make me. Please don't make me. *I'm afraid.*

"There's nothing to be afraid of."

"There is."

"Go to sleep. Hush now. Go back to sleep."

44

Annie's wisdom was home grown. It came to her naturally, seeped in like tea leaves, infused with the secret ingredients of her faith and good humor. She grew roses in old coffee cans, and set twin pans of homemade bread in the sun to rise twice a week. In a box, under her bed she kept all of her son's baby clothes. She claimed she could still smell his baby scent on them, and showed me how well kept they were, with a layer of tissue pressed between each year, from one to five. At six, she said, he announced he was no longer a baby and was far enough along to bein' a man, that he didn't want any more hand-mades. He wanted store bought. She still makes all of her own dresses though, chosen from sensible colors and only the best materials, sure to withstand the strongest detergents and wash cycles. "Double stitched seams," she said, "was the secret to a long lasting, house dress."

In Annie's house everything was cleaned and dusted, with things seeming to just fall into their own natural order and place. Somewhere just past the hem of her skirt, that when she walked, trailed over lost things found, that when she sat down, covered up the patched up holes in chairs, and tucked back the shedding rug that had lost it's color, faded back to earth tones of brown and ash. She still had the first pot holders she made when she was married, and Tom's clothes, even five years after his death, still hung in the closet, pressed and ironed, as though he might walk in one morning and take off a shirt from one of the wire hangers.

Annie was everything that was full, and soft and warm hearted. She was always saying things like, "Lay back, take a moment and just sit right here..." She would pat the spot beside her, and one just couldn't help but to go there, and sit in the sun, just to hear her voice, smell the baking bread from the kitchen, and the sap of pine trees coming through the open windows, or look through boxes of nothing but buttons. Each time, I saw her, I noticed more, from her house full of everything she'd ever owned, or been given, or found, to the way she talked about her life, or gave advice to those around her. There was always more to Annie than one could ever hope to know.

. . .

"A good meal does more than feed the body." she said. "It feeds the soul." Annie reached up and took down a huge bowl. "It smells good, looks good, tastes good, even feels good. That's something that does more than stop a hunger. Like chicken soup—not that can stuff, but homemade, where everything that goes in is real. That's made from the heart. Just saying *homemade chicken soup* makes you feel a bit better. Your mother might never have made it, but you can learn how. Smell your house up with it and see how much you'll feel better, and everyone who comes in too. There's a hidden art to cooking, it heals what ain't right in other places.

"Don't get tired, Katherine." she told me. "Once you do, you'll follow it to the end. Till there's nothing." She looked long and hard at me, then broke two eggs against the glass side of the bowl. "I've seen it happen. They'll say, 'I'm too old to change, too many years have passed. I'm set in my ways, and I ain't moving!'— Ho'de'ho—" she said. "Set in the grave, is more like it." Between the two yokes, a large clump of butter slid down, separating the pale yellow. "After awhile, they become too tired for love, for change, even for conversation. They don't care much about anything. Lily was that way. Even Tom and I some. He didn't stop caring. He mostly cared about other things, mostly God. It took up a lot of his time, and didn't leave much for anyone else. It made me tired sometimes." She added one cup sugar, one teaspoon salt.

"First, you run. Run so fast the years race by unnoticed. Missed before you even knew they were there." A dash of baking soda went in unmeasured. She stirred it fast, whipping the sides of the bowl, then pulled out the flour sack from overhead. "Then you slow down, tired from all the years of effort and struggle, of trying to keep up. Then the ache in your bones come, and you slow down even more, like you were hollow, an old, brittle cookie that crumbs up at each bite. One that was once moist, and so sweat— so as you couldn't wait to taste it, but with each bite, another piece falls away. You'll be too tired to pick 'em all up..."

One and threeforths cups of white all purpose flour form two hills in the center of the bowl. I clicked the beaters into the mixer and handed them to her. "Then, one day you stop." She looked at me again, beaters raised, white hills waiting. "Anger Katherine, is sometimes good. It might be just enough to make you stop running— at a time when it still matters. Make you walk around awhile. Take your time, kick off your shoes and feel the grass between your toes!" The beater was on. A tornado of steel stuck down between the mountains, shooting powder, eggs, and sugar into the sides of the bowl. She turned it off, licked her finger. "Try Katherine, with every bit of your being—try. Don't let them hold you back."

I traced the edge of the bowl with my finger, tasted it too. "My mother doesn't like facing truth or facts." I said. "When the psychologist started in for both— she high tailed it out of there, cried all the way out of his office, and away from such things." Annie opened up the cabinet and began putting things away. "Then came the psychics. They told her what she wanted to hear, qood stuff, blame it on a past life sort of thing. 'It's not your fault...' they told her. But even their good words ran out eventually, so she turned to God. God forgives everyone and everything without question or price. You don't have to fix it. Just box it. Put it on a shelf and forget about it."

Annie pulled out a box and said, "Like this cereal everyone wanted, and no one liked after I bought it... Shelve it to heaven and close the pearly gates behind it! Out of sight, out of mind, all is forgiven in the *church of God and grocery.*" We both laughed.

"Jessie's the one who lost." I said. "She paid the price. She's like her now."

Annie said, "Some people won't be reminded of their mistakes. Jessie's on some dark back shelf in her mind probably." She picked up the bowl and poured the thick batter into a pan, spread it quick with the back of a spoon. Each little hill she patted down, then put the whole thing in the oven. We both watched it for awhile. It seemed like I could actually see the heat making it rise and form. A wonderful smell drifted from it.

"I guess so." I said.

As Annie put the dishes in to soak, some of the dish water spilled down the side onto the floor. It made a dark imprint down the side of her dress. I picked up a dish rag and knelt down to clean it up off the floor. When I sat back down I said, "My grandparents spent half of their lives changing things around, trying to make things better. Moving from city to city, every few years or months, a new place." I pictured my mother, drifting through sluggish water, dragged behind like a barge. "Maybe that affected her in some way? Made her unsettled?"

Annie used the same rag to dry the counter, twisted the dress part that was wet, smoothed it down. "When you get angry," she said, "you want to stop and look around for someone to blame. But the person is right there, in yourself. So get hoppin' mad! Let it out. Jump around like a crazy dog. Yell if you have to... *Life's exactly where you left it.* Her life is hers. Your's right here. It doesn't have to be a race. There isn't a finish line waiting out there someplace, and there are no prizes for getting there first. It's just a long, long journey between the first breath and the last. Don't hold her in. Fear's what does that, and that's what makes you run. You don't need to catch up and you can't turn back."

"I'm not crazy, am I?"

"You're just inside, like in a shell, trying to chip your way out. I know it's hard. But you got to keep chippin'. You got to, if you ever want to see what's outside."

"I don't want to be like them."

"You won't, as long as you're still trying."

45

"The Devil owed me a debt. He paid me off in son-in-laws." Grandma says this to me when I am older. She is on her hands and knees, weeding her garden. Handfuls of crabgrass are pulled out by the roots. "That's all it seems willing to grow—weeds." she says to the moist ground. The flower seeds she planted have never grown out of their tight shells. To me, she has been digging down into graves, dead things, since they have never grown up out of the soil, not one stem, or leaf, or bud.

Vermilion.

"Your sister's in town." Grandma makes this sound like a normal thing. "She looks terrible." she says, making this sound' normal too. "She's thin as a rake, looks starved, miserably depleted. All she does is praise that man— talk about all he's done for her. I think she's a little crazy? All she can talk about is how much he takes care of her— while we can plainly see the scars all up and down her. She acts like it's a reward or something to be proud of."

"Maybe, to her, it is?" I say.

"Just like her mother—"

"Maybe she'll leave him?"

"She won't. She loves it." She punctuates the last word with a shovel rim.

I wonder if she means him, or what he does? "I doubt that."

"You watch— she's in, till he kills her."

"You sound like you can't wait?"

"Maybe your mother will appreciate her mistakes now."

"I don't think she'll even notice."

"She will."

"Jessie has feelings too."

"Only for being stupid and wanting everyone to feel sorry for her. She's not a child anymore. She's as old as your mother, when she got married. Now everything's the same! I'm going to give up on this family. Not one straight line in the bunch. I'm embarrassed to go anywhere. Someone might ask me about it? I could never lie. It'd show in a heartbeat. No good lying, best not to say anything. But, as they say, 'You can choose your friends, but you can't do anything about your relatives'— *or son-in-laws.*"

"What about John? You think this way about him too?"

"Did I say anything about him? No. But he could get a better job than that one he's got now. There's no money in it. Why doesn't he look for a better job?"

"He likes the one he has just fine."

"What about your job? You still at that same place?"

"You know I am."

"It's a shame you spent all that money on school and not a thing to show for it now. Repaying that school loan? I guess you would be. How about teaching? You could be a teacher."

"It doesn't matter what kind of job I have. I'm a painter."

"How many shows have you had?"

"That takes time."

"When will you have the time? You've been married a long time now. What about kids? You putting that off too?"

"I want kids. I just don't think it's a good time yet. Neither of us do."

"I'm surprised he'd want kids. He can be so childish himself. He'll probably be supporting all of you too, if you become an artist. You have seemed rather unstable lately. You did just leave." I can see her staking me up beside the tomato plants, tall and gangly. She frowns at the way I bend.

"I didn't leave the city."

"Most people don't usually drop everything without warning and disappear. Would you do that if you had kids?"

"No, of course not. That's why I did it now, because I don't have kids yet."

"I just want to be sure you're OK. I'm not trying to argue about it."

"I'm fine. I want to know where I am with everything, so I can decide where to go from here?"

"Have you?"

"I know where I've been. I know where I am now. The rest is still being worked out."

"Well, I hope you figure it out. Not like your sisters though, or your mother. You were the only one who might have a chance."

"They all had the same chances. They just didn't make very good choices." Incompatible soil.

"That's what they all say."

"I'm sure Jessie knows she made a bad choice."

"You could sure fool me."

"She's not a fool. She's stubborn."

"She sure is trying hard at it."

"We all are."

. . .

I am hungry. I say, holding out two dirty hands to her. I would eat anything she might offer, dirt, rocks, red clay, new grass, tough roots spread out around me like a thousand strong arms to hold me back. I am weak, feed me, make me strong.

I would eat through anything now, to get to the surface. To break my shell in half and slip a pale hand out, snake thin in hunger, greedy for a drink of the sun. I wouldn't stop drinking, I tell myself, till there was nothing left. Till I was full to the top— with her golden, hot pancake syrup. That is what she is made of, the gold mixed, flower pollen that bees feed to their young, the sweetness of nature, hidden down deep in the throats of forest trees. I take for granted her generosity, or steals, like a bear steals, ignoring the hundreds of stings meant to protect it. Her pale, white hand, reaching down the throats of flowers, down into graves, digging with a gardener's shovel, pale against the dark soil, like her own searchlight. Peering into holes, cursing the devil for rotten, good-for-nothing son-in-laws.

Patiently, she pulls each of them out, one at a time, and throws them over her shoulder in a pile by the concrete steps.

. . .

"No whales today— Katherine!" Amos yelled over to me and waved. It had become his daily report when I came out to paint. They sat facing the bay in their rocking chairs. Only the back of Annie's head and one arm was visible from the angle I was in. Amos was in profile, his white hair slightly lifted in the wind, one of his hands motioned as if in deep conversation. The horizon edge beyond them, I put just below the center point on the canvas, with the water's darker colors of brown and blue shadows, making the lighter colors of their old rockers stand out. The shape of the chairs, the direction of the plank angles, the lifted hand of Amos, all drew the eye towards the horizon, then back down on the right, to them. The composition was circular, receding and coming back up close. I knew what I would call it even before I had begun. I picked up a brush, looked at it a moment, thought of a shovel, then dug down into the first color, brought it up to, *The Whale Watchers*.

46

Pushing against my fear of things, of not knowing for sure, I walk in dark rooms to see how much I know? Everything I run into is something, I didn't know, or forgot. Or to see how long can I stand it— before the fear becomes too much, and I have to reach for the light switch? In the dark, proportions alter, grow larger, more threatening. It is easy to be overcome by fear. The whole body succumbs to it. Hands, feet, pounding heart, suddenly all my parts, have a mind of their own.

When I tried to go back, it was too soon. At night, I drove back to the city several times, past the apartment. John was always home. The light in the upstairs bedroom was on. I could see his shadow pass by the window, or in the kitchen. Part of me had hoped he would stop and look out, but he didn't. Each time I drove away telling myself I wasn't ready. Each attempt left me feeling worst, not better. But, in an odd way, feeling worst was better.

Then one night, sitting there in the car, the darkness no longer a comfort. Not knowing what was going on inside did not make me feel safely lost. I simply reappeared in the doorway, surprising him. But like most surprises, it was on me. I betrayed myself, dragged back the past within the first ten minutes. By twenty, he was not so happy to see me again.

Indanthrone Blue.

"She told me to leave." he says. "That's it. There's no more to the story." I keep moving away. I don't want to listen. I try to block him out, but can't. "I loved somebody besides you." he says. "I've already admitted this." He talks down to his hands, or shoes, one or the other. His voice is fragile, weakening me, so that at the same time the sound of it, pulls me towards him, his words shove me away. "She could cry the tears you couldn't. It was easy to love her for that."

Tears are running down my face, but I am turned away. Anger covers the weakness I feel. "Then why did you?"

"She told me to go find what I was really looking for."

I laugh. "And this..." I lift my arms to the room. Hold them open. "Here it is! How do you like it?" Spinning around, tears now concealed, to face him.

He only looks back sadly, says, "What is it going to take?"

"For what!" I scream.

"For you to realize— you're not the only one who feels?"

"Maybe, I should have asked her what she felt—"

"*Love.*"

"You should know." stinging. "You have so much of it to give..."

"And you had none."

"I know what you're doing." The door, I want to leave. I want to run for it, not to hear anymore... "You're trying to make me think I'm crazy. That this is all my fault."

"That is not what's happening."

"I can see right through this—"

"You have never had to be afraid of me."

"I wasn't afraid."

"You *wanted* to be." he said. "You wanted me to turn into some terrible monster... then hated me for not being one! You had feelings for me once— then suddenly, it was gone and you became this closed off, angry, hating face— who couldn't stand even look at me! What was it I supposed to wait for?"

"You can't put that on me!"

"It's not the way you want to see it— but it is. A part of it was yours, just as much as mine! You can't pretend to have just lived in a shell, doing nothing, having no part in what happened between us. Is that the evil thing you wanted to know from me? You—hurt—me. Here is what you waited for... I said it. *Truth!* Painful, hard to take, truth. That's the slap in the face you were hoping for. Hurt's, doesn't it?"

Hand pressing into my mouth, lips trembling, I am backed into a corner, turned away, fighting rage and hurt all at the same time. But, he is so close, I can feel him standing very near.

"It made you feel...something." he said, "For me? God, if nothing, it made you hate me— It took that much to move one inch of you. I wanted you to see me." His hand touches my shoulder. I jerk away. "I did love you then. But I could not love what you were becoming."

"Then why did you come back?" my voice is rough, punishing. "You could have stayed with her—" All the lines of my face exactly where I want them, I look at him, condemn him. "Or, maybe, you were too busy breaking her into pieces too? Who really lost more— me or her?" He is struck by the words. It is too late to take them back. He turns away.

"Go then." he tells me. "Go back to your nice, little hole. Wall yourself in. If it's really you, you're looking for— I hope you find it. But take a long, hard look at what you do find." His eyes have me finally. "Make sure it's you who comes back here. Leave your family— drown the whole god damn pack! But don't come back here seeing them in me." Tears are running down his face, two long trails, flowing out of him, making up for what I could not give. "Take as long as you want. I'll be here. Make up your mind. But, at least, give me the courtesy to let me know, one way, or the other... If you want me, or not!" The look in his eyes, sends me stumbling foolishly at the door, the safe blackness beyond. I am running. Just as he said I would. I hate it, that he is right, that he can know just what I will do, want to do. I didn't. Except to get away. Not to think. Not to know. Just *away.*

. . .

Find me, the darkness said. Alone, out here, I was wrapped in it, in a place without street lights, or city glare. I could see John in this darkness. We were both searching now, passing each other completely at times, stumbling and bruising, trying again and again to really see each other, but without our eyes. Seeing with other things than eyes, the heart maybe, or the body's fear, tingling, listening, straining to hear, afraid to find what was left of us, before it was too late.

Reaching forward, I lifted my arms. "Help me." I said to him.

Things come out of darkness, out of hiding, when they will come out no other way.

This is true for people too.

47

"Why did you never have children?" I ask Mary Cassatt.
"I never believed I could do both."

"Would you have liked to?"

"I don't know. Children take time. Painters never have enough time."

"True." I say. "And they're noisy, get into everything."

Mary Cassatt looks at me. She knows I'm lying. "Would you like to have children?" she asks me.

I see in her painting, a mother and child, arms encircling each other. The colors are pale, their skin brushed over with pure white, the shadows muted and gentle. A look passes between mother and child. My eye is drawn to their faces, where I cannot turn away. Beneath the skin tones, colors of red and blue show through, flushed, translucent skin. I imagine the life within, each of them pausing to listen to the contracting sounds of valves and chambers, the roar of rushing blood that they both share. In their touch they feel the pulse of the other. It becomes so loud, nothing else in the world can disturb it.

"I am afraid of children." I say.

Flesh Tint.

"I'd rather have something than nothin'." Jessie says. She takes only a small bite of her sandwich, then pushes it away. I had already put mine aside. Too much sun to eat. Even the plastic chairs are too hot to sit in. The outdoor table is glaring white in the sun, reflects against her face, so that every mark and scar cannot be missed. Her eyes are red, her face pallid, expression shifting. She looks at everything around us, except me. And, everything is so bright, I have to squint to see at all. I watch her through narrowed spaces.

The heat does not seem to bother her. She is laid back over her chair, one leg kicked up over an empty one. Everything is hung loose about her, her hair, her clothes, the way she talks. An attitude that wants to seem full of something, but all I see is the opposite, full of nothing. Nothing in the clothes to make them fill out, just skin and bone thinness. Nothing to hold together what she says either, only left over bits and pieces that she is trying to make something out of. She wants me to believe she knows what she is doing. "Even if it kills you?" I ask.

She flashes a half smile. Forcing a softness, where only hard cut edges look back. "I'm going to die one day. Why do you have to make such a big deal of when?"

"When you could have more."

"Ha! That's what I got don't I?" The edges fold back up on itself, closing in, the way metal does, all sharp angles and jagged points, a car wrecked face.

"Just more shit."

"So when is that so bad?"

"There are better guys out there."

She pulls out a cigarette and lights it in a quick motion with a beat-up silver lighter. Gray-black fingernails become metal on metal, slams it back down on the table. "Look—" she says. "If he leaves me, he'll come back and I'll be waiting. I don't want anybody else. That's the way I am, you could say. It's not as bad as you think. He loves me." *Like no one else ever has...* her eyes say. Eyes, that are lined in black, like picture frames. The conviction wavers in her, in her too red lips, cheeks that are blue tinted and yellow from fists she says love her.

"That's what you're willing to live for?" I ask. "Ten minutes of love? There are people out there who'd love you for more than ten lousy minutes, and they don't beat the crap out of you first."

"I don't want anyone else." The gray-black nails tap ashes into a pile next to her plate. "We're trying to have a baby." I flinch visibly at this. "God, you kill me—" she says. "Do you treat everybody like this? Or, just those you think can't get up there with you on that chicken shit rooftop you live on? What, you think you can just *give* me some other life and tell me it'll work better? You don't know anything—" She pushes her plate away. "I thought today would be nice. A nice, little get together and all, but you always end up making everyone feel worst." Her voice cuts right through the pretend, older tilt of her face. The words sound made-up, too much in control, every move, coordinated and deliberate. "They're right, you know. You think you can just paint a little picture of how it will be, and everything will be the way you say. Crap Katherine, you're just living in a nice, little world of your own aren't you? Don't tell me nothin'. Save it for some other shoe shit! I got better things to do than sit around here with you." She quickly grabs out another cigarette, lights it, sucks in the long smoke. She turns the worst of the bruised skin away from me, faces the strangers who are staring at us. "What you looking at—" she says to them, turns again, blows out the stale breath. Clouds now, between us.

The waitress passes, looks at us, and keeps going.

Jessie taps the cigarette rapidly against the side of the table. She is looking straight at me through the smoke. One eye half closed, peering at me, as though she can see right through everything I have said. "You so perfect?" she says finally. "You so happy? Why don't you mind your own business and leave everybody else's alone. Just once. It would be nice to see you, without hearing you run over mine. Hell, I can't even eat with you, without you trying to shove something down my throat."

I would like to think of something to say that she would hear. The silence, at least, lets me be near her, to see her. Every time I try and just look, without knowing, so she won't run away. Every time, something slips out. Maybe it will one day slip in, is the hope— into her thick skull, which I can't help myself but see as fragile, and white, shell thin, and soft as babies are— and that one day he just might put a fist through, if she doesn't listen.

Framed eyes are turned away, blinking rapidly, suspended in the smoky haze. They must be circled to show where they are, so that they will stand out, isolating the rest of her face, perhaps a trick to divert attention.

We sit, saying nothing, over uneaten food. But, eventually, the silence becomes too much for her. She gets up, slings her purse strap over her shoulder, one hand grab for the lighter and cigarettes. "Thanks for lunch." she says. Her voice, loose again, smart-mouthed. "And *nothing.*"

She starts to walk away then turns back, tapping cigarette, falling ash. The sun is behind her, shielding her face in darkness as she looks down at me. "You know," she says, "you've been married longer than any of us. You don't got no kids. You're still stuck in a no-where job, in the same old city. I never heard you doing no waltz with your husband. What you got, that I don't?" The cigarette follows the ash to the ground. She steps on it, then walks away. She doesn't wait for an answer. And I have none to give her.

Every child I see now, is my little sister. She is frozen in time. Her face— the way I remember it, turned up to me, looking for me to help her. She will never really grow old. She will haunt me. Elusive as a vision is elusive, always just out of reach of understanding, frightening to look at, to behold at any time, night or day. In locked away rooms where I think I'm safe— there she'll be. On crowded streets, where I alone will witness her screaming face, picture without words, the nightmares I see her relive over and over. No matter how hard I try I will never be able to take her away, wake her up, or make things better.

Section Five

Is there no way to ease into our lives?

48

"They say, when it rains, the devil beats his wife—" Paul Gauguin says this hungrily. "But this is not true. These are not her tears. They are his. She broke his heart by calling him a fool."

No man is an island, but Paul Gauguin was in body, a man and an island. It was only his spirit, that never mastered the art of being alone. He had abandoned his real family, so his muses pasted themselves over to be his new one. He painted them thickly to give them substance and form. Mother, child, missing father, absent men, lovers not yet arrived, bathing villagers, bodies at rest— they all gathered before him on the canvas. He was the secret listener of private conversations, his face pressed close to hear their voices, to understand the strange tongue that always an outsider, looking in, must try to interpret.

He ragged war on them with his brush. Angry, because he could not entirely believe they were what they seemed. They always kept certain things to themselves, secrets in a turned back, eyes looking to the side, closed hands.

"Drink," he says, only the cup he hands me is empty. "Drink in the storm!" he says. "Make pain your wine. Let it fill your cup! It will. Oh, it always will—". He cradles his against his chest like a drunken man. "That's the beauty of this poisonous life." Dips his fingers into the cup, sucks each one. "Toast! To the lightning— may it one day strike me down, so that I can have it at last! The secrets of life and death are right here, in this cup." He takes a drink, then lets it fill again. The eyes that look back at me over the edge, are those of a wild man. "Because these are the tears of the devil and they'll make you burn in hell. I don't give a damn what anybody says about me. This is what I want. I have a wife who hates me and a lover who loves me!" Over flowing cup, spilling onto the ground. "Ah, sweet rain... Look at me— the devil's fool. Ha! Toast to fools of wives! Toast to fools of fools!" He opens his mouth and the rain pours in. Tropical tastes, rising steam stirred out of the palms of leaves, wild tastes lined with mud paths, thatched roofs, and color, always the taste of color, and exotic named oils that could kill me with their poisonous ingredients— but with laughter, it goes down, harmless as rain.

. . .

It is that this pain has nothing visible to mark it's place. I cannot point to this spot and say, 'This is where it hurts.' There is nothing to show for it or prove it is really there. If it were *just* a thing of the past, I might could lay it aside, but this pain has wound itself around me entirely. Like a vine that has climbed around the inside of me, dangling leaves in front of my eyes, it is influencing how I look at everything, present, past, and future. It is as if, it is a pain simply to see...whether my eyes are open or closed. If it were a lie, I could cure it with a truth. But my past is not a lie either. It is just a pain, a weight. At some point, at least once a day, I wonder how can I live with this, and move on, and walk with my eyes open, seeing things as I do?

The tangled forest inside me, did not turn out it's leaves to the sun here. The wind did not spread it's flowered seeds, or grow out to new reaches. Mine grew deeper, sending it's roots chasing through my veins, knotted, blood red roots that grounded me into the earth, as a sewing needle does, pulling down the sinewy threads that follow it. Was it an illusion that I seemed free to walk around at all? A great fist of wind blew up from the water, uncurling itself across the steps where I was sitting. "I don't know." I said to it. I just didn't know how to live with it?

Amos was making his way over the rocks, coming up the beach towards me. When he reached the steps, he took one look at my face and said, "Come with me." I got up and followed. He headed back the way he had come. He said nothing and neither did I. I watched the ground instead. His large brown shoes beside mine, scuffed with dust and wet sand. Each step was guided by the wooden thrust of his cane. He leaned heavily on it, pushing it deep between the rocks and soft ground. He was watching the ground too, gray hair hung down straight around his face. It swayed like old ropes hanging off the side of a boat. He looked like he could have lived his whole life beside the water.

As we left the shade of the pines, I felt my skin already turning red. This was what I must resemble, sun-fried to a crisp. Living under the sun with years of asphalt and air-conditioning, city crust that crinkled like pine bark, crunched like fried chicken, or dead leaves. The Florida heat pressed in from all sides at once, always relentless. Walking through it, was like pressing against a wall that gave way just enough to allow the body through. I felt it moving across the surface of any bare skin, imagined it closing seamlessly behind me, solid again after each step.

Amos walked with his mouth open. He was breathing heavily through it. Over his skin, glistening salt, perspiration ran down in little streams. At the dock he stopped suddenly, turned to look at me, and asked in all sincerity, "What is my name?" The ropes had fallen to either side, angled face plunged through the middle. Over his nose, the skin was peeling. I wondered if I should answer such an innocent question. He looked down again, slowly lifted up a foot to get up the one step to the dock.

"Harold Amos Tenor." I said.

"How long have you known me?"

"Nearly three months."

"Just a drop in the bucket!" Both feet up, he went on down the dock, his cane hitting against the wooden planks. "I have *known* my name seventy-one years." he said. "I have asked myself, "Just what does that name make me? I am the son of a father and mother? Am I the ancestor to a tribe of people I have never met? Just who the hell is Harold Amos Tenor?" He stopped to watch a Blue Heron fly past the end of the dock, down to the shore. "I have spent my seventy-one years trying to figure it out, and I know little more than what you think you know of me in just three months." The heron landed gracefully, wings extended, legs stretching downward beneath him. "Do you wonder if that's what they do?" He motioned to the bird, who was standing at the edge of the water now, watching for a fish. "Looking at their reflection— asking, 'What the hell *is* that?'" He watched the bird for several minutes. "I dreamed once, that they were burying their prayers in the sand." he said. "Over there, where that one's at. Each prayer was a little, black marble. I don't know why they were marbles? But that's what they were. They dug a hole with their beaks, put the marble in, covered it up..." The heron caught its fish and flew off into the trees, out of sight. Amos rubbed a thumb over the top of his nose, scratching slowly, stared at the empty shore. "I've seen it." he said. "Death." I was staring at his peeling nose. I had thought, 'dead skin', just as he said the word, 'death'. It sent a shiver through me. He went on, "Empty houses. Dead end streets. Faces without names. Bones." He held up one hand, looked at it. "Held it, talked to it. Death said, 'Names won't keep you here.' So I asked, 'Then why do I have a name?' Amos looked at me, asked, "Do you know what death said?"

"No, what?"

"Nothin'. Didn't utter a word after that."

"Names don't mean anything." I said.

"Might be. Or could be, death is just a selfish son-of-bitch. "

"So, what did you do?"

"Turned around and went right back where I started. Dead ends don't lead anywhere. If I didn't know the face, made-up a name for it. Buried the bones. Kept right on walking. I traveled across more state lines and back porches than you can imagine. Out there, unsettled as a dog with fleas, till I got here. I do know this though, I've seen it— that the pain of living is in every square inch of land, and sky, water. Traveling teaches that as a rule of thumb. You can keep trying to get away from something, or you can face it, and get along without it. At the end you will die. This is promised. Every ill or pain will be gone, lifted from your spirit as though it were never there. You'll wonder why the heck you spent so much time worrying about it all instead of doing other things!" He hits his cane on the dock to make the point. "That—is all there is to it."

I listened, struggling between wanting to believe, and that the stubborn refusal not to. He went on, pressing through the stubborn set face I knew I had. "As a child, you thought the sun had two sides. You must be like the sun and turn inside yourself. Look out the other side, the inside. Use your light to see what you could not see before in the darkness."

At the end of the dock, we both stopped and looked down at the water. "You never found what you were looking for?" I asked.

"I found more than what I was looking for." he said.

He took his cane and tapped the end of my foot. "What is your name?"

"Katherine Eve Wells."

"Who is she?"

"I have no idea."

He tapped my foot again. "A woman with a past, a present—and a future. A history."

"No big deal."

"A mystery."

"I don't care for mysteries."

"Look behind you." he said. I did. "Do you see any chains dragging behind you?"

"No."

"Any ropes tied?"

"No. "

"Anything?"

"No. "

"No, is right." He pointed his cane down at the water, then out toward the ocean, then up at the sky. "There is your future."

Out loud I asked, "Why do I have a future?"

He turned away, his ship-like face moving through the wind, ropes swaying. His cane sounded against the wooden planks, keeping time and rhythm to the walk of a man who had walked across a nation, to get to here, this moment, this place. He left without another word.

What he said was simple. Nothing was holding me back, except me. Afraid of the future because it was something I could not see, I did not know what was out there. I could only see where I'd been before. I sat down, hung my feet over the side, stared at the reflections on the water. They are waving like candle flames, pressed flat over the bay. A cloud passed over the sun and the water below faded into a cool, bluish-brown. My mother was pressed down in the blackness. She was looking up at me, as I sat looking down at her, a reflection, a ghost. "I see you mother." I said.

Then the sun returned.

. . .

I am the circle inside the square. I can turn inside myself and see backwards, to the beginning. If I turn further, I will be back where I started, then further and further, until maybe, I'll go on from there? Out there...cut loose from rigging, and lines and anchors, like a sailor, looking up from ocean space, trying to find the words to say what I felt, then to send them off to all the right people....

Amos had said, "Life is a dream that can be interpreted by the symbols and images around the person living it. The whale is your symbol. Think about all the things the whale means to you. Ask yourself the question until you have no more answers. Then, you will understand the dream.

"What is the whale to you?" he asked me.

"My hope." I had said, though I didn't really feel it at the time.

Maybe it was. Maybe, it really is.

49

To speak of the spirit, one must glance away, to the side of things. It is too personal, too blinding, to know head on. The soul is not made of solid things. It resides within things, in surfaces and solid places. If one goes down into the earth far enough, you will reach first, the life giving waters, then further, to the center, fire— a core of molten rivers, reaching through the earth like veins. A life within, trembling, breathing, contracts and expands. It reaches out through the stone cracks, volcanic wells, icy flesh that is torn away, the size of mountains. Continuously reshaping itself, the earth is new-born every moment.

The spirit that is in me, knocks at the walls of my being, with heartbeats pounding— every moment wanting out, but forgetting the way how.

When I knocked on the door, Annie let me in. She said she working on getting dinner started, would I come on into the kitchen and sit with her? I followed behind, chose a chair next to the sink, then was given a bowl of potatoes and a peeler. I put the bowl in my lap, started peeling.

"How is everything going?" Annie asked.

"Fine, I guess." I said. The potato kept slipping out of my hand. I peeled up more potato than skin, and the feel of it in my hand made me think of a baseball. I was just as bad at sports as peeling potatoes. "I've been doing a lot of thinking." I said.

"What sort of thinking, good I hope?"

"The kind that sprouts up from too many questions, too little answers."

"Oh, that kind." She reached into my bowl and had three peeled and ready before I'd finished one.

"I was just wondering if there was one you might could answer for me?"

"What's that?"

"Well—" I looked at my whittled down potato. "I was wondering, what was it like when you had Joseph?" A baby's fist, that's what it looked like, my potato. "I've been thinking about having a baby." I said.

She ran her hands through the faucet water, lifted up some string beans, let them fall as they were rinsed. The space between her eyes was shaped in little hills, like one of the string beans. She thought about the question a long time before answering. "Well, I'll tell you." she said finally, turned off the water, dried her hands with her apron. "Just in there, in that room behind us, is where it finished up. And just here—" She looked down, took a step back, "is where it started." She reached back into the sink for the beans.

"Right here?"

"Just to the left of your foot there."

I looked down amazed at such an exact spot. She collected all the potatoes, put them in a pot, turned the fire on underneath. "Women were still having babies at home if they wanted then, and that's what I did, with two midwives. Two sets of hands, pulling and guiding and helping in all the ways midwives did, but in my case, it was a little different—they were men's hands doing the helpin'. My Tom— and my Amos." She smiled wide, looked at the floor again. "I remember being nervous at first. It happened fast, just after a pot full of breakfast dishes. I turned around and everything was in motion, me, the dishes, the floor, water comin' out in a flood, out of me, and down the sink, where all those clean dishes went back in! I barely made it to the next room, to the bed. There was a flurry of hands, helping voices, those two runnin' around trying to figure out what to do first. All I wanted was the bed and to lie down fast.

"Bless their hearts. It was a miracle they made it through all the pushin' and prayin". But, he came, just about on his own too, my beautiful Joseph, a slippery fish. Tom caught him right as he swam out. And there was Amos, all hunched over, sleeves rolled up, standing next to Tom with a basin full of water, as though it might just be a fish wanting go in for swim and he'd be there to help.

"All of us, I think, felt so many things at once, not a one could have been named. A life had come into the world, and we were the hands that carried it across. It's the hand the baby learns first. Just how it's held, the shape and grasp of it, it knows like it's first word. I held him to me so he would know me. Gently, I wiped off his face, his tiny closed hands, down his back. He was pretty gusted up. But he cleaned up real nice, turned the color of a raven's eye— wet and shiny. He went to sleep, and all three of us didn't say a word, or move, just watched his sweet form, sleeping there against me. I remembered Mrs. Minnie and her baby, the way they had looked at each other, smiling. He wasn't old enough to smile yet, so I was doing that for the both of us.

"It was a perfect made moment, all of us together. All that love in our tiny room, the waves outside gone quiet, hardly any wind, only a few birds in the distance. God gave me this tiny creature from love, Tom's love and mine, a miracle gone through me into this baby we named Joseph. I wanted to sing then, but hummed so he wouldn't stir out of sleep. Just a little something I remembered. Amos brought up the quilt to cover us as evening came on, Lily's quilt, with pieces of my dress in it. That brought everything together, made it just right and orderful. Just perfect..."

That was what made it so terrifying for me to imagine.

I told her how wonderful that sounded, how it would give me something to think about, but said I should be getting back. She told me to come back in an hour, have some dinner with them, so I said, I would.

Back at the rental, I turned on my lamp, sat down in the middle of my work area, looked at everything I had done.

My time here was ending. There was always that feeling, that I never had enough time. I would have to go back soon. My spirit asked me, in all the off to the side ways, if I have learned anything? I answered back, I *have*. I survived. All the visions and remembered things. I have taken up a collection of my parts, a collection of many. New skins over placed the old, growing as a tree does— in cycles. Parts in me say, I am ready to have children. Feeling pieces, that stir up longing when I look at babies, want instinctively to call one my own. But, then the thinking part takes over and says, 'What kind of life could you offer?' If I cannot give them what I've known, or seen, and have no idea what a good thing then to give would be? How would I know— *if I was ready?*

I imagine the baby knowing when. To turn upside-down to fall head first down the deep well. Falling towards the earth, a sense of being pushed in from all sides, like the city, or long office hallways, falling to the ground with dirt in the face. There becomes suddenly, no room, no way to move freely, forced to move. You cannot stay inside forever. I thought that way now. Here, I had found a way in. Now, it was time to follow the path that would take me back. A new birth.

I wonder at the point I crossed into my mother, swimming beneath her surface like a fish— a circular expression, divided into parts. The complexity of division, multiplication, parts growing into more parts, enclosing the walls of my spirit, growing to imitate the body of my mother, like her, but not her, like him, my father, but not him.

. . .

When I called John later, he was very surprised to hear from me. I invited him to a dinner Annie was giving for her son and granddaughters. It was awkward at first, talking to him. Our last fight had seemed so final, as every fight always seemed like the last and final one. He asked me how I was doing? I told him, I wasn't running. When he asked what I meant by that? I said, I had decided to go around barefoot from now on, and did he like chicken soup? He said yes and yes he would love to see where I had hidden myself these months. What time? Sevenish...Fine. Was everything OK now? Yes, everything was fine.

And for the first time ever, it was beginning to sound like the truth.

What is the whale?
—The whale is my rope. It's what pulled me through each day.

50

*L*eonardo wonders why the weight of man does not equal the weight of the man's life?

Proportions have made him solid in the center, rooted as a tree is, through time, and to the place the man is born to. As the seasons change, the tree and man can do nothing but change with it— standing tall, blooming, bearing fruit, bending to the forces of age, withering and falling back to the same earth that gave him life. He studies the shapes of arms and cannot help but see them as weak branches, twig fingers, easily broken. He measures and compares the mathematical significance of size and weight, the distance between parts.

In secret, Leonardo determines that flesh alone, will not know angelic perfection.

He draws the man inside the circle and square. The figure touches all sides, equally. He draws wings on men and they become angels. He designs around the man ways to make his weight equal to that of a bird. He desperately wishes to uproot the man and send him soaring into the heavens.

On the cliffs, high above the fields and farm houses below, I take his hand. "Trust me." I say, as though it were an answer to something. The experience draws a neat line around itself, closing us in together. We step off the edge. The valley flashes by with the speed of our thoughts, blurring the way bee's wings do, weightless, fast, and free. Out of the well of his voice is the sound of laughter. I drink it in, *flying* through the dreams of Leonardo da Vinci.

. . .

When I was a child, I thought the sun had two sides. At night, I believed, it turned inside itself and looked out the other side and became the moon— and lit up the sky like a night-light. It was by this light, I looked inside myself and saw the secret, hidden places, behind closed lids, to underskin places such as the heart, or bones, or thought spaces where things were kept like kitchenware, or spare blankets. Things that might have gone unnoticed in cast off ways and reasons, because they were common things lacking in obvious beauty, or so beautiful they could not be looked at for long. Once-in-a-lifetime moments that will never happen again.

Katherine Eve, do you take this man to be your husband?

Yes, I do.

John Patrick Wells, do you take this woman?

Yes, I do. Forever.

He had added that word. *Forever.* Already, I felt I had done less, promised less. From the first, my love proved less than he expected. And his, not as eternal. The love we promised in the beginning, was not what we had now.

. . .

"She said that?" John asked.

"She did. Annie said, 'Good food does more than feed the body. It gives it something more.'" We sat next to each other on the rental steps. He had arrived early for the dinner, wanted to see where I had been staying, see the paintings.

"Have I given you something more?"

"Absolutely."

"Enough to ask you to come back?"

"Do you want me too?"

He reached over, put his hand on mine. "You know, I do."

I could feel the warmth of his shoulder, hear his breathing, Comforting sensations, as though they were shaped familiar things, held in the hand, that I didn't have to see to know. There is a touch of unease about him. He glances at me, blinking, turns away. He seems not to believe his own eyes, in seeing me here, beside him again. "Sometime in the future, after I save back up the money I spent—" I said, "I do want kids."

"Don't worry about that."

"I just want you to know."

"Anything could happen in the future."

"I know."

"You could be a famous artist."

"And a mother—"

"Anything you want." He leaned against my shoulder; put his hand on my knee. "Can I ask you something?"

"Sure."

Eyes opened and closed several times. "If you love me," he said, "why do you act like you hate me so much?"

I could feel myself evading the question. I did know the answer, but kept looking off to the side, unable, or unwilling, to see it directly. Inside, I felt crushed, like tin foil, getting smaller and smaller all around. I repeat his question in my head. Nothing. Then the words are there, coming out. An answer. "—because you say, you love me."

He let out a deep, tired breath. "I'm not lying when I say it."

"I know."

"Then why?"

"I am a hateful person. I must have tricked you into seeing something lovable in me. I thought your love was a mistake."

He took this in, considering. Finally he said, "Do you know what I think about you?"

I knew. "Someone who works too much. Someone who never does things the way you want. Someone who can't trust you."

"These are all bad things. Don't you think I see anything good?"

"No."

"Well, I do."

"If you say them, I'll think you're lying, making them up on the spot."

"If I don't say them, will you still believe me?"

"I'll try." He took my hand in his, rolled the wedding band between his fingers.

"No one can guarantee the future." I said to him, breathless, slowly unfolding. "There is no guarantee that love will last as long as we want it. Even Annie says, 'That God's love won't last forever, not on guarantee'. She says, 'Eventually we all pay up."

"We've paid for it." he said. Then he put his arm around me, held me tight. Something, deep inside me, flushed warm, then hot.

I know what love is. I thought. It is the feeling I get when I reach for a color, open it, smooth it out across the surface with my brush, blend it with another color, harmony, complimentary colors that fall together without thinking, hues working together with all their uniqueness and individualness. Struggling, until the two work together within the composition. There are so many conditions to loving people. I was afraid that I did not know all the ways? "I'm not the same person I was." I say to him.

"Then I'll learn to love the new one."

"You'll still think I'm a bitch."

"But a loving bitch, married to a loving bastard."

"Wouldn't it be easier to have found someone else?"

"Not any easier."

As I hold his hand back, there is a kind of stirring inside me, a ball of string that had been slowly unwinding itself for years, bouncing down a steep hill, down through the time it took me to walk away from my childhood. It feels good that it is doing this.

"There is one part I have always loved about you." I said.

"What's that?"

The string is something I have just realized. It unravels completely, to the end, and I let go. It is a good thing to let go of.

"I have always loved, hating you."

. . .

What is the whale?

—The whale is a memory that appears and recedes from a darkness. It is immense. It is powerful. It is weightless, floating.

. . .

Annie uncovered the last dish of steaming food. "Fix your plates and go on out to eat." she said. "Anywhere on the porch is fine. Just make yourself comfortable."

Plates and silverware in hand, every face was leaning over breathing in each temptation. In the center of the table were three large bowls, surrounded by smaller ones. Boiled shrimp overflowed the edges of one. In the second, with a pair of tongs hanging over the side, were huge pieces of fried mullet, coated golden brown with a grit batter. Amos's specialty was in the third, boiled crab legs. Bits of onion and what looked like ham spilled around the legs, a hill of white rice. There was also seafood gumbo in a pot still on the stove, Annie told us. Then she pointed out the other dishes of green beans cooked whole in butter and bacon grease, yellow corn bread and hushpuppies, cole slaw— I had never seen so much food, or smelled such smells that made my stomach ache just for a bite.

When plates were filled, everyone grabbed a drink from the ice chest John had brought, made their way to the screen door and into the cooler air outside. John was smiling, sitting next to me. Bits of mullet had already fallen down his shift front. Annie had asked every person if they got enough? "Yes, yes..." we all told her. "Have you tried the gumbo? Is it too hot?..." There wasn't anything that hadn't been tasted. Joseph finally had to tell his mother to sit down and eat, when it looked like she might not ever reach her chair. "If everybody has what they need...?"

"We're fine. Now, sit down mom, enjoy it with us."

"Here grandma, you can have my corn bread. You don't have any." one of the twins said.

"Don't you like it?"

"I love it. I'm going to get two more pieces..."

"You eat what you have first." her father told her. Then to his mother, "Eat..."

"All right—"

Amos reached over, put a crab leg on her plate. She picked it up, snapped it deftly in half. Took a bite. Then to the corn bread, granddaughter smiling, mouth full. For half an hour hardly a word was spoken. Everyone seemed content to eat slow and savor secret ingredients and the unexpected hunger that seemed hard to satisfy. And through out the dinner, John and I exchanged looks, brushes of hand to wipe away crumbs, directing of a napkin to the right spots. Annie took this in too, as did Amos, but they let it go without comment.

When it looked like no more bites could be had, or forks lifted, Annie sprung to her feet and began collecting plates. I jumped up too. "Annie you just sit right there. I'll get everyone's dishes."

"A cook inspects her dishes to see how everyone liked the food."

"There is no way you'll hear any complaints, much less a leftover crumb." I told her.

"Amen," Amos said.

"The best I've ever had." John said.

"No better food anywhere mom—" Joseph patted his stomach.

"Um Umm good." said the girls.

"See—" I told her. "No complaints."

She smiled. "Well then, I'll just have to do with making some coffee."

I collected the rest of the dishes. John took up the glasses and empty cans and we followed behind her. When the coffee was done, Annie took down her blue and white china cups and placed them on a large wooden tray. "I'll get that, Mrs. Annie." John said.

"Such a nice, young man."

He took the tray and coffee from her. "Not so young." he said, backed against the screen door and held it open for her.

"You young people— always worried about your age."

"Well, he is getting pretty thick around the middle—" I said, poked his ribs.

"With food like this, who could wonder?"

"Now, now." Annie said. "Take this handsome thing on out of here—Katherine. The sun's about to fall on it's heel. We can't miss the best part."

Everyone was down at the dock. Amos had lit his pipe. A seagull feather, hanging down from one end, swung back and forth each time he went forward in the rocking chair. He was telling Joseph, who had settled against one of the posts, something about the government going to hell in a hand-basket and that he should teach the girls at home instead of sending them to school. As soon as Annie sat down one of the girls was in her lap, the other in Josephs. John and I poured the coffee then he went and sat down on the edge of the dock to hang his feet over. I pulled the last rocker over by him and sat down too. He leaned over, put his shoulder against my leg, held onto my foot.

"Look, grandma, what we found." one of the girls said.

"Let's see?" Annie put out a hand. In it her granddaughter placed a handful of delicate shells. "Ah yes." Annie said. "Angel wings. Do you remember these, Joseph?" She handed him some of the shells.

He smiled. "I must have collected hundreds of these when I was a kid."

"Do you remember the story I told you about them, when you first brought them to show me?" He smiled again holding one up to the fading light. "You see," Annie said to the girls, "while they're alive in the shell, they are like two hands in prayer, together." She cupped her hands together to show this. "When they die, they open up and become two angel wings; connected in the center." She opened her hands into two wings, side by side. "Your father here, asked me as a boy, 'Why the angel's wings were hidden in the sand?' And I said, when God sends one of his angels to earth, they have to leave behind their wings. They take them off just as they cross over and hide them here. This is why, when you meet an angel here on earth, he won't have any wings..."

"And then, I asked," said Joseph, "why are some broken and only one left?"

"Some angels, when they came down and started to live again as people, forgot what their purpose was, what God had wanted them to do in this life. These angels can feel the missing part, even if they don't remember what it is they lost? They are looking for their other half. They spend their whole lives looking for something they can't quite remember."

"How do you know who an angel is, grandma?" one of the girls asked.

"Well, that's the secret." Annie said. "We all have the potential of being an angel; some are just more along at finding their wings, and remembering their purpose. An angel is the inner life of God showing itself on the outside."

"Why are their wings so small?"

"Well, they don't use them to fly with like birds do. They are more like reminders to do something, of where they came from, and why they are here. When you find two wings together, that's an angel who's remembered what his purpose is."

"Then we shouldn't keep them?"

"They can find them no matter where they are. You take it with you and maybe one day you'll meet the one it belongs to?"

"Is grandpa an angel now?" the second girl asked. Annie's son looked at her.

"I'm certain of it." she said.

Everyone settled into comfortable positions to watch the sunset. I leaned down, placed a chin on John's shoulder. He reached up, touched my hair.

A layer of rusty color moved slowly over each of us, drawing the shadows around us like a blanket before a huge bonfire. Amos didn't address his mother; instead, he quietly picked up some of the angel wing shells, swung back his arm and tossed them high into the glowing sky. Each one, falling into the water sounded like drops of rain. He said no words, only sat back in his chair, took a deep, long puff on his pipe, and blew out the breath to the wind. Each of us, in turn would breath a little of it in, then give it back out, sharing the light, the sounds, the smells, tastes, and especially, in the warmth of a family gathered together.

"*Yes.* " I whispered softly.

"Yes, what?" John asked.

"Nothing. I was saying it to myself."

"Yes, you love me?"

"Of course, I do."

"You don't have to say it." His fingers traced the side of my face, lips. "Show me."

I looked at him by the last light of my last day. His smile, was slow and warm, drawing me back from an edge of the past and forward to a hopeful future.

"Kiss me." I said. "But slow, so I can remember."

51

Twenty-five years a Navy man, grandfather was. All he ate and dreamed were stars and the sound of oceans. Deep in the metal belly that rocked him to sleep each night, where he wrote the letters to his wife back home, attempting to tell of his dreams of stars and ocean, and how they rolled like the Captain's walk rolled, past the men in line, topside, portside, in the narrow spaces down below deck. He never could find the words that felt like sea legs, or rationed food, or the smell men made, closed up together, the sounds they made at night, womanless sounds, homesick breathing. Tears that weren't tears, but pillows pressed too close to slammed shut eyes.

At times he was sick of it all, all the nights and days of it. But before he could find the words to tell his wife, wrote— 'Doing well. Hope to see you soon, Love.' He wrote that word fast, scribbled out, so it looked like it was spelled with only the first letter and a long line behind it. His name. Period. Closed the letter. Folded it. Plain white envelope. One stamp. Address printed carefully in block letters.

Grandma, twenty-five years a Navy man's wife, and all she saw was how much dirt the new place had. How the corner store was now four corners farther to walk, and a growing child ate more and more everyday. A weight that drew down her shoulders by the pound, caving her in over the things she carried, to the post office, for the hopeful, thick letters she never got, to the grocer, laundry mat, dime store. Making money stretch in as many ways as possible, she'd count and recount her change to make sure it was right, tucked it in the little, inside pocket of her purse so it wouldn't get lost, next to the letter she could recite by heart, it had so few words, so little he spent on her and always the same. It never made her feel better, or helped her understand, or get through the days and nights that were her life. Shifting the two bags against her hip, she walked into the wind hunched over, tried to remember the exact shape of his face, couldn't. Took hold of her daughter's hand. "Come on." She said. "We still have a long way's to go."

My mother's feet were wore out walking beside her, one arm stretched up, to hold on, keep up, stay beside me now. Don't fall, pick up those feet— both of them walking together, their shoes mapping out lengths of time like a shipman's rope, between what was left behind, and everyplace they'd yet to go, floating from city to city by land, as he did by sea. My mother was afraid of angels and of seeing too much the same things. Inside, she must have known when it was time to leave again. When the pull of the road and packing boxes, sent her time and again out into the unknown, or hiding under beds.

When my mother grew up, she walked as little as possible and never holding hands. Her boyfriends carried everything for her, and told her anything she wanted to hear. She let loose change get lost, and bought things on whim. On her charm bracelet, she added a memento for each boy she dated. She could go from end to end and tell what each one meant. Circled back, the story would change and become something entirely different. Telling her own fortune by following the lines and faces. It didn't matter to her to keep things in their right order, or place.

My two mothers argue what to do with me. This was before I was born and before my mother was first married. Already, I am causing trouble, angry heartbeats. Already, without trying, I pit them, one against the other. My mother's knees go weak the first moment she knew where I was. Her first thoughts to me, were hoping I'd wash away, but I was a stain that could not be scrubbed off. I was too far in, too stubborn. Too strong to be got out.

When I stretched out her skin, so that it would never go back to what it was, she learns to hate her visible parts. When she can no longer hide me, she tells me hideous things, hoping I will become so frightened I will runaway from inside her. I am the first to cause her such pain as she has ever felt. Her shameful tears, her loss. Such as one tiny heartbeat can do, create a gaping hole between flesh and blood, and draw a clear line, between my mother as a child, and the motherless woman she felt.

All her real fears were born inside of me. Fear of being seen, of being found out, afraid of what will happen, of what it would mean, and to who? I was not a charm added to her bracelet. I made no tinkling sound when I brushed against her. I was not something she wanted to remember.

Inside her. Small and white, full of words and sounds, a thinking child, not yet feeling, moving to navigate the channel, narrow spaces, rolling gravitational pull, strong tides— a match-head striking against her inside, to burst afire, when I leave. Floating in the space made for me, kerosene, instead of water, inside her, inside her metal belly, to ensure a good strike. *Hot love. Strong light.* These are the things given a child at birth, seeking warmth to comfort us, and cool things to soothe our natures.

"Hush now. Hush." a stranger says to a child. "It was only a dream." But to a child, the images were there. The colors and sounds. How could that not be? When was the world divided and people learned not to see what the child sees? To *know* it?

The mother does not know. The grandfather and grandmother cannot say. So I am the child, and I wander on all fours, crawling around the furniture, learning about pain and dark corners. Struggling to right myself, reach out, hold on, steady, steady, rolling feet, unsteady legs, following the light to a window where outside there are stars. Struggling to find a way in which to map the world, a way out— *They all are.* A porthole view at least. Side by side, people pressed together like hands in prayer, or men at war, the wives and children— hordes of people, families, lives, histories! *Still*—everyone of us, without knowing it, same unsteady steps, no idea how, or when, or even if— but still, struggling for a rose-lived life, beyond.

What is the whale?
—*The whale is all people who have passed through my life, changing it in only a moment, then are gone.*

52

In the second moments of life, we learn to look around,
to see. We are still afraid. But now, our voice is more than a
scream. It calls out to the lights, and movements, and sounds
which still charge out at us, at rough hands we can now
name. The monstrous sizes we can cut down to size, by our
own size, and the shapes we can separate by color and
meanings of dark and light.

The sound of my voice is an echo. I hear it twice, once inside where it is right, and once outside, upside-down and backwards, and wrong. My voice flies from me saying, "I won't let you do it." It comes back, "Yes, you will. You can't stop me." I throw out again, "I hate you." It comes back, "You'll do as I say. Get in the car!" I don't move. The voice moves away from me, twisting among the walls and narrow streets until it disappears.

I see now what it is I am afraid of.

I am afraid of things I cannot change, and never could, because I could not forget all the things I saw, and heard, and felt, and could not change. I saw my mother in this way and I touched her and became frozen at the sound of her voice.

These things are over. I do not have to listen anymore. I do not have to believe what I hear coming back. And I can walk away.

. . .

"Still-born." Grandma reveals this. In her face I cannot tell whether there is sadness, or relief. "He didn't even show up." She says this too. "You should go in and see her. Don't mention how she looks. It makes her furious. The doctors have already been in three times to calm her down." Her voice is nervous, ticking off information in a rapid, under-her-breath way. "They put seven stitches in her forehead when she came in. Wouldn't say how she got it. Flat-out refused. Don't mention it. It makes her upset." Adds, "The baby was a boy."

"I'll be the first to have a boy—" Karen says.

"For god sakes shut up!" Grandma snaps.

Karen's mouth shuts, clutches her purse like a weapon. Grandma walks away, out paces her own reflection in the window glass. Puts rows of plastic chairs between her and Karen.

Over by the candy machine Jenny stands with granddad. He puts in quarters, selects different choices, fills Jenny's held-out hands, then they sit down and he helps her open each one. Karen and grandma continue to size each other up from a distance, grandma looking more tired, her face sewn up completely now. Karen's younger, but meaner face, has a pinched place between the eyes, a quilted pucker, that narrows her face into the thick edge of an ax handle. The look she swings at me says, Chop, Chop, Chop!

It takes me a long time to walk to Jessie's room. Everywhere there is harsh light, sharp edges. I walk carefully. Everything seems made to cut. In each room I pass, the sheets are folded to a paper-cut precision. Door edges if touched, could slice a finger. Doctors talk of incisions, look at the transparent ghosts of bones. And everywhere— all that light pours down from the ceiling, so that everyone is can peer into the sick and wounded. Nothing here is left hidden.

Beside the window, is Jessie's bed. She is looking towards the dark sky outside. She does not see me standing in the doorway. Her arms are laying on top of the sheets, at her sides. Folded around each, dark layers of bruised skin. In the center, the mound shape of her stomach. Nothing inside. The tiny soul had gone out. Left an empty place behind.

Finally, she turns and looks at me. "Hey." she says carefully, pulls her arms under the cover. Her lips too, are swollen.

"Jessie"

"One of these days he'll learn to listen. I told him something wasn't right."

"Jessie, don't."

"Not that he could have fixed it. He sure was happy he was going to be a daddy."

"I don't think—"

"I know. I should have done it a little differently. Kept my feet up more. Done it right to start with."

"Please, listen to me?"

"Don't start with me!" Her voice is thick, blurred with different emotions. "I'm tired. I'll rest up a few days. That will help things."

"You need help."

"That's what these doctors are for, not you." she says. I can feel myself shaking inside. In my throat is a fist of words that won't come out. I hold them back. "I hate places full of sick people." she says slowly. "It's always so cold."

"Why did he do it?" slips out.

"Do what?"

"Jess—"

"He didn't do anything."

"That's a little hard to believe?"

"He'd never lay a finger on me. I know what you're thinking..."

"He's going to kill you."

Her voice strains. "He loves me." she says. "What the hell do you know? You don't know anything." She'd said this before, that day. "This is none of your business— He's *my* husband. He'll be here soon and take me back. I don't need you telling me—"

"That you have a right to live?"

"I live just fine." she says, lowering her voice, in control. "Go away—"

I walk over to the window instead, look out.

As children we pulled together, now it was like someone had turned us, put us as two magnets, end to end, the wrong end, and now we forced each other back, never letting up. We can not help ourselves. We pushed each other away as a force of nature now. It shouldn't be this way, but it is.

"Why are you doing this?" I ask finally. A simple question.

"I don't need you." she says.

I lay a hand against the cold glass. Outside, it is a solid, black sky that pushed the city down below. I could see all the way to the tip of the bay, the bridge lights arching out over the water, the dark water looking like a black mirror, streaked with too many colors. The vision of the sky blurs, and I see only my reflection. I am transparent and pale. "You're right." I say. "You don't need me to show you anything. I was just hoping you'd change your mind?" When I turn around her hands are clenched, holding the edge of the sheet to her. She won't look at me. "I hope you get better."

"I don't take nothin' from no one." she shakes a thin fist at me. "You just remember that!"

"Get better, Jess." I move towards the door.

In the hall is my mother. For a moment, I am shocked at seeing her again. She takes a step backwards, looks at me as though, she is certain I will speak, watching me, careful not to make a sudden move. Now, when I look at her, it's like I'm also looking at Jessie, there's the same repealing force. The same feeling that, if I just look hard enough, below the surface, then I'd find out who you really are? Hopeful thinking. They keep changing. They keep hiding from me, make me look for them. Jessie is no longer just Jessie. She is an extension of my mother now, a smaller, lesser part, that has attempted to be her, and partly succeeded.

Standing there in the doorway, she is about to change into someone else. But, deep down, way, way down, in that place no one else ever sees, will she think to herself, 'I know how you feel, Jessie?' Talk about lost children, empty feelings. She has yet to move from the doorway. She seems to wait for me to say something. Only seconds pass as we stand there, facing each other, but I view her slowly, seeming to have huge lengths of time to see with. Her eyes are watery and red around the corners. There is one strand of hair flat against her forehead. Her hair is oily and dark, without shine. The edge of her collar is bent up on one side. Her body is slopped forward, even though she seems to be leaning back, away from me. If I reached out with my hand I would touch her. That's how close she is. I imagine what her skin feels like, not warm or yielding, but cold, slick like metal.

She doesn't seem as huge as she used to. There is a frailness about her now, as though her bones were made of glass and they had been broken down long ago. I imagine they must cut her from the inside when she moves. I can also smell her house on her this close. The smell of it always stays in her clothes. It smells faintly of dust, and worn out things, old closets, or the smells that are under beds that haven't been vacuumed in years. But these are really places I remember as a child, smells from places I would hide in, where I would think only of her.

She thinks I will speak to her. It is something she wants. Her eyes tell me this.

I do something completely unexpected. I reach for her hand. Pull it to me. She is frozen silent, says not a word. Her skin against mine, tough skin, warm fingertips. Not cold, as I would imagine it to be. I turn the palm up, look at it closely. I trace the heavy lines with my finger, lightly, trembling. Then I turn my own palm up, put it next to hers. From out of a vague memory, I remember her telling my future.

I say to her then, "Only the past is written in stone. Never the future." The lines, in each of our hands, showed how our past had sewn us together, in each, were difficulties and pain. I did learn about loneliness and losing everything, just as she had said I would. Two hard women. In her hand, I could feel the pulse of blood. Her heart. When I look her in the eye, they are wide, startled. She is holding her breath. I tell her what I see in the lines of her hand. "You were almost right..."

I almost didn't make it away.

Then I reveal to her, a secret that I had learned. Something I could give her. Something, whispered so that she would be able to hear it. "Mother...one feels, first with the eyes. Then with the hands. Then with the heart."

I let go of her hand. It drops heavily back to her side. I move around her, walk on.

First, with the eyes. Then with the hands. Then with the heart. My heart beat strongly now, fiercely and alive.

I don't turn around to see if she's watching me. I walk slow, not like I'm running to get away, but on purpose, as though I know where I'm going. I'm conscious of how my arms swing naturally, not stiff or rigid. I walk on as though I am unaffected by seeing her, as though it was the most natural thing in the world for me to do this. 'Did I know that woman I just passed?' my body might convey. 'No...' and I keep going without turning. 'I'm certain I don't know her'.

I move towards the light. Away from the darkness.

What is the whale?
—*The whale is my mother. I have been calling her.*

53

It was just after sunrise, when I rowed the boat out on the bay. 'Amos beckoned', Annie said, though I still could not hear him. I rowed, pulled the oars through the thick water, listened for Amos's voice.

"Here'll do, I think." she said.

"Do you want me to drop the anchor?"

"No, let us drift. Let the water carry us on it's own."

I tucked the oars in the boat beside me, waited. Over the morning water, the air was damp and gray. A white brush of fog hovered, slowly fading as the sun rose. Somewhere, to the left, gulls were crying out, being answered.

"You ever seen a man tune up an instrument?" Annie asked. "A string guitar or a banjo? He has to listen real close. Puts his ear right up to it, so he can hear the slightest change. He turns each knob real slow. And each time he turns it, he listens. He gets close by taking his time. He has to develop his ear and wait for the right moment. He plucks each string, then listens, then turns it a little more, until all the strings work together. They make music only when they work together. This is how, I believe, God makes a soul work. He fine tunes it a little at a time, until he can run his hand across all the strings and make music."

The wind was lifting up the sides of her hat, like wings. Fly, fly— it said. But Annie held herself down along with the hat, her hand on top, her feet squarely placed in the bottom of the boat. The wind blew up off the bay only stronger, kicking up sprays of water, formed little pools of water along every surface.

"We had one of the nicest mornings together." Annie began. I placed a hand onto my shoulder where the old pain was. "He was in a rare mood." she said. "We talked about his father. We talked about Tom, old times. Then, all of the sudden, he just out and said, 'Annie, you are the finest woman I have ever known! A damn fine cook too. Tom was a lucky man.' Ate himself a second helping of blackberry pancakes, cleared away the dishes for me, then said he was goin' back down to his place, said he had some things to finish up... Can you believe he pulled that big, old chair of his onto the porch? That's where I found him. *Just like that.* I'd never seen him look happier."

Gathered around her in the boat, were Amos' s most personal things— a bundle of feathers, his pipe, his tobacco pouch, cedar walking stick, a worn pair of shoes, and laid very carefully across her lap, the feather headdress. Each dark, blue-gray feather, I knew, he had found while walking the shore, and for each one, thanked a heron for leaving it. Annie said it was time to send along his things, to return back what was his.

When the gulls had quieted and the fog moved further away, she said softly. "I *know.*" Then was silent again, until she said the same two words again, as though she were agreeing to something someone had said. "I *know.*" Her voice was so low, it could have been a whispered prayer. I listened, watched the fog disappear, thought of Amos being gone. In my mind, I pictured him. He might be a bird now, I thought, and know what it feels like to fly, feeling the clouds from the inside out.

"There ought to be ways to let someone know how much they mean, while they're still here." she said then. "More than what you try to show. Some for sure way."

"He knew." I said.

"No, no." she whispered still.

I turned around as far as I could, so I could see her. Her eyes were closed. She tapped her heart gently. "God won't mind if I keep a little bit of him here. In a pocket, safe inside." she said. "The heart needs a keepsake of it's own." A tear was at the corner of her eye. She opened them. The tear ran down her cheek. Then stared out at the water for a long time, stroking the heron feathers in her lap.

"This, here, is *Harold Amos Tenor.*" she said. "Part Indian, part white man, part fool and friend." She looked back towards the shore. "He is full blood in spirit now, more than friend in memory. Lord...as we are here with you today, remembering Amos... The land— his body, the water— his spirit. When they came together you granted him life. When you pulled them apart you gave him death. I am a grateful woman for knowing this man. I know his mama is a proud woman to know her son at last. I know she is. I know it..."

She reached over the side of the boat, let her fingers just touch the water. Then she looked at me and said, "He was right. I owed them nothin'. Not one cent of nothing." Her voice sounded tired. She lifted the hand, looked at the water that ran from the fingers. "It was hard to keep from singing, hard to keep it in. It always seemed to want out more than I did. Sittin' right behind my ears, humming, like bees in an old barn roof. That's just what Amos always called it, when he'd hear me humming some tune— '*Those happy bees.*' he'd say. He even called me Honey Bee when Tom wasn't around." She laughed softly.

"I pretended for so long, I couldn't sing. That I couldn't fight. I pretended I didn't know how to live any other way than what they gave me, but I could. Tom showed me that. Amos too. Life was always there. Bubblin' up inside me, trying to rise out of me like it did the first day. Like the first day it was in me when I born, or the first day I sang. I kept it all down, like my head was down, whenever I went past anyone back then. I didn't want people to see me. It cost me too much.

"Amos said to me once, 'Annie, you hum a tune real nice. Why don't you put them words with it?' and I said, 'I couldn't sing a note to save my life—'. He said it was a real shame. I said so too.

"They thought they'd killed the song right out of me. But they were sure fooled." She rocked back, looked at the sky. "Amos—you kept it alive for me, all this time. I should have done it long ago. Amos—" she said, half smiling, half dreaming someplace else. "This is for you. I hope you're listen'n?" Then she leaned back against me, took two, long deep breaths, reached behind her, took my hand in hers, and started to hum. Testing her voice a little, she reached out with the sound. The happy bees gathered up together, rose in one long, honey sound. Then, seeming to find the right place deep inside her, the wings changed, became a voice, and flew out with the first words. As her voice traveled up against my back, I could feel each breath she pulled in and each note she let out. The song was low, and sweet, and deep as a tree is deep, rooted in the earth where all things began. Those first words rose up towards the sun, growing arms and branches, leaves that bloomed full with the pollen flowers that fed her soul and mine.

Kept in so long... I could hear that as she sang. The sound of life, just released, her second birth into the world. And, as she sang, she placed Amos's things in the water. Some floated, others sank below, bumping against our little boat as we drifted. Her voice moved us along the waters of the bay, through the fog that was now lifted, our hearts rising with it. If I was ever close to a spirit, it was then, on that song, through Annie's voice that I was closest. I don't know if it was Amos that I felt, but it came down on us, maybe sitting beside us, looking at us now. I could feel it's touch inside and out.

She ended her song with the same words she started with, "I know—" she sang. "I *know*." Still, she held the last piece of Amos to her, the heron feathers. Then, very carefully, reached out and placed it in the water beside her.

After some time I said, "Annie, there's not a soul alive who can sing like you."

"That's the voice God gave me." she said.

"I know Amos heard it."

"He did."

Then we watched as a school of dolphins rose around us, our little boat turning in a slow circle as they passed. They were playing with the headdress still floating on the water, pushing it towards the ocean with them. I took up the oars to steady us and return us to shore, but we both watched, until we could no longer see them. Their sleek, morning gray bodies, moved away through the water taking Amos with them, to the place that spirits went and babies began. That's the way I saw it— out there, in the blue-black darkness, that always waited just out of reach. But in our hearts, our minds, our bodies, and on the song that would keep on going, as sound does in space, traveling by ocean waves, always outward, forever. It was fitting to see him go like that. Fitting in the way he died too, death on a doorstep, at the beginning, on a stomach

286

full of blackberry pancakes, and loving words to the woman he loved, though neither had ever admitted it. She knew. They both knew. I was lucky to be near enough to see them as I did, and to know too, what their love had set free.

Annie sighed, held my hand in her warmth. "There is no choir in heaven." she said. "It is here. All around us— the voices in the way we are, the way we live.

"We are all here to find our voice— *and sing.*"

The End